FUNNY

THEY SAY I'M **PRETTY FUNNY** FOR A GIRL

REBECCA ELLIOTT

PENGUIN BOOKS

PENGUIN BOOKS

UK | USA | Canada | Ireland | Australia
India | New Zealand | South Africa

Penguin Books is part of the Penguin Random House group of companies
whose addresses can be found at global.penguinrandomhouse.com.

www.penguin.co.uk
www.puffin.co.uk
www.ladybird.co.uk

Penguin
Random House
UK

First published 2020
001

Text copyright © Rebecca Elliott, 2020

The moral right of the author has been asserted

Set in 10.5/15.5 pt Sabon LT Std
Typeset by Jouve (UK), Milton Keynes
Printed and bound in Great Britain by Clays Ltd, Elcograf S.p.A.

A CIP catalogue record for this book is available from the British Library

ISBN: 978–0–241–37462–7

All correspondence to:
Penguin Books
Penguin Random House Children's
80 Strand, London WC2R 0RL

MIX
Paper from
responsible sources
FSC® C018179

Penguin Random House is committed to a
sustainable future for our business, our readers
and our planet. This book is made from Forest
Stewardship Council® certified paper.

For Clementine. Always for Clementine.

ONE

Dressed in a tight, gold, sequined, off-the-shoulder catsuit, I have my leg slung over the shoulder of Ron Weasley as we dance the salsa in front of an enthusiastic studio audience made up entirely of penguins.

Not real penguins. Penguin chocolate bars.

The dance finishes and the judges – Lady Gaga, Paddington, Winston Churchill and Darth Vader – all give us a ten. Ron Weasley kisses me on the cheek and says it's all down to me, that not only am I the best dancer, who moves across the floor like a goddess, but I'm also hilariously funny. I blush and crack a joke. The crowd howls with laughter as he drags me back on to the dance floor and we salsa the night away.

It's possible I'm dreaming . . .

I'm a bit suspicious: chocolate bars aren't normally the size of people, Winston Churchill is actually dead, Ron Weasley's a fictional character and my normal body couldn't actually move like this even if my life depended on it. But then my normal body is fat, and in this dream, as with all others, I'm not fat. I'm not thin either – I'm just me. Just the inside me, the *me* me. Although, judging by my current dream, the *me* me might not be fat but it is pretty weird and seems to have a crush on Ron Weasley that I was unaware of until now.

I try to hold on to it, but the dream floats away, and rushing in to take its place is the realization that the music I've been dream-dancing to is actually my phone screaming 'La Cucaracha' next to my head. It's my alarm telling me to wake up for school.

Meaning, urgh, I actually have to get up.

Which means moving.

Which seems impossible.

Eyes still clamped shut, I concentrate all my efforts into one of my arms. It slowly rises into the air before manoeuvring over to my bedside table and hovering above it. Like one of those claw machines at the arcade, I repeatedly lower my hand and grab wildly, hoping to chance upon my phone, still loudly singing the most annoying tune ever written.

Why, oh why did I think that song was a good idea for an alarm? AND a ringtone. Must have thought it was funny. I'll change it later. (Except I know I won't. This exact same thing's been happening every morning for days now.)

On the bedside table, books, glasses of water and jars of moisturizer (used only once or twice before I got bored with the whole idea of a 'facial routine') go flying until I finally locate the phone with my fingertips. I clasp it tight, trying to strangle the thing to death, then yank it towards me.

I prise open one eye just enough to squint at the time, inconceivable as it is: 6.45. No one should be awake at

6.45. It's ridiculous. I blindly paw at the screen and eventually manage to turn off the alarm.

The next thing I know Ron Weasley shouts my name in a high-pitched voice as he punches me in the stomach for messing up the foxtrot.

'Haylah!'

My eyes fly open as I realize it's actually my four-year-old brother, Noah, who's just jumped on my stomach to wake me up.

'Haylah! Hay . . . Hay . . . Hay!'

'Ow – Noah! What are you doing?' I mumble.

'I'm hungry! I want breakfookst!'

I make a sound halfway between a sigh and a sob as I look at my phone, still clenched in my fist. It's 7.30. I've slept in. Again.

I stayed up way too late watching comedy on the internet. Again. Why is my midnight brain incapable of thinking, *You know what? I'll watch that next video tomorrow and go to sleep now, when I choose, rather than keep watching the next clip, and the next clip, until I slump into a coma and my phone hits me in the face.*

'Stupid midnight brain,' I groan as I hide my face back under the duvet and squirm around, trying to shift Noah off me. But, like a tiny champion rodeo rider on a bucking bronco, there's no way he's coming off, no matter how much I thrash about or alert animal welfare organizations.

Noah giggles, loving our new 'game', so I give up the thrashing and slowly emerge from the duvet, squinting at the blinding daylight like a disgruntled tortoise woken early from hibernation by a psychotic squirrel.

'Fine, OK,' I say. 'I'll get breakfast – just get off and give me a minute, yeah?'

'Now, now, now!' he shouts as he bumps up and down on my belly.

'Ow – stop! Noah, that really hurts!'

'But it's like a big bouncy castle!' he says, still merrily thumping up and down.

'Thanks,' I say, raising my eyebrows. Body positivity is not exactly one of my little brother's strengths. Or perhaps it is – to him, resembling a bouncy castle *is* a body positive. After all, the ideal body to a four-year-old *would* be bouncy, or have a tail, or five arms, or be covered in rainbow-coloured fur. It wouldn't be anything as boring as thin and beautiful.

He looks confused, but keeps bouncing. 'Thank you? What for?'

'I was being sarcastic . . .'

Noah stops bouncing and leans his little round freckled face down towards me.

'What's "star cat sick"?'

I prop myself up on my elbows so our noses are nearly touching. 'That's a very good question, Noah,' I say seriously. Then I grin. 'Come on, let's get breakfast.'

'Yay, break-fookst!'

A small laugh escapes through my nose. There are a few words Noah doesn't quite say right yet. Mum says we shouldn't laugh at him, but sometimes it's extremely hard not to.

'It's breakFAST,' I say.

'Break-fookst!'

'No, look, try saying it slowly. Break . . . fast.'

'Break . . . fookst.'

I give up. 'Yeah, that's exactly it. C'mon.'

We plod down to the kitchen, past the toys, clothes and books that Mum continues to optimistically pile on the stairs for us to take to our rooms. We ignore them of course and head into the kitchen, where every surface is covered with dirty dishes, pans, empty microwaveable cartons, half-eaten tins of beans and, well, you get the idea. It's a mess. And I know I should clear it up, but clearing up's just really, really boring. I mean, no one ever lay on their deathbed thinking, *I wish I'd cleared up the kitchen a bit more.*

Saying that, there probably are people who lie on their deathbed thinking, *I wish I hadn't contracted that deadly virus from my unsanitary kitchen.*

Look, I'll clear it up tonight, OK?

'Bring me food, woman!' says Noah, grabbing a spoon from the drawer and then sitting on his favourite chair at the kitchen table, a dark wooden thing with a bogey-green, stained velour seat pad. None of our furniture matches, and not in a trendy, eclectic way, because not only does our furniture not match any other furniture we have, it also doesn't match anyone's idea of what attractive furniture looks like.

'What do you fancy this morning?' I say, fumbling around in the cereal cupboard. 'Cornyflakers? Rice Krispicles? Chocopops?'

We never have the real makes of cereal, only the cheap, supermarket-brand knock-offs, but Mum insists they come from exactly the same factory, only some get boxed for stupid rich people and the rest for smart poor people.

Noah ignores me, instead giving all his attention to his upside-down reflection in the spoon as he pulls tiny gargoyle faces at it.

'Come on, Noah – decide quickly. We're in a bit of a rush,' I say.

Eventually, Noah shovels two 'Wheaty Bixits' down his throat while I pile anything handheld and edible into his lunch box. After putting in all the normal lunch-boxy stuff, I grab a jar of Marmite, hold it up to the light and put that in. This is one of our favourite games. We've not really got time, but I can't resist.

'No!' he shouts, his spoon halfway to his mouth. 'I can't eat that!'

'No?' I say. 'How about this?' And I put a potato in his lunchbox instead.

'Not that either!' he says, laughing, but still shovelling in the cereal.

'No? Oh, OK. These though, surely?' I say, putting in a tea bag and a couple of dishwasher tablets. He's got the giggles now, and, by the time I prepare to sprinkle Bisto over the top, he is spitting Wheaty Bixits across the kitchen in full-on hysterics.

'Noah!' I say, wiping up the mess. I'm not annoyed though. I love being able to make him laugh so much that cereal comes out of his nose.

'Do it again! Do it again!' he says as I wipe his face.

'No, we really haven't got time, Noah. Come on – finish your bowl.'

I'm on a diet so I just have a yoghurt.

And two pieces of toast.

And a Twix.

Then I install Noah in front of Mum's iPad while I take a shower.

In the bathroom, I step on the scales. Then I realize I'm still wearing the T-shirt I slept in so I take that off and get back on again.

Then I realize my hair's tied back in a scrunchy so I take that out, and consider shaving my head, as long hair's got to weigh a fair bit too, right?

Then I remember long hair's more flattering on a round face and I get back on the scales again.

Then I realize I haven't been to the loo yet so I sit down and squeeze out what I can and then get back on the scales again.

Then I realize I should have weighed myself *before* breakfast, not after – everyone knows that – so I figure I can probably take around six pounds off the reading anyway.

Then I realize I ate pasta last night and they always say you shouldn't weigh yourself the morning after eating pasta as it throws the result completely off. So I ignore the reading entirely and hide the scales behind the laundry basket to stop them looking at me with their evil, judgemental glare.

While exfoliating in the shower (and surely all that exfoliated dead skin weighs a couple of extra pounds too?),

7

I am alarmed to find a gold sticker firmly adhered to my outer right thigh. It reads MADE IN CHINA and probably came off one of Noah's toys. It takes some serious scrubbing to get it off, making me wonder how long it's been there.

Oh God, was it there last night when I went swimming?

My meddling aunt bought me an annual pass for the local swimming pool for my birthday. She said it was to help me get fit, but of course she meant it was to help me get less fat.

Now I think about it, I do remember a severe-looking middle-aged woman staring at my thighs as I got out of the pool last night. I just thought she was a weirdo, but she was probably thinking, *Good God, do the Chinese make everything now, even our fat kids?*

I guess at this point we ought to properly address the elephant in the room. The room being whichever room I'm in and the elephant always being me. Because elephants are fat. And so am I.

I'm not *crazy* fat though, if that's what you're thinking. I'm not the kind of fatty who inspires Channel Five documentaries or makes the news for rolling over and accidentally asphyxiating a cat and not realizing for two weeks. I'm just regular fat. Round, wobbly, that kind of thing. And I'm not one of those fatties who's all up top or all down below – nope, I'm fat all over, me. Big stomach. Big bum. And in recent times big boobs too. My norks came in around two years ago, and since then my body's just been a collection of perfectly round, overlapping circles. Like a living Venn diagram or a really basic and badly drawn Spirograph pattern.

So, yeah, I've got a great rack. But even before the chesticles I've always been big. My mum used to call it 'puppy fat', but now I think even she realizes these puppies aren't just for Christmas, they're for life.

The truth is, whatever I *look* like, I don't *feel* fat on the inside. Non-fat people think fat people must feel differently to them, experience the world in a different way, that everything we think and do must be affected by our fatness. But I feel normal (whatever 'normal' is). I don't feel weighed down or like I'm wearing extra padding. I actually forget that I'm fat until I walk past a mirror or get called a name, and suddenly I'm reminded, *Oh yeah, I'm fat*. And I don't eat all the time either. Or daydream about food. Or sit and devour a cake in one sitting or binge and then starve myself.

I just get hungry. And I like eating.

Eating quite a lot is normal for me. It's my normal. But this story isn't about my weight. So if you're thinking there's going to be a 'happy ending' where I have an epiphany and become a slim, sexy health freak who's into yoga and mung beans (they're a thing, right?) then think again, sunshine.

This is me. And these are my massive boobs.

Take us or leave us.

TWO

After a considerable amount of persuading, begging, tickling and jelly-bean-based bribery, I finally prise Noah away from the iPad so I can get him into something resembling a school uniform. He's pretty big too, so he's in elasticated 'sturdy-fit' grey shorts and, when I discover all his white polo shirts still covered in mud, playdough and snot, I grab a plain white PE T-shirt from the back of his wardrobe. As he dances around the living room, I can feel time running away from us and desperately glance at the faded floral wall clock for support, but it glares back at me with the news that, yes, once again I'm going to be late for school.

Dammit.

I hold the T-shirt up in front of him. 'OK, let's get this on quick, Noah, cos we're *really* in a bit of a hurry now.'

He stops dancing and stares at the T-shirt with a look of disgust on his face.

'But it doesn't have a thing!' he whinges, folding his arms over his round pink belly.

'A what?' I ask.

'A thing!' he shouts, putting his podgy hands round my neck and wiping soggy Wheaty Bixits all over my school shirt, which had, for once, started the day clean.

'Oh – a collar. OK, wait a minute,' I say.

I run off and come back with a black permanent marker pen, which I use to draw a collar on his T-shirt.

'Happy?' I ask.

'Happy,' he confirms as I pull the shirt down over his head.

There then follows a frantic ten-minute search for his shoes (which we finally discover are in the freezer because yesterday his 'feet were hot'), followed by a slathering on of suncream, which is no easy thing on a Noah who refuses to keep still. It's like trying to spray-paint a hyperactive monkey.

I grab our school bags and shove a cap on Noah's head, then we make our way past the mountains of shoes, coats, scooters and junk mail in our diarrhoea-coloured hall until finally we emerge from the house. We're late, but if we get moving quickly we might be OK.

'I need my water bottle,' says Noah just after I lock the front door.

'Right. Fine,' I say, trying to hide my annoyance as I go back in, grab the bottle and fill it. 'Anything else?' I yell.

'Nope!' he says.

I lock the door again and hand him the bottle with a forced smile.

He stares at it then says brightly, 'I can't do zip.'

'OK, yep,' I say, grabbing his bag, unzipping it and shoving the bottle in. I grip his hand. 'Right, let's go!'

'My reading book!' he squeals.

'Argh! Noah, we don't have time – you'll have to go without it!'

His face begins to scrunch up and I know I have to get the damn book because otherwise we'll be stuck here while he has a massive meltdown.

'OK, OK!' I say, and I'm back in the house and grabbing the book and stepping outside and locking the door again, and all with a false grin plastered on my face so he doesn't get upset.

I try to speed-walk him to his school's breakfast club, but as always Noah's pace works on a reverse sliding scale in relation to mine. The quicker I want to move, the slower he does.

'Come on, Noah!' I try to say in a breezy tone as I yank him along the pavement. But he senses the urgency in my voice and stops dead.

'Why are you angry?' he says.

'I'm not angry!' I say in what I had intended to be a jolly voice, but actually comes out slightly hysterical and strangulated. And I know I've got about two seconds before the boy explodes. 'Just . . . in a bit of a rush,' I add in a 'funny voice' that masks my frustration about as well as putting a trilby on a dog disguises it as a human.

'Why?'

'Because we're late, that's all. C'mon.'

I rub his back and give him a smile, which seems to stop any impending explosions, only now he thinks playtime can resume.

I try to grab his hand again, but he raises both his arms out in front of him and lets out a loud groan as he takes a painfully slow step forward.

'Noah, now what are you doing?'

'I'm . . . a . . . zombie . . .' he moans.

'Brilliant. Could you be a *quick* zombie?'

'Zombies . . . aren't . . . quick . . .'

'Well, what if you'd eaten the brain of a really fast runner? Then you'd be a quick zombie.'

'It . . . doesn't . . . work . . . like . . . that.'

'*Could* it work like that today though?'

'No.'

I bend down towards him, look him in the eye and try to talk in a steady, patient voice, like Mum would, but it just comes out fierce.

'Noah. This is stupid. We need to walk quicker. We are going to be SO late. Now come on!'

His bottom lip starts to quiver. *Oh God, here we go.*

'It's OK, it's OK,' I say through gritted teeth. 'I'm not angry, see – happy face!' and I force my lips into a grin, which is way more sinister than jolly.

He lets out a loud cry as he sits heavily down on the grass by the pavement.

'I KNEW you were angry!' he wails.

'Well, I AM NOW!' I spit as I turn away, my fists clenched in frustration. And I want to scream. I want to

13

grab his little hand and drag him along the ground if necessary, all the way to school.

I mean, *seriously* – people go on about how cute and innocent little kids are, but they can also test the patience and understanding of a sodding saint. Surely even Mother Teresa would find it hard not to lose it big time with this kind of dumb-crappery.

Ready to burst forth with a massive rant, I turn and look down into his little pink face, all screwed up and wet with tears. His big sad brown eyes look up at me. And immediately my anger fades, and my heart melts, and I just want him to be happy again. So I scrunch my eyes up tight for a moment, gathering any patience I have left in me, and sit on the grass next to him.

'I'm sorry,' I say as his sobs continue. 'What if we play I-spy?'

'No.'

'What if we . . . pretend to be trains?'

'No.'

'What if . . . I give you a chocolate bar after school?'

He sniffs. 'A Milkybar?'

'Yeah, OK, a Milkybar.'

'Pinkie promise?' he says, extending a little finger.

'Pinkie promise,' I say, curling my little finger round his.

'OK,' he says, before springing up and carrying on the journey like nothing's happened.

And I feel bad because Mum says we have to improve his diet. But Milkybars are made of milk, right? And cows make milk. And cows eat grass. And grass is basically a vegetable so, if you think it through, it's basically one of his five-a-day. Basically.

After dropping Noah off at his school, I start to run the rest of the way to mine – until my boobs hurt, and then I just power-walk the rest of the way. And by 'power-walk' I mean balling up my hands into fists and then walking *slightly* faster than I do normally. In truth, it's less a 'power-walk' and more a 'determined stroll'.

So of course I get to school late.

As I walk into my form room, my fringe sticking to my forehead with sweat, my teacher's just about to finish taking the register, so at least I don't have to make the walk of shame to the office to sign in.

'Late again, Haylah?' bawls Mrs Perkins, pointing her sharp nose and severe cheekbones in my direction. If I have a body made up of circles, hers is made up of triangles and straight lines. She's like the Eiffel Tower in a cardigan. Though, for all her thin, upright boniness, she somehow has a voice louder than gunfire.

'Sorry, miss,' I pant. 'I did try but –'

'It's OK,' she says with a patronizing, teeth-sucking grin. 'Just try and make it the last time this week or I'll have to make a note of it.'

I nod. And I'm grateful to the woman for letting me off, but I also kind of wish she wouldn't. She might as well write on the whiteboard and get everyone to copy down that 'Haylah Swinton is just a loser from a needy, broken family who couldn't possibly be expected to function on the same level as normal folk'.

I make my way to the back of the classroom where Kasia and Chloe are sitting, as always. The three of us have been BFFs since primary school, when the only deciding factor for choosing your best friends was who lived nearest to you and who shared your love of My Little Ponies and friendship bracelets. Now we've been together so long we're like an old married couple; we might be better off and happier without each other, but it's just not an option any more: we can't remember how to exist without each other. Or perhaps, because there's three of us, we're more like an old married couple and their faithful old fat dog.

Which would obviously be me.

As I walk past some of the boys, Dylan, a big loudmouth who never misses an opportunity to make fun of me for a laugh, wolf-whistles ironically. His mates snigger. So I turn to them and do a curtsy. Which makes everyone laugh. My insides swell with excitement. This might turn out to be a good day after all.

There's no better feeling than getting a laugh. Nothing beats it. I mean, I've heard a rumour that snogging feels pretty good, but I can't imagine it would make my brain light up nearly as much. Plus, when you make someone else laugh, you don't have to swallow their spit.

Unless you tell a joke to my fat-tongued Auntie Pam.

'Just sit down, Haylah. We don't need a dramatic entrance, thank you,' bellows Mrs Perkins.

'Nice curtsy, Pig,' says Chloe with a giggle as I sit down next to her.

Yep, so there's something I can't keep hidden from you any longer: everyone calls me Pig, OK? I'm all right with it, so you need to get over it quickly so we can move on. It was kinda my doing anyway.

It started when we were all new to 'big school' and trying to figure each other out. Year Seven is like the birth of a dystopian society. Still suffering the aftershock of the cataclysmic event of finishing primary school, we're thrust into fending for ourselves in an unknown and brutal gated community. All individuality is suppressed as, dressed in the Regime's standard-issue uniforms, there's a mad scramble to assign everyone to predetermined categories: geeks, populars, bullies, losers, brains, princesses and so on. Our past lives are forgotten, and in this new dog-eat-dog world we must find a place for ourselves, and fast, otherwise we'll be left alone, friendless and hopeless in the dusty wasteland of the all-weather pitch.

And, when you wear what people see as part of your personality on the outside, like I do, people are quick to jump to conclusions. I was big, so the conclusion drawn was that I was a loser, easy prey for bullies who wanted to get ahead of the game and prove their own strength and superiority over their classmates.

It was standard name-calling at first: Fatso, Fatty, Chubster, Big Fatty Boom Boom – you know, the pre-dictable wit of the underdeveloped Neanderthal brain.

But it wasn't long before one of them made the link between my surname – Swinton – and swine, meaning pig, of course. I started to hear people snorting and whispering 'Pig' as I walked down the corridor. Chloe and Kas said I should just ignore it, but I decided on a different approach. So one day I asked them both to start calling me Pig.

'What? Seriously?'

'Yeah. I actually think it's pretty cool,' I said. 'I'm rebranding myself with a one-word name, like other awesome women before me such as Beyoncé or Pink. Or God.'

'Erm . . . God's not a woman,' said Kas.

'Oh, come off it! Handmade and ran an entire universe while single-parenting a polite and well-behaved son? There's no way a bloke could pull all that off.'

'Fair enough,' said Kas.

'Yeah, but PIG?' Chloe said.

'What?' I'd replied. 'They're intelligent, cute and they taste amazing – I can live with all that.'

After that I made everyone call me Pig, and whenever I heard someone whisper it in the corridor I would turn to them, offer to shake their hand and loudly say, 'Yeah, that's right, my name's Pig. Did you want something?' And they'd realize there was nowhere else to go with the joke. As they shrugged and walked off, my mates would laugh as I threw my hands high into the air and proudly yelled, 'That's right, I *am* Pig, and don't you forget it!' It worked. The bullies gave up on me and moved on to the next obvious prey as I'd made it clear I was no victim. I make the jokes. I am not the joke.

I do remember though that the day I decided I was going to be Pig, I cried myself to sleep.

Now I'm just used to the name. I don't mind it. Not really. At least it's a punchline I wrote.

'Right, class, it's a house assembly now so gather your things up and walk QUIETLY down to the hall, please!' booms Mrs Perkins.

We all take note of her request for quiet for around two seconds, but, as the sound of chair legs scraping the floor and bags being zipped up increases, so too does the laughter, chatter and eventual hysterical yelling at each other across the classroom. Unsurprised by her defeat, Mrs Perkins trots out of the room, rolling her eyes as the class begins to trickle out after her. That's the cool thing with a crappy school like mine – the teachers are about as interested in enforcing the rules as we are in following them.

I notice Chloe's still sitting down, doing her make-up. She wears a lot more than the rest of us. To be honest with you, I haven't really got a clue what I'm doing with the stuff. The last time I tried to put on eyeliner, I sneezed and headbutted the mirror so hard Mum had to take me to A & E with concussion. That was bad, but not as bad as Mum rambling on in the car, saying that the wearing of make-up goes against our feminist principles.

'You're perfectly pretty as you are, Haylah,' she chuntered. 'I don't know why you'd want to plaster your face with that crap just for the sake of what boys might think of you! I mean, come on, we're all about girl power in this family, and then you go and knock yourself out trying to make your eyes look "sexy" because heaven forbid that a boy should look into a girl's eyes and see she's not at least wearing mascara. I mean, *shock, horror*! However would the boy recover from such a gruesome sight?'

I didn't point out to her that, if you follow her argument through, then surely we shouldn't do *anything* to look more attractive to anyone. We shouldn't wash, or wear a bra, or get our hair cut, or wear nice clothes, because true feminists should just present themselves as bedraggled, grotesque, stinky, hairy, saggy scummers. Problem is, you can't really expect anyone to want to be near you then, let alone fancy you.

But I didn't point that out, or the fact that I hadn't actually been putting make-up on to attract boys. I was just bored and was also going to eyeliner on a little Jack Sparrow-esque beard and moustache before sending a selfie to Chloe and Kas with the caption, 'You guys always say I should try wearing more make-up, is this right?' But instead I just softly groaned along to the throbbing in my head.

My mum's a nurse so the injury must have been really bad for her to take me to hospital – you've got to be pretty close to death before she'll give you a bit of Calpol, let alone bother her colleagues with your suffering.

Chloe really knows what she's doing with make-up though, even if she's doing it for dubious reasons (in Mum's book at least). She models herself on her older sister Freya, who's training to be a beauty therapist and is also an actual model. Well, I mean, she says she's a model, but all she's really done is posed for a flyer for a local garage and done some dodgy stuff online under the name 'Booty McTooty'.

Anyway, Freya taught Chloe everything she knows about foundation, contouring, multi-masking, muck-spreading and steamrolling. OK, so I made those last two up, but I mean, what the hell do I know? Feminism and the risk of brain damage aside, until they invent a blusher that makes my cheeks look less like two spacehoppers squashing a ping-pong ball, there seems little point in me wearing make-up.

Chloe always looks gorgeous though. Well – a bit tarty, but gorgeous. Underneath her perfectly styled short blonde bob she has cheekbones you could crack an egg on and her eyebrows are a work of art in themselves. Like two elegant wings of a dove, rather than my unplucked beasts, which look like two hairy caterpillars gearing up for a fight.

While Chloe piles on the eyeshadow, Kasia produces a hairbrush almost the size of a tennis racket from her bag and starts brushing her long dark hair. Kas isn't knock-out gorgeous like Chloe and she doesn't think she's pretty either, but everyone else does. And, yeah, I guess she has a slightly larger than average forehead, but her little chin makes her face heart-shaped, and her permanently narrowed eyes make her look like she's always on the verge of bursting into hysterics.

'Oh God, I forgot it's assembly today. Who's doing it?' she says in her gently accented voice. Oh yeah, she's also Polish and lived in Poland until she was, like, five, and although most of it's gone you can still hear the twang of a distant land in her speech. So she's got that sultry-foreign-accent thing working for her too. It's so unfair. I mean, would it have been *too* much to ask for Mum to make me live in an Eastern European country for a few years when I was younger until I picked up a sexy accent?

'Oh, please say it's not Mr Jacobs talking about the war again,' says Chloe to her reflection in the mirror.

I immediately do my best Mr Jacobs impression – low-voiced, mumbling, wide-eyed and Scottish. 'Imagine yourself there . . . in a trench . . . knee-deep in poop . . . and mud . . . and more POOP . . . You don't know what day it is . . . You can't think straight . . . You can't hear anything above the great rumbling sounds of death and destruction all around you . . . You haven't slept in days . . . That was one hell of a weekend at Glastonbury, I can tell you.'

Kasia and Chloe both laugh, which makes me smile and twinkle a little bit inside.

'Come on, we'd better go,' says Chloe.

In the hall, we're all relieved when Mr Humphrey, our head of house (who tries to make up for his lack of personality with the loudness of his ties), announces that it's the annual house talent show. Basically, each of the school houses picks some idiot to go through to the whole school 'Castle Park's Got Talent' (apparently, not an ironic title) competition at the end of term. And if you're think-ing, *Oooh, 'houses' – how la-di-da*, believe me, it's not. It's just a random splitting of the whole school into three clumps and then calling them 'houses', as if that's going to fool people into thinking this is a posh school like Eton rather than a trashy comprehensive in an under-privileged arse end of Suffolk.

To make matters worse, the houses are named after famous people who lived here, which is fine if you're in Orwell House or Britten House, but they decided to name the third house after a woman and the best they could come up with was Elisabeth Frink, who was some sort of sculptor. Problem is, no one's ever heard of her and Frink is just a naturally funny word. 'Did you get into Frink House?' has now turned into a gross, euphemistic way of guys asking how far their mates got with their girlfriends the night before. So everyone wants to be in Orwell or Britten. Obviously, I'm in Frink.

The competition is all a big embarrassment really. Still, it's better to sit through this than have Mr Jacobs getting us to imagine all our friends being shot or disfigured by shrapnel.

First up is Henry from Year Eight, who's a fellow Frinker and was chosen simply because he was the only one who volunteered. If you're wondering why I didn't, well, in my dreams is one thing, but I could no more get up onstage in front of a room full of people than I could get Noah to eat a plate of broccoli. Both would end up with me crying in a humiliated heap on the floor while being pelted with vegetables.

Henry from Year Eight, on the other hand, was happy to volunteer as he confidently believes he's a great magician.

And, to be fair, he probably would be a great magician if he had normal social skills, a voice that could be heard from more than a metre away, decent props and some actual talent for performing magic tricks. Unfortunately, he doesn't have any of those things.

Words are mumbled, props are broken – and at one point his belt buckle gets caught on the black tablecloth and reveals the stuffed rabbit that's supposed to appear out of a baseball cap in the finale. Instead, he changes the ending to reveal a folded, oversized playing card from his pocket that's supposed to match the card Mr Humphrey randomly chose from a pack earlier. Only when Henry produces the card, it turns out it isn't the right one.

He stares at the card.

We stare at the card.

For a moment, it looks like he's going to cry, so I start clapping loudly, which luckily starts everyone else off and prompts Mr Humphrey to shuffle him offstage saying, 'Well, thank you, Henry, or should I say the Amazing Henry!'

No, everyone thinks, *you really shouldn't*.

Next up is Jinny, a Britten House girl from Year Ten who sings an Adele tune to a karaoke backing track, and it isn't too bad. Not great either, but after the Amazing Henry even a Mediocre Jinny manages to impress.

And then lastly there's Orwell House's offering which, to everyone's surprise, isn't one of the geeks or princesses – it's Leo. A murmuring of wonder and admiration swells around the room as he stands at the side of the stage, waiting to be called on.

Ah, Leo. Everyone knows Leo. He's two years above us and he's just this big, easy-going, cool dude who has a smile that could bring about world peace and a smooth voice you could spread on a crumpet. *Ahhh, Leo.*

'Oooh, it's lovely Leo!' whispers Chloe.

'He's *sooo* yummy,' purrs Kas.

'Ugh, please – you guys sound like the voiceover for a yoghurt advert. Just stop it now,' I say. I mean, sure, I fancy him too, but I'm not going to humiliate myself by owning up to such a hopeless crush. 'What do you think he's doing?'

'Oh God, I hope it's dancing,' says Kas.

'As long as it's Magic Mike-style dancing,' says Chloe.

'Of course,' giggles Kas.

'Seriously, ladies? I mean, how would you like it if boys talked about *you* in that way?' I say.

'Oh God, I hope they do,' says Chloe, with a smile that says she knows she's winding me up.

'Oooh, me too,' says Kas with an equally evil grin. 'I'd love to be objectified.'

I play along. 'Well, it's good to know Emmeline Pankhurst's efforts weren't wasted on you two,' I say in my most over-the-top, sarcastic voice.

'Emmeline who?' says Chloe.

'Pankhurst! Suffragette! Women's Lib!' I whisper-shout. Then, as she and Kas giggle, I realize they're still winding me up.

'Oh, ha ha, very funny,' I say, before we all have to stifle our laughter as Mr Humphrey introduces Leo.

I bet he's going to sing too, I think. *I mean, a popular guy like that doesn't even need actual talent. He only needs to open his mouth and bark, and most of the audience in here will melt.*

'And next up we have Leo Jackson, who's going to perform some stand-up comedy for us this morning.'

Wait, what? I sit bolt upright, like I've just been fully inflated, my eyes wide and fixed on Leo.

'Looks like this is more a show for you then, Pig!' whispers Chloe.

'Shh!' I say as I edge to the front of my chair, eyes never straying from their target.

And, yes, partly it's because it's nice to have an excuse to stare uninterrupted at Leo Jackson, who *is* undeniably (amazingly) good-looking, but mostly it's because I've never seen anyone actually do stand-up comedy live. I've only ever watched it – a *lot* of it – on TV and online before now.

Truth is, I'm kind of obsessed with the funny. I spend hours and hours with comedy and comedians every day. Watching their stand-up acts on the internet, listening to their podcasts and reading any book on comedy and comedians I can get my hands on. And, when I'm not watching and listening to comedy, I'm secretly writing my own material, and (even more secretly) dreaming that one day I might have the courage to actually perform it. Which I probably never will, but I'm hoping that, maybe in a decade or so, I'll have had a complete personality overhaul and be able to stomach the idea of publicly baring my soul onstage, only to have it potentially shattered and rejected.

And funny *is* my soul – it's the core of me. I look for it in everything around me, listen out for it in every conversation. And, when you find the funny in this serious world that is so often full of pain and cruelty, it's like discovering a diamond in a cave of crap. It's precious. Maybe more precious than anything.

Money, beauty, fame, power? Not interested. I just want to get people laughing. To be able to say something, just words, that shoot into someone else's brain, making them feel nothing but happiness for just a moment ... never mind the Amazing Henry – that's *true* magic. And suddenly I find that someone else here shares my love of the funny, and it's only Leo-ruddy-Jackson!

'I didn't know Leo did comedy,' Kasia whispers.

'Shh – shut up, I want to hear!' I whisper-shout back, not taking my eyes off him.

'Oooh, I think Pig's in *luuurve*,' says Chloe.

'Give up now, Pig – he's mega popular. He'd never even speak to us,' says Kasia.

'I know that! Now shut up!'

The hairs on the back of my neck stand up as Leo clears his throat and grasps the microphone. It's a situation I've imagined myself in so many times, and yet even in my imagination I can barely hold the microphone I'm so nervous.

I feel what he must be feeling as some of the butterflies from his stomach make their way through to mine. It must take nerves of steel to stand up in front of a room of people, with no music, no props, no one else to fall back on if you forget your lines: just you, a microphone and an audience you hope to God will find you funny. If you're a bad singer, or magician for that matter, people will still clap at the end, but if you tell jokes, and people don't laugh, no amount of clapping can make up for that.

To be a stand-up comedian you're basically volunteering for possible total public humiliation and shame. Which is why I'm sure I'll never have the nerve to do it.

But Leo does. And, as I watch him bravely grab the microphone, it feels like someone has just scooped out my insides and replaced them with warm, energetic kittens, which is horribly unnerving yet oddly pleasing.

I've never met anyone who loves comedy as much as I do. I've never met anyone bonkers enough to want to put themselves through this, just to make people laugh.

It's ridiculous, I know, but in this moment I feel that I *get* him, probably more than anyone else ever could, and that, if he knew me, he'd definitely *get* me too.

And I realize that if he's good, if he makes me laugh, I may well fall in love with Leo Jackson right here and now.

Which, what with him being the most popular guy in school and me being, well, me, probably isn't the best idea in the world.

Oh, please don't be good, Leo. Please don't be good.

THREE

But of course Leo is good.

More than good. Amazing.

He must be nervous, but you can hardly tell. With one hand in his pocket, he casually takes the microphone out of its stand and holds it underneath his big warm grin. It's a smile that starts at one side, and then there's this adorable beat before the other side rises up to join it. It's a smile accompanied by his expressive upturned eyebrows that turn it from arrogant to vulnerable and cheeky. It's not a smile that makes you think he's full of himself, it's a smile that makes you think he's full of you. It's a smile that makes everyone in the room think it's especially for them and them alone. It's a smile that makes you think everything's going to be OK. And it immediately gets the audience on his side. Of course everyone's already on his side anyway. It is Leo after all.

He takes a deep breath and unnecessarily says, 'Hi, I'm Leo.'

His friends at the back of the hall break in on cue with whoops and cheers.

He begins talking slow and low, not rushing it, not tripping up over any words and not afraid to use his arms in massive gestures to emphasize certain phrases or leave big pauses at the end of jokes which the room happily fills with laughter and cheers. I knew Leo was popular, but I just thought it was because of his looks. Where the hell did he get this comedic confidence from? And, if he has any going spare, can I have some?

He starts with a few one-liners, funny ones, but it's when he gets into the anecdotal stuff that he really hits his stride.

'OK, so recently I turned sixteen . . .'

His friends whoop. He nods, encouraging them.

'Yeah, thanks, but I dunno, I'm not so sure it's such a great thing. I mean, I'm not an adult yet – that's eighteen, right? So instead I'm in this weird *twilight* zone between childhood and adulthood.

'I'm like a half-man, half-kid mutant. Like, I still play video games, but I've started to tidy up the consoles afterwards.

'I still eat Coco-Pops sandwiches, but now I'm a *little* bit disgusted with myself when I do.'

Oh God, he's deliciously pathetic and self-deprecating too. If only he'd been totally up himself, then I could have shrugged it off as a git-crush, but this . . . Now I just wanna crawl into his school jumper with him and be his permanent hug.

The laughter's coming thick and fast now from all around the hall.

'Wow – he's really good!' whispers Chloe.

'Yeah, stop drooling, Pig – it's never gonna happen!' says Kasia, nudging me.

'*Shut up!*' I hiss, not wanting to miss a word from Leo. And also maybe wiping some drool from my chin.

'And I have some "rights" now,' he continues. 'Like, legally. Yeah, I was checking this stuff out online. I have a list and everything.'

He delves into his pocket, and produces a scrap of paper.

'It's exciting stuff. I mean what fifteen-year-old doesn't desperately look forward to their next birthday when they can finally join a trade union, choose their own GP and buy premium bonds. Rock and roll, right?'

He throws a hand in the air, then paces along the front of the stage as if it's his natural habitat, like talking to a room full of people and trying to make them laugh is the easiest thing in the world.

'OK, so they're mostly a bit dull, but there's a few that *are* interesting, like this one – I can't drive a car yet but *legally* I *can* pilot a glider. That's right, I can *fly an aircraft* in the *actual* sky above people's *heads*. I mean, whoever wrote that law had *clearly* never met a sixteen-year-old boy. Cos I'm guessing that to be a *successful* pilot – and by "*successful*" I mean one that doesn't crash, killing everyone in a huge fireball – I'm thinking you need to be quick-thinking, alert and intelligent.

'Hello! Sixteen-year-old boys are the *opposite* of this! We're uncoordinated, grunting, hyperactive apes! We take stupid risks – we think we know *everything,* but we don't actually know *anything*!

'I mean, seriously, does this sound like someone who should be piloting an aircraft? PEOPLE ARE GOING TO DIE!'

I glance around the room as everyone explodes into more laughter. And, even though I don't know him and have had nothing to do with this, I kind of feel weirdly proud of him.

'But another pretty cool, though completely mental "right" I've got now is that I'm legally allowed to change my name – to anything, pretty much. I mean, I can just fill out a form and – *boom* – change my name to Handsome McSexy or Lord Massivepants or Wolverine Lovebeast. Or, just to piss off my dad, I've been thinking of changing my name to, like, the *whitest* name I can come up with. My dad's a very proud black man and I'd just love to see the look on his face when I tell him I've changed my name to Horace Ponsonby-Smythe.'

Everyone's in hysterics now and Leo's mates are whooping and hollering as he thanks the audience for being 'so awesome'. He's smiling and he looks at ease, like this is what he was made to do. Like the laughter is feeding his soul. And, as he walks offstage, I realize I don't want him to go.

I want to see more of him, hear more of him.

I want him to make me laugh again.

I want to make him laugh.

An electric shiver runs down the length of my spine at just the thought of his eyes on me, his laughter being the result of something I've said. I want to make him laugh more than anyone else I've ever known.

I clap so much my hands sting, and just before he reaches the stage curtain he turns, and I swear he looks right at me. Which seals the deal.

I'm in love with Leo Jackson.

Hopelessly,

        stupidly,

                in love.

Balls.

FOUR

Of course I remember quite quickly after leaving the hall that this is ridiculous.

Leo is good-looking, popular, two years older than me, and is no more likely to look at me, let alone talk to me, than he is to sprout wings and declare himself the Fairy King.

And the thing is, that didn't bother me yesterday. Yesterday I was quite happy admiring him from a distance like everyone else, but now . . . now it's different. And all because . . . what? He made me laugh? I mean, is that how it's going to be from now on – I fall in love with every guy who makes me giggle? Because that just sounds exhausting.

And, look, I'm just not *that* girl – I'm not the girl who has pathetic crushes. I'm not the girl who draws pink love hearts in the back of her schoolbooks with boys' initials inscribed in glitter pen inside them. I'm REALLY not the girl who fantasizes about a Disney ending where magical sparkles surround my floating body as it transforms into a beautiful princess and the prince puts down his microphone and picks me up instead, passionately snogging me while fireworks explode behind us. Seriously – I AM NOT THAT GIRL!

But, oh, he was funny.

In fact, he was *the* funniest person I've ever seen in real life. I mean, sure, Mum's funny, Noah's unintentionally hilarious and my friends make me laugh a lot – but Leo was different. He was actually *doing* comedy successfully, and I just, I don't know, I guess it's like suddenly this world – the world of comedy that I love and always dreamed about being a part of in the future, when I'm at college or whatever – has just zoomed in closer like a rocket. A Leo-rocket I want to jump on and let it launch me right off into space.

No, wait, that sounds wrong.

'Are you all right, Pig?' Chloe asks me as she leans over to copy my work.

'Leo-rocket!' I blurt before my brain tells my mouth to shut up.

'What?' says Chloe.

'What? Nothing! I didn't say anyth– What?'

She laughs as I look back down at my maths book and struggle to stop my cheeks from glowing red.

Stupid cheeks.

I always let Chloe copy my work in maths. I'm not great at it or anything, but I'm OK, which is a lot better than Chloe. Kasia's *really* good – so good she's not even in this class with us: she's been siphoned off into the advanced maths set. In fact, she's in the advanced set for everything. I'm not sure if it's because she's an actual genius or because she just works really hard, but either way we massively take the piss out of her for it. As all good friends should.

Mum says I *could* be in the top set for everything too, if I only 'knuckled down' to my schoolwork instead of thinking up jokes all the time. But then where's the fun in that?

'You don't mind, do ya?' Chloe says as she scribbles down into her book exactly what's in mine. I don't even think she reads what she's writing. I genuinely think I could write 'I, Chloe Jenkins, smell of rotten hamster poo' over and over and she'd still happily copy it all down and proudly hand it in, possibly with a 'nailed it!' wink to Mr Haynes as she did so.

'Course I don't mind. You can't help being a big old thicko,' I say with a wink.

Chloe twirls her perfectly styled hair between her fingers and laughs.

'Oh, don't look now,' she says suddenly. 'Stevie's looking this way.'

Of course I do look now, which is exactly what she wants me to do, and, sure enough, over the other side of the classroom, staring at Chloe, is the tiny, spiky-haired Stevie. A boy neither of us has ever heard speak, let alone had a conversation with. He's holding his maths book up in front of his face and peeking over the top of it. Dylan, at the desk behind him, seems to be doing exactly the same thing. They both look away sheepishly when I glance over. *Pathetic.*

'Yep, you're right,' I say.

She gives a tiny squeal of excitement. 'It must be working!'

'What?'

'My sister says if you want the guy of your dreams . . .'

I gape at her. 'Hang on. Seriously? *Stevie's* the "guy of your dreams"?'

'Yeah!'

'Little Spiky Stevie?' I glance over at him again, tilting my head to the side and squinting, trying to work out what it is that Chloe sees, but I just can't. I'm still just looking at the pocket-sized, nervous boy with ridiculous mountain-range hair on a head hunched lower than his shoulders as he cowers behind his maths book. When I look at him, my overriding feeling is not one of passion, but rather one of concern for his welfare as I notice that the window above his head is open and I can only hope that a gust of wind doesn't rush in and flatten the boy.

'Yeah! I must have told you I fancied him?'

'I may have chosen to block it out . . .'

Chloe sweeps her hair behind her ear, gracefully ignoring me. 'AS I WAS SAYING – to get the guy, you do this thing where you kind of ignore them, then give them just a sideways glance every two days. Drives them *crazy* apparently. Must be working.'

'Yeah,' I murmur as I look over at him again. And I really don't think this frail boy could be 'driven crazy' by anything – though possibly, at a push, mildly unhinged.

I sometimes wonder if Chloe intentionally makes dating more complicated than it needs to be. Unlike me, she's pretty and popular and could easily go out with who-ever she wanted, but where's the fun in that? Much more interesting to pretend there's sport in it.

'The thing is, Chlo, ignoring him, not ignoring him – I don't think it's going to make all that much difference, to be honest. I think what you're missing is the fact that you could pick your nose and wipe it on their faces, and most guys in our year would think that was just adorable and want to date you more.'

'That's rubbish, Pig,' she purrs, glowing from the compliment.

'It's not, and FYI I think Dylan might have the hots for you too,' I say.

'Eew, not Dylan.'

'What's wrong with Dylan? I mean, he's a bit of a loudmouth, I guess, and he seems to hate me, but he's kinda funny and he's gotta be more interesting than *Stevie*.'

She waves this away. 'Dylan's way too big for me – he's like six foot, right? And pretty wide too. Which is weird because he's Chinese.'

'And?' I probably don't want to know where this is going, but, like a 'top seventeen pictures of bad celebrity facelifts, the last one will make you heave!' list, I can't help but click for more.

'Well, they're normally pretty . . . compact, right?'

'I gotta tell you, Chlo, I've got a worrying racist alarm going off in my head right now.'

'What? I'm not being *racist*. If anything, I'm being the opposite of racist – I'm saying he's not Chinese *enough* for me. I think his mum's Chinese and his dad's English, so maybe he gets his size from his dad. I'm saying that if he was more, you know, *fully* Chinese he'd be smaller and *more* my type, got it?'

'Wow,' I say.

'What?'

'Just wow,' I say, shooting her one of my most disapproving stares.

'OK, you're right, I'm sorry!' she says, her hands held up in surrender.

Shocking racial stereotyping aside, it doesn't seem to cross Chloe's mind for a moment that judging boys based on their *size* might piss me off a little bit. And this just pisses me off more. Especially now I've got the whole Leo thing on my mind. It reminds me that looks, body shape and size are what matter to most people. I don't stand a chance. Not with Leo. Not with anyone probably. And Chloe doesn't get that – how could she? The world of boyfriends and dating: for her, it's all there for the taking. All the pop songs we listen to about gorgeousness and perfection, and love at first sight and being sexy on the dance floor, they're written for her. She can be a part of that world. Not me. I don't belong there. Never will. And, thanks to being a strident feminist, I used to be totally fine with that. But now, with Leo . . .

'Seriously, though,' she says, 'you OK? You've been . . . *weird* since this morning.'

'Weird? Weird how?' I say, weirdly.

She leans back in her chair and looks me up and down as I try to look anywhere but in her direction. I do *not* want her to know about my Leo thing. It's a hopeless, pathetic lost cause. *I* know that, but the last thing I need is to be told that by Chloe.

'Guilty-weird,' she says, 'and maybe a little bit creepy-weird.'

'I don't know what you mean, Chlo,' I gabble. 'I'm just, y'know, getting on with my Thursday. Feeling all Thursday-ey, I suppose. I mean, Thursday's a weird day, isn't it? It's neither one thing nor the other. Friday's got that Friday feeling, and the weekend's the weekend, right? Monday and Tuesday have the fresh, beginning-of-the-week vibe going on, Wednesday's the hill of the week, then you get past that and you know things are picking up. I mean, it's all feet off pedals coasting towards the weekend, right! Except then you've gotta get through the Billy-no-mates dullard that is Thursday. So, you know, if I'm being weird, then that's all it is. I'm lost in the half-baked cloudy crap of the nothing that is Thursday.'

She laughs. 'OK, now you're just being normal Pig-weird again. That's fine,' and she carries on with the copying.

But, with Chloe thrown off the scent, my mind drifts back to Leo. And suddenly – without my permission – it concocts a Leo-based daydream.

He's onstage at a big comedy club, bringing the house down, and at the end of his set he introduces me as the next amazing act. I smile as I pass him and grab the mic.

Stop! This is tragic and ludicrous.

I snap myself out of my imagination and get back to dividing fractions, knowing that whatever I don't get done in the lesson I'll just have to finish as homework tonight.

But it's only so long before my brain tires of reality and slips back into the warm embrace of the unreal again.

This pattern repeats itself all day. Every time my thoughts are left to their own devices, they delve back into the daydream, each time making edits and improvements.

In English, daydream-Leo winks at me, having spent longer introducing me than on his own set.

Stop it.

Instead of concentrating on faking parental letters to get five schoolmates out of PE in the afternoon (my ability to fake grown-up penmanship regularly earns me two quid a letter), the daydream fills my mind again, and the audience chants for me before I come onstage, with Leo longingly reaching for my hand as I pass him.

Stop it!

I say goodbye to Chloe and Kas and head off to pick up Noah from after-school club. But the daydream gets more detailed and enjoyable with each step, and now has the beginnings of an elaborate subplot involving various famous comedians all begging me to be the next presenter of *QI*.

By the time I've picked up Noah I'm being presented with an award for Best Comedy Newcomer by Leo morphed into compère. As I come onstage, he holds my hands and we kiss for ages to thunderous applause from the audience, before I have them all in stitches with my first joke.

Seriously – just stop it! I really try to will myself as I indulge in this final version while walking Noah home. All the while, Noah does his best to yank me back to his own twisted version of reality by firing his nonsensical questions at me.

'Why do dogs not wear shoes?'

'Why don't bald babies wear wigs?'

'Can Jesus fly? And does he live with Santa?'

And on and on.

My annoyance with him at least makes me feel less guilty about dragging him a slightly longer way home that happens to pass by Leo's front door.

I only know it's Leo's front door because me and the girls almost gatecrashed his party last year when it got out to everyone that his parents were away and it was an open house. When we got there though, it was really quiet. So, like a spangly, crop-top-wearing James Bond, Chloe led the way as we stealthily crept up to Leo's window. Our adrenalin-fuelled giggles were soon dampened as, through it, we could just see Leo and a handful of his mates sitting round a table playing poker. Not even strip poker, just poker. Or it could have been any card game, I suppose. They might have been playing Snap for all I know.

Chloe swore a lot and called them all 'a bunch of dullard fun-sponges' and we all stomped off back to hers to play Scrabble. Which, yes, OK, sounds as lame as Snap, but at least it was our own version called Blue Scrabble, which is basically Scrabble, but you can only put down rude words. I remember laughing uncontrollably as Kas tried to convince us that, in the right context, her word 'gazebo' could be extremely filthy. So actually it turned out to be a pretty good night.

And, now I think back on it, I find it so cute and classy that Leo *could* have yet *didn't* throw the big, clichéd, wild teen party. But at the time it wasn't quite the high-school, rock-and-roll, life-changing evening we, or at least Chloe, had hoped for.

Anyway, that's why I've been here before. Not because of some seedy stalker intentions. They're new to today.

And it's only now that I notice that this is a much nicer road than the one we live on. But then this is Leo – of course he'd live in a road where people don't have their Christmas lights up all year round, a road where stolen, wheel-less bikes aren't left in bushes, a road that you can confidently walk down without being called a 'slag' by an eight-year-old sitting on a vandalized postbox.

'But why are we going this way?' Noah moans.

'It's a short cut,' I say.

'What's a shot gut?'

'It just means it's quicker, OK?'

'My legs hurt. They feel heavy,' he says, reaching down to grab and raise each knee at every step.

'Look, I'll take your bags, all right?'

He hands me his huge assortment of book bags and rucksacks stuffed with the soft toys and plastic figures he insists on taking into school every day, along with stacks of today's 'drawings', which will be crap as always yet Mum will stick them on the fridge anyway, and a library-load of books we're supposed to read with him before tomorrow. Like that's gonna happen.

And now that I'm laden, sweaty and panting, like a knackered old bag lady, I'm beginning to regret my decision to walk home via Leo's house, but here we are all the same. Luckily, he's nowhere to be seen. I mean, it's not like I'd talk to him even if I did see him.

So what the numbnuts am I doing here? Idiot.

We pass by Leo's front door. A lovely, modern wooden thing. Not like our dirty white plastic, flowery-patterned glass monstrosity. I allow myself to stare at it for a moment. It's his *actual* front door. He's probably in . . . I mean, I don't know but . . . probably. Just the thought that he might be makes my stomach thundercrack into a thousand tiny, beautiful, vomiting butterflies.

Oh, for the love of God, stop it.

FIVE

When we finally get home, I haul Noah's bags through the front hall and remind Noah to 'shh' in case Mum is asleep.

'I know!' he shouts back.

I'm about to shush him again when I hear, 'It's OK, guys, I'm up!'

Mum's in the living room. I can't see her yet, but already I know she'll be lying on the sofa in her checked pyjamas, listening to Radio 4, dozens of weight-loss-company branded food wrappers scattered around her.

Noah runs in ahead of me, yelling, 'Mummy! Mummy!' before launching himself on to her.

I follow after him. She's wearing her pyjamas with the stripes rather than the checks, but other than that I had the picture spot on. Still, the sight makes me smile as I flop down on the sofa and cuddle up to her just as Noah's doing. There's plenty of her to go around, and for a moment we're just one big bubbly warm ball of squidge.

'Aww, I missed you guys!' she says, throwing her thick arms round us and drawing us closer until her brushed-cotton-clad boobs are squashed up against my face.

'Aww, Mum!' I complain. I can't breathe all that well, but actually it's oddly comforting.

I always feel sorry for people with thin mothers. Slender, minimal-chested, angular women may be what the catwalk prefers, but what use are they when all you need is a warm, bosomy, healing Mum-hug? I guess it's just whatever you're used to, but I'll take my soft and cuddly mum any day of the week.

Even if it does mean an awkward faceful of tits every now and again.

'Anyway, how could you miss us?' I say, easing myself out of her boob folds. 'You only saw us last night, crazy woman.'

'I know, I know, but these night shifts, they seem to go on forever, you know?'

'I know,' I say. 'You on again this evening?'

''Fraid so, darling. That OK?'

'Yeah, of course. How was work last night?' I say.

'Oh, you know, same old. Oh, except . . .' Mum starts laughing at her own story before she tells it.

'What?' I say, already laughing a little myself, even though I have no idea what she's about to say, but I love Mum's funny stories. Her eyes light up and she always starts talking really quickly, like I do most of the time, and she does the voices brilliantly.

'So this posh woman came in with some serious "water-works" issues,' she says and starts laughing hysterically.

'Mum, I've gotta say, as punchlines go, that's not your best.'

'No, I know, bless her – but I had to get her to give a urine sample, and she took one look at the little bottle and said, "Are you seriously expecting me to channel a tsunami into a pipette?" So I explain that even if she can catch *some* of the downpour, that's good enough for us, so she tuts and waddles off to the bathroom and returns ashen-faced. When I ask what's wrong, she says, "There's something you should know. I consumed a Berocca earlier. And it *may* have had a *slight* effect on my . . . output."

'And then, I swear to God, the tube of wee she hands me was *glowing* bright yellow and I couldn't resist it so, in my best Yoda voice, I said, 'Peed a lightsabre, you have.'

Mum and me both lie back on the sofa in hysterics as Noah looks on, a little confused but chuckling along indulgently anyway.

'And what did she say?' I manage to get out.

Mum's still laughing so hard, she can hardly get her words out. 'I don't know – I had to duck down behind the nurses' desk to hide my laughter while Sue took over!'

'Well, it's good to know you take your nursing responsibilities so seriously, Mother!'

'I know, I'm terrible, but you've got to get through the nights somehow, right? Especially as I really do miss you guys so much. How're you both doing?'

Her tone has changed a bit now, and she's not laughing. I wish she wouldn't worry about us; we manage just fine.

'We're OK, aren't we, Noah?'

'I'm starving!' he yells. 'What's for tea? What's for tea?'

Mum makes a noise that's part groan, part sigh, part laugh; a noise which means, 'I'm exhausted, but I'll do this because I love you.'

'Don't worry, I'll make something,' I say.

'Do you mind, sweetie?' She's clearly relieved, and settles back down on the sofa, with Noah scrambling all over her.

'It's fine,' I say, walking to the kitchen.

The maths homework can wait till later.

After we inhale some fish fingers and baked beans in front of the TV, Mum gets ready for work and I get Noah in the bath.

'Have you ever seen a chimpanzee in the bath?' he asks as he gets in.

This is completely out of the blue. We haven't been talking about chimpanzees. We haven't watched any TV shows about chimpanzees. We've been living in a totally chimpanzee-free environment, but this seems to be how Noah's four-year-old mind works. Totally randomly.

'No,' I say, 'I've never seen a chimpanzee in the bath.'

'Me neither,' he says wistfully as his little round belly disappears underneath the bubbles. 'Can I have a biscuit when I get out?'

And I wonder if the whole cute chimpanzee question was just a way to soften me up so I'd OK a biscuit.

'No, it's bedtime after the bath, Noah. Mum said no more food this evening.'

'I want a biscuit.'

'No.'

'Bis-KIT!'

'No!'

It occurs to me that this exchange could go on for many hours, so I think of a way to change the record.

'Hey, Noah!' I say, like I have something really interesting to show him.

'What?' he says, trying to remain angry about the whole biscuit thing, but finding it hard to hide his interest in whatever I'm offering.

'What noise does a chimpanzee make when he's getting into a hot bath?'

'I don't know, Haylah. I told you, I've never seen one!' he huffs.

'No, no, it's a joke,' I explain.

'Oh!' he says, the anger and biscuit frustration fading away in an instant. He doesn't understand jokes but loves them nonetheless. 'OK . . . what noise does a chimpanzee make when he gets into a hot bath?'

'*Ooo ooo ooo ahh ahh ahh*,' I say.

Silence. Then eventually:

'Ohhhhh, I get it!' he says. 'Because when the water's hot I make that noise, and chimpanzees just make that noise anyway . . . so it's funny!'

'Well . . . yeah. I mean, ideally you'd just laugh rather than deconstructing the joke, but yes.'

'I have a joke,' he says.

'Oh great! Go on then,' I say, knowing full well he hasn't. He likes the idea of them, but hasn't actually got a clue how they work or what they're for. Much like me with exercise equipment.

'What . . . does –' his eyes go up to the ceiling as he thinks of something that to his mind sounds like a joke – 'a chicken say when it gets into the bath?'

'Noah, why do most of your jokes involve chickens?'

'They're funny!'

'OK. I don't know. What does a chicken say when it gets into the bath?'

'*Bok bok bok bok bok.*'

He looks at me expectantly for a laugh.

'Hmm, that's not *really* a joke, Noah,' I suggest.

'Why not?'

And, like an idiot throwing pound coins into a change machine at an arcade and thinking, *This time I'm bound to win big!* I have one more go at explaining the concept of comedy to him.

'It's just not – it doesn't work. You've gotta take one expected thing and turn it into something unexpected that still works. Urgh. Look . . . OK . . . a chicken and a frog walk into a library –'

'Then what happened?' he asks as if I'm telling him a factual anecdote from my day.

'The chicken points around the room saying, "*Bok bok bok bok*," and the frog says, "*Reddit reddit reddit*." '

'Then what did they do?'

'No – that's the joke! Because they're in a library. Full of books. And the chicken sounds like he's saying, "Book,

book, book," and the frog sounds like he's saying, "Read it, read it, read it . . ." Get it?'

He stares at me and then actually laughs for a bit, though it's clear he doesn't really know why he's laughing.

'Kind of!' he says, still laughing away merrily. 'OK, OK, I have another one!'

'Have you thought of it already?' I say.

'Yes,' he says confidently.

'Go on then.'

'Knock knock.'

'Oooh, a knock-knock joke – classic. Who's there?' I answer.

'Chicken Poo,' he says, already giggling at his own comedy genius.

'Chicken Poo who?' I say.

'Ha ha haaaa! You said chicken poo!' he says, splashing his hands down in comedic triumph.

'Brilliant,' I say as Mum bursts through the door, her hair tied back, glasses on, looking proper nursey . . . although also somehow different, but I can't put my finger on it.

'I'm off now, sweeties,' she says, leaning down to kiss us both. 'You lock the door after me, OK, Haylah? You know the drill – call me if it's an emergency, and there's always Hal next door if you need someone quick, OK?'

'I know, Mum! It's fine – go, go nurse people. Ya big-boobed hero, you!'

She smiles. 'Love you guys!' Then I realize what's different about her.

'Hang on, Mum. Are you … did you know you're wearing lipstick?' I say as if pointing out to someone that they have spinach in their teeth.

She immediately looks shifty. 'Well, yes …' she stammers. 'The shop was giving them out for free when I bought my foot-fungal cream and a Venus lady razor. Just thought I'd slap some on. Anyway, gotta go – love you both, byeee!' And she quickly sweeps herself out of the door and down the stairs.

'A lipstick AND a razor?' I shout after her. 'You're shaving your legs again! Does that mean I can start now too?'

'No!' she calls brightly back to me before we hear the door closing behind her.

Mum never normally shaves her legs, or wears make-up, at least not since Dad left. And whenever I've begged her to let me start shaving my legs, as it's bad enough that they resemble two wide tree trunks, to the point where if I dare to wear shorts in the summer small children do bark rubbings on them, so it might be nice if they weren't covered in a thick layer of fur as well, she's always said no. Then given me the old faithful, 'a true feminist doesn't conform to society's pressures of physical beauty just to please the male onlooker' routine. Which is fine until you get changed for PE and your mates compare your bushy legs to their dad's. Or Chewbacca's. Or Chewbacca's dad's. But, before I can consider Mum's traitorous preening activities any further, Noah starts squirting me in the face with a miniature water pistol.

'Aww, Noah!' I say, wiping the soapy water out of my eyes, but he stops my anger in its tracks by poking out his little bottom lip and doing his big sad-eyes face. 'What is it?' I ask.

'I don't want Mummy to go,' he says.

'I know. But she's only at work, and she'll be back in the morning. Come on, let's do your hair and get you out.'

I finally manage to persuade him to let me shampoo his hair by saying the word 'shampoo' very slowly, with a big gap between each syllable. It's truly amazing how much mileage you can get from the word 'poo' with a four-year-old. Then I dry him and read a book and he asks for one last joke before sleepytime.

'OK, one more,' I say. 'What does a cat like to listen to?'

'I don't know – what does a cat like to listen to?'

'Meow-sic.'

'Ha! Like "meow" because it's a cat and music so . . .'

'Meow-sic,' I say again.

'You funny, Haylah,' he says as his eyes start to droop. 'You should be a comedy.'

'Do you mean comedian? Do you think so?' I say, a bit too thrilled and possibly taking the career advice of a four-year-old a little too seriously.

'Yeah, you should . . . do more funny.'

'Yeah, I mean, I always wanted to, one day, you know. But you're right, I should just go for it.'

Remind me why I'm putting so much faith in the counsel of someone who thinks cheese is a fruit . . .

'Yeah,' he slurs with his eyes firmly shut.

'Because how else is Leo going to notice me, right?'

'Right,' he mumbles.

'OK, I'm going to do it. I'll find a way to make him laugh, to show him I'm funny too. Then he'll notice me. You're a genius. Thanks, Noah.'

And I kiss him on the forehead, but he doesn't know because he's already asleep.

SIX

I sit at my desk in my room, a fresh page of my notebook in front of me, pen poised over it. Every day since I was about ten, I've written down the funny stuff that happened that day, or funny stuff that was said, or funny stuff I thought of. A bit like a diary, I suppose, but without the serious and boring bits.

I flick through the last few weeks, stopping to read a few of the entries that make me smile.

Tonight Noah referred to Lemsip as 'Calpol Coffee' and his big toe as the 'thumb of the foot'. I think he might be a genius.

It occurs to me today that burps are worse than farts. We all know where farts come from so frankly it's unsurprising that they smell bad. But burping, that's from the place we eat, talk, kiss, smile. At least a fart is honest: it knows what it is and where it comes from. There's an integrity to a fart. But a burp is basically just farting through your face. And there's something truly gruesome about that.

Noah's joke today — 'What does a wee in the morning?
A chicken.'

Kas after a jogger ran past us — 'If I ever wear patterned
leggings, just shoot me.'

One-liner idea:
  Everything's going wrong at the moment. Even our kettle isn't
working. Oh well, when it rains, it pours.
  Just be nice if it worked in nice weather too, y'know?

Noah in playground talking to the mum of a small boy.
  Noah: 'How old is he?'
  Mother: 'Three.'
  Noah (wistfully): 'Ah. I used to be three.'
  Surely you have to have lived through at least a decade before
you're allowed to be nostalgic?

I write down Mum's 'peed a lightsabre' story and Noah's
random 'Have you ever seen a chimpanzee in the bath'
question and then I stare at the page. Normally, what I
write down comes pretty easily, but now, after seeing Leo's
set, my mind's a blank. Nothing in this notebook is
anywhere near funny enough to make Leo laugh, to make
him notice me. I need to write some new stuff, proper
stand-up stuff, something that *he'd* find funny. And that
seems impossible.

Funny, think funny, think . . .

I need a snack. That'll help me think.

I go to the kitchen, eat some toast, come back to my desk, sit, hold my pen . . . *think funny, think funny, think* . . . and before I know it I slip back into a Leo-daydream. Only this time we're at school. I crack a killer joke to my friends in the corridor just as he walks past, and he doubles up with laughter, pushes past Kas and Chloe and takes my hands, tears still streaming down his face. 'That was the funniest thing I've ever heard – you're a comedy genius! We should totally hang out and maybe get married and stuff.' And on 'stuff' he winks at me and . . .

What the hell am I doing? This is bat-crap crazy!

I mean, what's the actual plan here? I just run up to him in the hallway and tell him a joke that makes him laugh so much he'll immediately propose? And since when is that even a thing I want anyway? As we've already established, I'm not the misty-eyed, sappy girl who wraps a white pillowcase round her head, imagining bridal bliss – that is NOT me!

Plus, it's unlikely I'll ever have the courage to look him in the eye, let alone get a sentence out, let ALONE make it funny. At best, all he's going to see is a random fat girl waddle up to him and mumble something before fainting and falling heavily to the floor.

This is just stupid. Numptiness on an epic scale. What was I thinking?

So I get my maths book out of my bag and do my homework instead until my phone rings. It's Chloe asking to copy my maths homework.

'So, how about we do a swap?' she says, almost singing the word 'swap'.

'What kind of *swa-ap* . . .?' I sing back.

'You give me the answers –' she puts on a strange, steamy voice like a bad drag act – 'and I'll give you some information you might like.'

Oh God, it's going to be something about Leo. This is mortifying.

But I pretend to remain clueless and breezy.

'Sounds interesting – what information? Cos if it's a new skincare routine, forget it. I already have an amazing one – Noah comes in every morning and smears random gloop and snot over my face, I scream and then wipe it off with a sock. Works wonders.'

'No, no, it's good – it's about *Le-o*.' She sings the word 'Leo'.

Ugh, I knew it!

'What? Why would I be interested in him?' I bluster, my stomach swooping all over the place. 'Leo who? Why would I – What are you talking about? What information? Not that I'm interested, but what? I don't care – whatever – WHAT?'

She's laughing now. 'Well, obviously you're not interested at all or anything, so I guess you wouldn't want to know that his dad runs a music and comedy open-mic night once a month at his pub on East Street! AND that apparently Leo always performs there, so, if you wanted to watch him onstage and drool over him *again*, he'll be there next Friday night!'

I try to get my jaw to ascend and rejoin the rest of my face.

'I thank you,' says Chloe. And I can almost hear her bowing. 'Now pay me in maths, woman.'

'OK, but wait. Firstly, how do you know that?'

Chloe sighs, but I can tell she's enjoying every moment of this. She loves knowing stuff before everyone else. 'You know my sister's going out with Jake?'

'Sulky Jake, yeah . . .'

'Well, he plays guitar at this pub sometimes. He had a flyer for next Friday night and it says at the bottom, "featuring the comedy stylings of London Young Comic of the Year runner-up, Leo Jackson".'

'Young Comic of the Year? Wow,' I say, even more in awe of Leo.

'Well, *runner-up*, but yeah, pretty cool, right? Doesn't it just make you *luuurve* him even more!' Chloe's stupid, low husky voice now sounds more like a late-night, cheesy radio DJ.

I roll my eyes. 'Shut up. And anyway it's in a *pub* – those places where adults drink and schoolkids aren't made to feel all that welcome.'

I really can't see how this is going to work. But I SO want it to.

'Look, it's a family-friendly pub – as long as we go in with an adult and don't try to order beer or anything, it's fine! Tell your mum you're coming round to mine for the night and my sister will take us.'

Like a puppy when his owner shouts 'walkies' I can barely contain my excitement as we make our plans, though I manage to stop myself weeing on the carpet. We're going to get Kas to come along too and, as long as Mum lets me out for the night, we're totally going to a pub to see Leo perform!

Obviously I don't let Chloe know I'm quite so obsessively enthusiastic.

'I mean, yeah, sure – it sounds like a laugh, right?' I say.

'Uh-huh, whatever, Pig,' she says, not buying my nonchalance. 'It's gonna be so much fun! Now pay up. C'mon, question number fifteen . . .'

I read her my maths answers. She ribs me a little more about Leo and tells me she hopes Stevie will be at the pub that night. I don't tell her that I'm still totally flummoxed by her obsession with a guy who shows little signs of life, let alone personality. Whatever floats your boat, I guess. And Stevie's nothing if not a floater.

Kas and me have never had actual boyfriends, me because no one's interested so I've never been interested back and Kas because, for all her talk of boys and fancying them, she's actually pretty shy around them and wouldn't really know what to do if she got one. Like when I really wanted a Suzy's Salon Hair Crimper for Christmas because all the other girls had one: I soon realized it was actually just a stupid bit of tat I was scared to turn on. All it did was make me hungry for crinkle-cut crisps.

But Chloe has always had boys from our year dashing up to her and saying, 'My mate fancies you!' before running off, and sometimes she'll agree to 'date' one of them, but that normally means holding hands with the guy at lunchtimes and an occasional snog at a party. The fact is, none of us really know what we're doing with boys, although Kas and Chloe always seem to have their eye on some guy or another and gossip about how utterly 'dreamy' their unsuspecting prey is. But me, well, it's probably just another clichéd consequence of having a selfish prick for a dad, but I've never really seen the point of boyfriends.

Until now. Until Leo and his comedy came into my world and turned it all upside down. And the thing is, there's no point telling Chloe and Kas about it because I know I haven't got a chance. I'm not a complete spanner – I don't think for a moment he'll ever be my 'boyfriend'.

But if I could just make him laugh. If I could just get him to *see* me, to notice me, because I'm funny, like him . . . maybe that would be enough. Maybe that would be amazing.

But it's never gonna happen. Still, to see him do stand-up again, at the pub, would be something. In fact, that would be chuffin' brilliant.

I feel a bit better. I go back to the notebook and actually manage to write down some half-decent jokes – stuff I could say onstage (if I ever had the balls to perform); stuff that maybe Leo might like, might laugh at (if I ever had the balls to talk to him).

And I keep trying to tell myself that it doesn't matter. That it's enough to write this stuff down, just for me.

For my daydreams. For my imaginary comedy life.

Still, I wish I had the balls.

God I want balls.

No, wait, that sounds wrong.

SEVEN

The next day at school, Kas and Chloe are all hyper about our pub plans next Friday. They're already talking about what they're going to wear and which shoes would look best with Chloe's new lipstick, but I'm just concentrating on trying not to sound too excited so as not to start up the whole 'Pig *luurves* Leo' thing again.

'You do want to go, don't you, Pig?' says Kas. 'You don't seem that up for it.'

'Yeah, sure. I've just got a lot of other stuff on at the moment and it's, well, it's still a week away. I mean, I'm sure I'll be excited nearer the time.'

'What stuff?' Chloe scoffs at me with a grin.

'Just . . . stuff.'

'Like . . .?'

'Like . . . hobbies and stuff. I have a very busy life. It's not all about you guys!'

'Since when do have you have a *hobby*?' says Kas.

'I have hobbies . . . erm . . . sleeping . . . eating . . . toileting . . .'

Kas laughs. 'They're not hobbies!'

'They're leisure activities that give me pleasure, so I don't see why not,' I say grandly, hoping to dismantle the conversation with another laugh.

'I think I know the *real* hobby you're into,' says Chloe with a grin that could rival the Joker's for evilness. '*Luurving* Mr Leo Jackson.'

Oh, for frick's sake.

As the two of them giggle, Mrs Perkins blasts over the class, 'Right, who wants to take the register back?'

I grab the opportunity for an escape route and shoot my hand into the air.

'Ms Swinton, I'm impressed! You're not known for your volunteering,' says Mrs Perkins.

'It's one of her new *hobbies*, miss,' sniggers Kas.

'Is it OK that I hate you both a little bit right now?' I whisper to them as I grab my bag and get up.

'Aww, Pig, we're only messing about. C'mon, you know that,' says Chloe.

'Yeah, whatever, you evil old hags.' But I say it with a smile.

Then, as I walk between the desks to the front of the class, Dylan puts on a loud camp voice and says, 'And coming down the catwalk now we have a glorious outfit from the latest collection by Jean-Paul Porkier . . .'

I grit my teeth, but I go along with the joke. What else can I do? So I strut down the classroom, my chin raised high, shoulders back, lips pouting, my hips swaying with each step and my body then my head snapping back to the room as I reach Mrs Perkins. The class falls about in fits of giggles.

Mrs Perkins is less impressed. 'Yes, thank you, Haylah, most amusing, but if you mess around like that again in my classroom it'll be detention, OK?'

'Sorry, miss,' I say, taking the register from her.

Dylan's such a cack-nugget.

I head to the school office, the flush leaving my cheeks with each step. Thinking back to the conversation with Chloe and Kas, I know I should just stop denying it and tell them that, yes, I have a little thing for Leo, and, yes, I know it's going nowhere. Try to make a joke out of it. But this feels different. This time the joke is very much on me. I know there's no hope for this crush. And they know it too. So if I own up to it I go from being the funny, strong one in the group to being the pathetic, heartbroken loser.

I drop the register off at the office and walk towards the history rooms for my first class of the day. But, as I go past the lockers, I hear a familiar voice booming its big warm laugh.

Leo. He's leaning up against his locker, talking to a bunch of his friends (mostly girls), all hanging on his every word. My heart begins to pound so loudly I start to think everyone can hear it.

Stupid heart.

I could keep walking. I *should* keep walking. Look at the ground, attract no attention. Instead, with what seems like no instruction from me, my feet walk into the rows of lockers behind where Leo's is. My locker isn't here, I have no legitimate reason to be here. So I fiddle with someone else's locker as I listen to Leo.

For the second day in a row, I've turned into creepy stalker girl. Maybe *that's* my new hobby.

'So your dad doesn't mind if we all come down the pub next Friday?' says one of the girls.

'Nah, he's cool with that, as long as you don't try to buy any drinks – Jax, I'm looking at you!' says Leo. 'And no heckling!'

'I'll only heckle you if you're not funny, mate,' says Jax as I continue to fiddle with the lock on my pretend locker.

Oh God, I'm an actual nutter.

Then I look round and realize there's no one down this aisle to see me anyway, so I stop and just lean up against the locker backing on to Leo's, willing my heart to stop clanging against my chest so loudly.

'Oh, no pressure then!' says Leo. 'Actually, I haven't got anything new written, and if I can't bang anything out by next Friday I won't be getting up at all.'

And now my traitorous heart skips a beat.

What? But he's got to get up and do his thing! So that I can be there in the audience. Adoring him.

As I flip out at the thought of Leo not performing, his mates take the piss, asking, 'How hard can it be to write a few knock-knock jokes!' But what do they know? Bunch of comedic simpletons.

I understand, Leo – I totally get how hard it is to write the funny.

Then they leave, apparently for art class, and as they go Leo puts on a ridiculous high-pitched voice and does an uncanny impression of Mrs O'Farrell, the art teacher. 'Use your inner eye, students. Don't draw what's in *front* of you, draw the spaces *between*. Don't draw what you *think* you can see, draw what you *feel* in your hearts. UNLEASH the artist within!'

They laugh. I laugh (quietly). He leaves. Then I do something stupid.

I don't know whether it's the thought of Leo not performing at the pub, the adrenalin from hiding making me go slightly insane, or the high of being so close to him that makes me do it. But whatever it is, with my blood pumping round my body at lightning speed, I get a pen and paper out of my bag and write down one of the jokes I wrote in my comedy diary last night.

One I could imagine Leo laughing at, but now I can also imagine him telling.

Man, it was hot the other day. So hot. I threw open the freezer, took great handfuls of whatever I could: frozen peas, Soleros, you name it, and just shoved it all down my shirt. And trousers.

Lay face down on the floor just enjoying the cold on my skin.

I mean, I know it's probably not great for the food or anything, but man, it felt good.

You understand, right? Cos Waitrose sure didn't.

I sneak round the corner, check no one's looking and then post it through the gap at the side of his locker.

And I stride triumphantly away down the corridor.

And with this one truly heroic act she saved humanity from the impending disaster of a Leo-less comedy stage!

Then the full force of my utter dumb-nuttery begins to hit me.

Oh . . . holy . . . crapballs.

And I walk to my class on shaky legs, the harsh sting of regret hitting me a little more with each step.

What, oh what the hell was I thinking?

EIGHT

For the rest of the day, I'm just a big sack of sweaty nerves. *Why, why, why did I think that was a good idea?* He's going to open his locker, read out the crappy joke to his friends, who'll all laugh along with him – not at the joke but at the strange, sad muppet who must have left it to try to get his attention.

Oh God, they might even know it's me!

'I bet it's that big girl – she looks just the sort of desperate weirdo who would do something that crazy,' they'll say.

Ugh! Why am I such an incessant ball-bag of muppetry!

But at the end of the day, desperate to somehow kill the turmoil in my head, I find an excuse to leave Kas and Chloe and head down to the lockers. Maybe if I see the look of hatred in his eyes as he reads the joke it will put a stop to this stupid crush once and for all and I won't care any more. Or maybe it'll miraculously fall out of his locker and land on the floor, and I can subtly pick it up and bin it before any damage is done. Or maybe there's a part of me that thinks I deserve to be laughed at for being such an idiot in the first place and I'll get some sort of closure on any hopes I might have of being anything other than a dumb-ass loser.

Who knows? But, for whatever reason, my feet have taken me here. To the lockers. There are dozens of students milling around, so at least I'm not noticeable as I lean up against the wall, staring down at my phone, pretending to be engrossed in something other than Leo's locker, which I can just about see round the corner.

The sound of squeaking shoes on the floor, laughter and chattering, and, cutting above it all, the opening and slamming of metal doors fill the air. Then Leo's voice. He's with a group, as always. My heart leaps. I try to keep my eyes fixed on my phone, but they keep flicking up to him.

Stupid eyes.

Still chatting to his mates, including a tall girl with shiny braces on her huge teeth who keeps touching his back (*who is she? How dare she touch him!*), he opens his locker door. My note doesn't fall on the floor. He picks it up. He looks at it.

Oh God, he's actually looking at it.

I can't hear what he's saying. I don't think he's saying anything. He turns. He's . . . laughing. Holding the note and laughing. Not a big belly laugh, just a cute, chesty chuckle. A private laugh. *Oh halle-frickin'-lujah, this is just amazing!*

He's looking around, maybe trying to identify the note's author. I stare down at my phone.

Don't look up. Don't look up, stupid eyes, I beg you.

Then I do. *Dammit.* But it's OK – he's not looking my way. He's putting the note in his back pocket. I can't quite

69

hear, but I think the tall, toothy girl next to him is asking what he was laughing at.

'Oh, nothing,' I see his lips say, a smile still on them as a leftover after his laughter. Laughter I gave him. Straight from my head to his. Just like I'd always imagined.

I turn and walk away, unable to stop the smile forming on my own lips.

That. Was. Proper. A-ma-zing.

My brain still glowing like I've been plugged into the mains, I pretty much skip home from school, actually quite glad that Kas and Chloe are both busy for the weekend with their families as I don't think I could hide my Leo-based mood from them. I pick up Noah from school, still on a high. I tell him the pictures he's done today are the best I've ever seen (though between you and me they are, of course, still really quite terrible). I tell him we're going to read all his books this weekend. And play whatever games he wants. And go to the park. And that tomorrow he can have an extra-long, extra-bubbly bath.

'Until my fingers look like brains?' he asks excitedly.

'Yes!' I answer. 'Until all your fingers look like tiny wrinkly brains! And you know why?' I ask.

'Why?'

'Because today is a good day!'

'I thought today was a Friday,' he says.

When we get through the front door, I can't wait to give Mum a big old hug on the sofa, and share my blindingly brilliant mood.

But instead I hear two voices from the living room. My mum's and ... a man's. A random man I've never met before.

He says something and then she ... *oh, my good Lord*, she's actually giggling. Like proper girlie giggles. All high-pitched and breathy. They say that laughter is the best medicine, but right now hers is causing me to feel nauseous.

'Mummy!' Noah shouts. 'Haylah, Mummy's here with a man!' and he runs down the hall towards her disgustingly girlie cackle.

'Right,' I say. 'Brilliant.'

NINE

Like a crime scene investigator arriving in dimly lit, ominous surroundings, unsure of what gruesome sight lies before me, I gingerly enter the living room to see my mother on the sofa hugging Noah while beaming a sickening, lipstick-clad smile at a strange man sitting in our armchair. I fight the urge to recoil.

'Haylah, this is Ruben.'

Well. Firstly, what the hell kind of a name is Ruben? I mean, has he just walked straight out of the Old Testament or something? We already have a Noah in the house – what's next, Nebuchadnezzar?

And, secondly, what is up with his facial hair? The man's face gurning up at me is all beard. I can barely make out any features behind it, it's so all-encompassing. It's like a matted squirrel landed on the man's face and he's never got round to detaching it.

Plus, everything about him is some shade of beige. The beard, the clothes, I assume the personality – and from his wrists at the end of the beige sleeves of his beige jacket sprouts thick beige hair. Like the straw stuffing of a badly dressed, poorly constructed scarecrow.

Of course I don't say any of this. I just give him a 'Hey' and then shoot a questioning look at Mum.

Determined to ignore my look, she sheepishly says, 'Ruben's a friend from work. I'm just going to go and make us a cup of tea.' And then she sashays out of the room, leaving me and Noah alone with this bearded nutter.

'Oh,' I say. 'Are you a doctor then?'

'No, I'm a Play Specialist,' he says, in absolute total seriousness.

You can't see his lips, so when he talks it's the only time there's any evidence of a mouth behind the beard. It's like someone poked a hole in a Shredded Wheat.

'Play Specialist? Is that an actual thing?' I say, suspicious of everything this man stands for.

'Haylah!' Mum screeches from the kitchen. She's trying to keep her voice breezy, but it just comes out hysterical. 'Of course it is! Sorry, Ruben!'

'No!' he says, laughing a big, deep, annoyingly Santa-esque laugh. I mean, it's not quite 'ho ho ho' but it's not far off. 'It's fine! It is an actual thing. I use play to help sick children on the ward. To help them understand what they're going through, or sometimes just to distract them from what they're going through, to keep them happy at a difficult time.'

'By *playing* with them?' I ask, with a frown.

'Yeah!' the beige man says, with an unnecessarily merry chuckle at the end.

'And do you need a qualification for that, or can anyone do it?'

'Haylah!' Mum shouts from the kitchen again.

'I have a PhD in Duplo management,' says the beard with a grin.

I can hear Mum giggling pathetically and I force out a slightly scornful 'Ha' in recognition of his 'joke'.

'Duplo! Duplo!' Noah shouts in excitement. We very rarely have any guests round and he can barely contain his delight in Mum's new 'friend'. The traitorous little wretch.

'Do you like Duplo, little man? You got any we can play with now?' says the bearded idiot.

'Yeah, yeah!' says Noah, dragging a big plastic box of giant Lego pieces out from underneath the coffee table.

Ruben starts asking Noah what he likes building, and kneels down on the floor next to him to play. And it's then that I notice, as his beige corduroy trousers rise up his ankles, that this freak isn't. Wearing. Any. Socks. And I almost spew up a little in my mouth.

I walk into the kitchen, open the cupboards and grab fistfuls of snacks.

'Hey, Mum,' I whisper, 'who the *hell* is that?'

'Haylah, seriously, love, what's got into you?' she whispers back. 'He's just a friend. I expect you to be nice to my friends – I'm nice to yours!'

'A friend . . . or a *BOY*friend?' I whisper-shout back at her.

'Well, I don't know yet,' she says with a disgustingly coy grin. 'I guess we'll have to wait and see! Look, we just get on well at work and we've had a few coffees together, that's all.'

'Coffees!' I exclaim wildly as if she's just told me they've had several children together.

'Shh! Yes, *coffees*. Well, lattes actually.' She whisper-giggles like a brazen hussy. 'Is that OK with you?'

'Huh. I guess,' I say, ripping off bits of baguette and shoving them into my mouth to ease the nausea.

'Anyway, I invited him round and we might go out for a proper drink later. If that's OK with you, of course, *Mother*,' she teases, with that horrible, glossy red girlie grin again.

So *this* is why she's wearing lipstick and – *eurgh!* – shaving her legs. For him. She's a traitor to the sisterhood.

With a swish of her nurse's uniform, which is frumpy and hard-wearing and bears absolutely no resemblance to the 'sexy' nurse's uniform people wear to fancy-dress parties, but has nevertheless taken on a whole new sordid meaning in my head, she grabs the two mugs of tea. I follow her back into the living room and she puts them on the table before slumping back on to the sofa.

'Thanks, Dawn,' Ruben rumbles, using my mother's first name like he owns her or something.

I stand in the doorway, stuffing my face with digestive biscuits as this stranger kneels up on *our* rug, one hand holding one of *Noah's* Duplo characters, the other gripping one of *our* mugs from which he slurps *our* tea through his gnarly beard.

I mean, what the hell gives this no-sock-wearing, beige-bearded Santa-wannabee scumlord the right to touch and consume our stuff?

'What you guys making?' asks Mum from the sofa.

'Well, I'm working on a house and . . . Noah, what you got going on there?' he says.

Noah holds up a random collection of coloured bricks and announces, 'It's a dog-powered wig-making machine.'

Evil Santa bellows his ho-hoing laugh and Mum chuckles into her tea.

'Well, that's quite an imagination you've got there, my boy!' he booms.

MY BOY?

And it's at this point that I lose it. Which I think you'll agree is fair enough, right? *Who does this stinkhole think he is, coming in here, talking to Noah as if he's his dad or something?*

My cheeks burn red and I explode with: 'He gets it from his dad!'

There's an agonizing silence and all the air in the room seems to go cold as Mum stares at me with a look so sharp I can feel its two points spearing into my soul.

Regret starts seeping into my thoughts as I desperately hope Noah didn't hear me mention the forbidden D-A-D word.

But thankfully neither Noah nor Ruben were really paying attention. Only in the silence now are they vaguely aware that *something* sinister just happened in this room. They look up for a moment, both with clueless expressions on their faces, like meerkats in the desert checking for danger, but Mum quickly removes her daggers from me and offers the simple creatures a comforting grin, which is enough to settle them back down to their Duplo.

The truth is, I'm not really sure why I was bigging up or even *bringing* up the guy who left us when Noah was three months old and ran off up north with his secretary. If Noah had heard me it would only upset him. So OK, yeah, it wasn't one of my best moments but still, I can't be expected to just put up with this crap and not say anything, right?

I sigh loudly, then storm off in the direction of my room, slamming the door behind me as I hear Mum saying, 'Sorry, Ruben. I guess she's had a bad day or something.'

'No, that's quite all right, I understand,' replies the sockless wonder.

I pace around my bedroom, kicking clothes and books across the floor as I go.

The thing is, I haven't had a bad day. I've actually had a super-awesome day, but now I come home to find this new man-friend invading our house, and in an instant Mum's not Mum any more, she's this giggling girlfriend in a nurse's costume. And, oh God, they're going to get married. And have kids. Little tiny, bearded, beige brats running around with their high-pitched Santa laughs.

I stop pacing and curl up on my bed. OK, I shouldn't have brought up Dad. That was stupid. It's the unwritten rule in this house. *Don't* talk about Dad. Don't even think about Dad. After all, he never thinks about us. When he first left, he used to see me and Noah every weekend, then every fortnight, then his new girlfriend got a job up north. Last I heard, they were trying for a baby and, well, now he doesn't even call us on our birthdays.

I shut my eyes. Shut it all out.

*

A few hours later, I wake from my nap to the muffled sound of Noah's usual loud complaints at being put to bed. I can make out his piercing whinges followed by Mum's calm bedtime-story-reading tones and then the boom of an irritatingly jolly Santa laugh.

He's still here then.

Soon after, Mum calls upstairs to say that they're going for drinks and to check on Noah. I grunt back a response and the front door shuts. Then the post-nap grogginess lifts and I feel stronger, fresher.

I'm not going to let this mountain-man twonk-womble spoil my day. Why should he?

Just think about something else.

So I think about Leo. Laughing at my joke. And the thought makes my insides go deliciously fuzzy. I want this feeling to last. I should write him a new one. Put it through his locker again on Monday.

I get up and sit at my desk, grab my notebook and start twiddling my pen around in my fingers. But, as much as I want to escape into the funny, my mind is blank. I know I've got all weekend to think up funny stuff but I really need something to come to me now, to lift me out of this brain funk. I sigh and swap the pen for my phone and faff around on that for a bit.

Then some sappy nonsense meme Kas has reposted sparks a thought. I turn off the phone and let the idea grow in the silence. And with it the familiar excitement that I'm just about to capture something funny.

I go after it, like the BFG chasing glowing dreams with a net before plucking them out of the sky, only with jokes. Instead of shoving it in a jar, I need to write it down before it floats away. I close my eyes for a moment, take a deep breath, then grab my pen and trap the funny.

Oh, I am so the BFG* of comedy.

* The Big Funny Girl, obviously.

TEN

Mum gets back late from her drinks with the woolly-chinned Duplo-twit. When she comes into my room to say goodnight, I pretend to be asleep. She gently kisses me on the forehead, and for a moment I feel guilty about the way I was earlier, but then I remember the hairy, sockless ankles that she brought into my world without even a heads-up. And the anger, along with a little bile, rises up in me again.

The next morning over breakfast it's all super awkward between me and Mum, and neither of us really says anything to the other. Noah happily fills the silences by rambling on about his favourite superheroes and what he thinks they'd have for breakfast. Apparently, Batman would never eat anything as 'wimpy' as muesli, but he'd happily lift his mask and nibble an almond croissant.

Mum leaves for a day shift and says, 'We'll talk later, OK, honey?'

'What about?' I grunt.

She sighs. Kisses Noah goodbye. And leaves.

I give Noah the bath I promised him yesterday, but my heart's not really in it.

'I like Ruben. Do you like Ruben?' chatters Noah.

'Yeah. I suppose,' I say, kneeling on the floor and washing and rinsing his hair a little more violently than I normally would. 'Right, stand up and hold your hands out.' I squeeze soap on to his palms. 'Now clean your bum and belly button.'

'Why do we have belly buttons?' he asks while scrubbing away.

'Noah, is this going to turn into a massive list of "whys"? Because I'm not sure I can be bothered this morning.'

'No. Just one "why".' He sounds certain. I fall for it.

'OK,' I say, rearranging my legs and sitting cross-legged on the floor. 'We have belly buttons because when you're in your mummy's tummy she eats food and some of it goes into your tummy down a tube that goes in through your belly button. Got it?'

He stares at me for a moment, his face screwed up as he ponders this, then he sits back down in the bath with a splash and ponders it some more as he drums his little fingers on the side of the bath. You can almost see that one original question exploding into a million others behind his eyes.

Oh, sweet baby cheeses, here we go.

'How was I in Mummy's tummy? Did she eat me?' he says.

'No, Daddy put you there,' I say as casually as possible as I lean back against the towel rail.

'How?'

Uh-oh. 'Doesn't matter. Just . . . magic.'

'Is Daddy a magician?'

'No, although he's good at disappearing acts. Now wash the back of your neck.'

Noah does as he's told, but the distraction doesn't have the desired effect. 'What's a disappearing axe?'

'Nothing. No, he's not a magician, he's a financial adviser.'

'Is that like a magician?' he says, lying back in the water.

'Erm . . . yeah, if you like. Look, I think it's pretty much time to get out now, Noah.' I am desperately trying to draw the conversation to a close as I stand up and start searching for the least-damp towel.

He ignores me and looks down at his belly, poking above the water like a plump pink island surrounded by a bubbly sea.

'So . . . if I have a belly button, does that mean I have a baby in my tummy?'

'No! I told you, you were fed *through* that when you were in *Mummy's* tummy. And only girls can have babies anyway.'

'Why?' is his inevitable response.

This conversation is getting wildly out of hand. I hold out Noah's towel for him like a matador trying to make the crazy bull change direction.

'They just do,' I say, struggling to sound breezy. 'Boys and girls have different bodies. Boys have winkies and girls . . . don't.'

And even before the words are out I realize I've just made it a whole load worse. In desperation, I reach down into the water and pull out the plug, which normally freaks

Noah out as he thinks he's going to be sucked down too. Apparently not today. Instead, he calmly steps out of the bath and lets me wrap him in the towel, though the conversation is, troublingly, still not over.

'How do girls wee then?' he asks, shivering a little as I kneel in front of him, rubbing the towel up and down to dry him.

'Erm . . . they have a . . . hole.'

What is wrong with me? I definitely shouldn't have said that.

'Oh, OK.' He looks around the bathroom like there's a sea of questions erupting within him and I brace myself.

This is bad. I don't know how to answer the questions he's about to ask. How I answer them could affect his whole future outlook on women, relationships, sex, marriage . . . everything . . . If I get it wrong, I might screw him up for life. An image of Noah as a depressed, middle-aged, lonely fat man sitting on a psychiatrist's couch, pathetically saying, 'You know, I think I can trace all my problems back to a conversation with my sister, in the bath, when I was four years old, and she graphically and inappropriately told me about the facts of life.'

Oh God, I need Mum. He needs Mum. *What am I going to say?*

Then he stops looking around, pulls an arm out from under the towel, points a podgy finger at the corner of the bath and says, 'What's that character on the shampoo bottle called?'

I look at the kids' shampoo bottle. It has a cartoon of a

bear dressed as a superhero on it. Nothing to do with boys and girls and babies and belly buttons. Noah's magpie-like brain has just seen something else that at this moment seems shinier to him, and he's flown off in an entirely different direction after it. God love him. I let out a small laugh of relief.

'It's not funny,' he says. 'I need to know his name.'

'Of course, sorry,' I say. 'I don't know what his name is . . . erm . . . Bobby?'

'No,' he answers firmly.

And the conversation is mercifully over. As he leaves the bathroom in his towel maxi-dress, I grab him and kiss him on the cheek. 'You're a complete nutcase, you know that?'

'You're the nutcase,' he says and shuffles off down the landing.

The rest of the weekend is spent looking after Noah, avoiding any serious conversations with Mum when she is home in case they turn to the subject of Ruben, writing as much funny as I can and daydreaming about Leo.

When Monday morning finally comes round I manage to drop Noah off at school early for once, and then rush on to catch up with Chloe and Kas. All weekend I've been bursting to tell them about Mum's new 'friend' but wanted to do it face-to-face as sometimes there aren't enough vomit emojis in the world to express your feelings on an issue.

'So I have super-gross news to share,' I say with a smirk.

'Oh God, yes please," says Kas, grabbing my sleeve desperately, "*anything* to take my mind off my weekend at my cousin's wedding – I had to sit at the kids' table with a bunch of eight-year-olds while my dad flossed on the dance floor. I was, like, kill me. Kill me now.'

'Well, I had to stay at my dad's all weekend,' says Chloe, 'which was a total snooze-fest, so yes, *please*, Pig, tell us something interesting, we don't care how gross!'

So as we walk I tell them all about the furry-faced loser, saving the best until last.

'And then I noticed –' I finish the story with the grand finale as we walk through the school gates – 'he WASN'T WEARING SOCKS!'

'Eurgh!' says Chloe, pretending to throw up. 'That is proper unforgivable.'

'That is not right,' says Kas, followed by a giggle. 'Though I bet you he's the sort of person who WOULD wear them with sandals. The twisted freak.'

And I love them both even more right now for their totally brilliant and supportive responses. In the warmth of the moment, I even think about opening up to them about Leo and the locker joke, but then I stop myself. Perhaps because I like that it's just between Leo and me. Perhaps because I know they'll take the piss. Or, worse, they'll get all serious and tell me I really don't stand a chance. Either way, I don't want to hear it. So instead, as we walk down the corridor to our form room, I start up a game of 'Would You Rather?'

'OK, so would you rather . . .'

'Oh God, I love this game,' says Chloe.

'Just don't make it too gross, Pig, all right?' says Kas.

'As if! OK, if you HAD to pick one, would you rather lick a stranger's sock or kiss the back of Mr Jacobs's hairy hand?'

'Eugh! Dude! Why would you put that in my head? Why?' says Kas, holding her belly and pretending to retch.

Chloe swiftly and confidently choses the hand, and sticks to her decision even after I point out that the hand she'll be smooching is still fully attached to sweaty dullard Mr Jacobs, rather than just floating there like Thing from *The Addams Family*, who, between you and me, I've always found a strangely attractive character. Kas, still ashen-faced at the very question, tentatively chooses the sock, even after I point out that it's a stranger's sock and God only knows what kind of oozing foot diseases they have.

'Well, what are we supposed to say then? You came up with this nightmare situation! What would you do?' says Kas, laughing.

'The question-setter doesn't have to answer. Them's the rules,' I say as we wind our way through the desks in the classroom to ours at the back, throwing our bags down as we collapse on to our chairs. I tear open a four-finger KitKat I've brought as a morning-break snack, though, like the *Titanic*, it was obvious it was never going to make it that far. *I'll just eat half and save the other two fingers for later*, I think optimistically.

'OK, I've got one,' says Kas, leaning across the table, resting her chin on her palm. 'Would you rather . . . own a talking cat or a tame polar bear you can ride around on?'

Chloe, inspecting her face in her compact, and applying more unnecessary foundation, goes for the bear because she reckons she'd look fabulous riding around on its back in fur and winter boots, even after it's pointed out to her that the choice doesn't necessarily require her to live in Antarctica, but she says you'd need to wear them anyway, to complete the look.

Me and Kas, on the other hand, reckon that the polar bear is all well and good, but, after you've ridden it into town and back looking 'fabulous', all you're left with is a massive scary bear in your back garden who could rip your face off if it's hungry enough. So instead we go for the talking cat, although I wanted to firstly ascertain what personality this cat has and whether or not it liked me. After all, what's the point of having a talking cat if it's boring and hates you?

'Got to be honest,' says Kas, 'I hadn't really put that much thought into it.'

Some of the rest of the class join in as we go on to cover other important questions such as 'Would you rather go to school without trousers or a skirt, or go into a public swimming pool wearing only knickers and bra?' (Generally, the girls opted for the swimming pool, as it's pretty much what they wear anyway, apart from me – I'd never be seen dead in anything resembling a bikini – and the boys opted for trouserless, apart from Dylan, who reckons he'd look 'damn hot' in a bra.)

Then it was 'Would you rather fart popcorn or sneeze gummy bears?' and 'Would you rather have octopuses instead of hands or guinea pigs instead of feet?' And then the question that Noah randomly asked me this week, which we all felt was the most philosophically challenging of the day, 'Would you rather be a potato or a tomato?'

The bell goes and Mrs Perkins shuffles in, making a couple of alarmingly loud yet painfully dull announcements. Chloe puts down her mirror, leans towards me and says with a worrying smirk, 'OK, Pig, would *you* rather . . . Leo thought you were the *funniest* girl in school or the *prettiest*?'

'Oh, shut up, Chlo! Like he'd ever think either of those things. And I couldn't give a diddly squit if he did!' I say, turning away from her and towards Mrs Perkins as if fascinated by her monotonous drone.*

Kas puts her hand on my shoulder. 'Aww, you have a really pretty face, Pig – everyone says so,' she whispers.

I turn to her, and she's got her head to the side and is giving me her most patronizing, teeth-sucking grin. I am more than a tiny bit annoyed.

I roll my eyes and shrug off her hand. 'That's just what everyone says to fat girls, Kas, because they think it makes us feel better. It doesn't, OK? Because what you're actually saying is, "You have a really pretty face *for a fat girl*." It's like saying to the Elephant Man, "At least you still have really handsome shoulders."'

Kas laughs nervously and whisper-shouts, 'You're not fat, Pig!'

'You're really not, Pig. You just have some curves on you! There's nothing wrong with that. I wish I had a couple

* (Obviously the answer is 'funniest' though.)

88

of your curves,' says Chloe, looking down at her own flatter-than-a-touchscreen chest.

'You can borrow some of mine if you want,' I say.

'How generous of you,' says Chloe with a grin.

'Well, fat people *are* known for their generosity,' I say, raising my chin, and they laugh again, but I can tell I've made them a bit uncomfortable. Good.

Mrs Perkins takes the register and, as we gather up our bags and books and sit on the edge of the desks, waiting to make our way to first lesson, we talk about the open-mic night at the pub and I'm relieved that the conversation has veered away (a bit) from Chloe's Leo question.

The plan is for Chloe's sister to take us, and me and Kas are going to tell our folks that we're going round to Chloe's for the night. There's no way Mum would let me go to a pub, not unless it was with her, in the day, and to a soulless 'family-friendly' place that gave out child menus with dot-to-dots of smiling vegetables and a beer garden with a swing hanging from a plastic tree. You know, somewhere classy.

'The problem is, if Mum's working nights then it's not gonna happen,' I say.

'Hey, but maybe now sockless dude is in the picture he'll look after Noah for the evening if she's out, yeah?' says Chloe.

'Maybe, I guess, but, eurgh, sockless dude,' I say, with my head in my hands. 'I don't know, maybe he is just a *"friend"*. That's what Mum called him.'

'My mum had a "friend" from work – now I have to call him Uncle Nick and he leaves his toenail clippings in the sink,' says Chloe.

'But Nick's all right, isn't he? You like him, right?' says Kas.

'Yeah, he's all right. Plus, even Dad likes him, which is weird, I suppose, but it makes my life easier.'

'At least you still have your dad around and you can escape to his at the weekends,' I say. 'If the sockless beard moves in, I'm stuck with him – and Noah's so young he'll start calling him Dad, which means I'll have to call him Dad and . . . urgh! That's just too gross to think about.'

Just then the bell rings and we all pile out of the classroom and start roaming the corridors to our first lessons.

'It's no better when your parents stay together,' Kas says as we walk. 'Mine are a nightmare.'

'Really? I love your parents – they always seem so happy together,' says Chloe, walking in between me and Kas, linking arms with us both.

'Well, yeah, they don't *fight* or anything, not really. It's far worse than that: they have little digs at each other, like ALL day, even when we're in supermarkets and stuff. Mum calls it "affectionate bickering", I just call it super embarrassing. *Then* they make up at the end of the day by drinking a barrel of wine in front of Polish soap operas and snogging on the sofa. It's disgusting.'

I guess we all have to put up with whatever particular parental horrors we're dealt. Which seems unfair as our parents have at least some say in what kind of child they have. They set the rules, design our childhood, decide on our clothes, our schools, our moral outlook, mould us and push us and pull us into the kind of shape they think their child should be, whereas we have absolutely no say in what kind of parents we have. We just get dropped randomly into the care of fully formed people, who may scar us for life, cripple us with embarrassment or make terrible decisions about bearded trolls. And there's nothing we can do about it.

'Parents, eh? Who'd have 'em?' I say. 'But, yeah, I'll see what I can do about Friday.'

'So, not long now till you get to stare at lovely Leo onstage again!' says Chloe, squeezing my arm.

I do wish she'd drop this, though the truth is, at the mention of his name my heart skipped a little again. Then I remember the new joke in my bag. The new joke for Leo. And I know it's crazy and SO risky putting another joke through his locker door, but the thought that we have this little secret between us, that I might make him laugh again, spurs me on.

'Look, guys, I'll see you in English. I've just gotta run to the loo first, OK?' I say, breaking free from Chloe's arm.

'We'll come too,' says Kas.

'Oh, er, no, I wouldn't if I were you.' I grab my stomach and lower my voice. 'Got a bit of a belly ache. What came out of me this morning defied science – it was a solid, a liquid and a gas all at once.'

'Eurgh! Pig, that's gross!' laughs Kas.

'I'll tell Mrs Kelling you're going to be a bit late,' says Chloe, grabbing a body spray from her bag and handing it to me. 'Best give that a bit of a spray around you afterwards, yeah?'

'Er, thanks,' I say, and when they've disappeared round the corner I eat the other two KitKat fingers because, well, why wouldn't I? Then I make my way over to Leo's locker. I get out the latest piece I've written for him, hoping it'll make him laugh just as much as the other one. Fingers crossed. Not KitKat fingers. They've gone. Mourn them if you wish, but I'm talking about actual fingers. Well and truly crossed.

This is the bit I've written for Leo. (In case you didn't know, 'bit' is what comedians call a section of their routines. Oh yeah, being a proper comedy writer now, I totally get to use their lingo.)

You know what I hate? So-called 'inspirational' memes. Sappy, supposedly uplifting crap in a bad font against a sunset background.

I mean, why do people repost this twaddle? There's nothing less uplifting than wading through your social media and finding:

'Life is what happens to you when you're busy making other plans.'

Really? Yeah, well, joke's on you because I'm not making any plans. I'm scratching myself and spending hours reading endless arse-drivel like this.

'I wish I wasn't so healthy . . . said no one ever.'

OK, fine, but equally, 'I wish I was friends with a
sanctimonious, gym-obsessed health freak . . . said no
one ever.'

'One small positive thought in the morning can
change the entire outcome of your day.'

Well, I guess that's true, especially if that thought is,
'You know what, I think I will get that face tattoo today.'

At the end of the day, I wait by the lockers again, surrounded by a bustling herd of students, then watch as Leo opens his locker and finds my joke. I crouch down at the end of his row, pretending to search around in my bag for something, and glance up at him out of the corner of my eye. My heart drums a steady, forceful beat around my body as the tall girl with braces who's always following him around – Keesha, I think her name is – leans over his shoulder to see what it is. He snatches it out of her view and smiles and laughs as he reads it.

And a great tide of warm sunshine floods my brain and I can't help but smile.

'So, you got any new comedy stuff for the open mic yet, mate?' I overhear his friend Mikey ask as he digs around in his own locker.

'Yeah, actually,' says Leo as he folds up the note and stuffs it into his pocket. 'I've got a couple of new things. Just not sure if I'm allowed to use them!'

He says this last bit loudly, and my heart bounces into my throat as I realize he's talking to me! OK, so he doesn't *know* he's talking to me, but he's totally TALKING TO ME!

My bent knees are now shaking a little as I slowly stand up straight, grabbing my phone out of my bag so I have somewhere for my eyes to look. I tap my slightly quivering fingers randomly on it, pretending to be doing something vitally important.

Oh God, is he looking at me? Does he know it's me?

Quickly, I shove my phone to the side of my face and loudly start up a pretend phone call. What else could I do?

'Hi, Mum, yeah . . . yeah . . .'

Why the hell did I choose my imaginary phone call to be to my MUM? I should have pretended to be talking to some hot boy called Brad or something. Urgh, I'm USELESS.

I pause while phoney 'Mum' talks back to me and look in the opposite direction while actually still listening to Leo.

'What you on about? Why can't you use the new stuff?' says his friend Mikey.

'Oh, nothing,' says Leo. 'They're just mostly jokes about your mama being so fat, and I'm not sure she'd be OK with that.'

'Oi!' says Mikey with a laugh. 'Although yeah, she'd probably be fine with it as long as you paid her in biscuits.'

'Oh! You made a funny! Everyone – Mikey made a funny!' says Leo, slapping Mikey on the back as they walk past me. Quickly, I enthusiastically resume the fake phone call to 'Mum' again.

'Yeah, Mum, OK, I'll do that, yep . . .'

And then, when Leo is *right* in front of me, my phone, held to the side of my face, actually rings. Loudly. 'La Cuca-ruddy-racha'.

My face burns red as he stops dead and turns to look at me, giving me a quizzical look as I fumble with my phone in a mad panic to shut it up.

Refusing the actual incoming call from Mum, I then bang the phone against my thigh a few times, as if trying to get it to work properly, then examine it again with a frown before looking up at Leo and saying with a shrug, 'Weird.'

He shrugs back with a pained smile that says, 'Yeah, you are,' and catches up with his mates.

And that's it. The one and only word I'll probably ever say to Leo Jackson will forever more be 'weird'.

And for a moment I'm mortified. Then I think about him laughing with his mates and wanting to use my stuff in his set, and again I can't stop the smile spreading across my face.

Jokes about fat people and idiotic fake phone calls aside, I feel a little bit fabulous.

ELEVEN

I pick up Noah from his after-school club and take him home past Leo's house again. I know I shouldn't. I know Noah's stompy little legs are tired and he just wants to get home. I know I won't see Leo anyway, and even if I did he at best only knows me as the weirdo with the imaginary phone calls, but still, here we are.

Why? Because I'm an obsessed, idiot stalker, that's why.

Halfway along Leo's road, Noah starts dragging his feet slowly along the ground.

'I'm *tiiiiired*. I can't walk properly.'

'You know that will only make it *harder* to walk, Noah? If you just walked normally, you'd –'

'I can't walk any more, Haylah – my legs are *broken*!' he interrupts.

I swallow down my bubbling frustration and, as usual, use my impeccable childcare skills to calm the situation with food-based bribery. 'No they're not. I'll tell you what, if you walk normally all the way back, I'll give you a packet of crisps when we get home.'

'Cheesy Puffs?'

'Yep, Cheesy Puffs. Now go, Cheesy Puff Man – fly!'

'Yay!' he says as he starts running. But he's quite spherical, so the momentum makes his body want to roll over in front of him like a ball.

Uh-oh.

'Noah, don't run so fast! You'll fall –'

But it's too late. He, of course, falls flat on his knees. And, of course, it's right outside Leo's house.

'*Owwwwww!*' Noah wails as he rolls around on the pavement.

And I think I can see someone in the upstairs window of Leo's house looking out to see what all the noise is about.

Oh God. *WHY IS THIS HAPPENING TO ME?*

But I can't blame the vindictive nature of the world for causing these close-proximity-to-Leo embarrassments. If I will insist on following him around like a psycho puppy dog, knowing that I and my family are prone to muppetry and numptiness of the highest order, I shouldn't really be surprised if he witnesses some of it. And I vow to avoid Leo from this day forward. At least until tomorrow.

I run up and crouch next to Noah, wrapping my arms round him, frantically hoping the screaming will stop.

'It's OK! It's OK!' I say in desperation. 'Be a brave boy – no need to cry. Here comes the ambulance! *Nee-nah, nee-nah!*'

Oh God, get up, Noah. I really do NOT need Leo to see me doing some kind of demented ambulance impression.

'MY LEGS HAVE SNAPPED OFF!' he hollers, claw-ing at his trousers and trying to roll them up his chubby little calves to assess his injuries.

'Your legs haven't snapped off, you've just grazed your knees. It's OK,' I whisper urgently, stroking his hair, possibly a bit too hard.

He grabs my face, wiping mud, gravel and God knows whatever else into my hair and cheeks. Brilliant.

'THERE'S BLEEDING BLOOD!' he sobs into my face. 'I N-NEED A DOCTOR!! I N-NEED AN OPREPRATION!'

'Shh, shh, it's OK. Come on, let's get up and go home. See how brave and *quiet* you can be, *please*?'

But it's too late. Leo's front door opens. O.M.Giddy-gosh.

I hear footsteps on the path behind me, but can't bring myself to look round. I try to keep cuddling Noah with one hand while combing through my hair with the other, but it's matted with mud and crap from Noah's hands.

'Everything OK? Is he all right? Can I . . . do anything?'

It's Leo. Right behind me. *What if he remembers the embarrassing phone thing? What if he realizes I've been following him around like a bat-crap-crazy, lovesick lemming?*

No. No. No. No. No. No. I take a deep breath and turn round.

'Thanks . . . No, it's fine,' I say, struggling to my feet, though one of them now has pins and needles from Noah sitting on it so I'm fairly wobbly. I swear it's like my body hates me and takes any opportunity to wreak its revenge.

I hobble a bit and then turn and face Leo, who's looking utterly gorgeous in a pair of jeans and hoodie. Wow. He actually changes out of his uniform as soon as he gets home.

That's so classy.

I try to keep my weight on my one loyal foot as I say, 'He, erm, well, he fell. Obviously. But he's fine now, aren't you, Noah?'

'I'M NOT FINE! I NEED MECIDON!' he yells.

'No, you don't need mecido— I mean, *medicine*,' I say through a forced smile. 'I'll get you a plaster when we get home, OK? Come ON!' And I try to yank him to his feet, but his hands are slippery with mud and tears and I fall backwards.

On to my butt. Which makes a heavy *oof* sound as it hits the pavement, and hurts so much I blurt out, 'Argh, flump nuggets!'

And that's when I really feel very strongly that death is the best option at this point, but unfortunately there's no obvious method of suicide to hand.

As I consider forming a noose out of my own hair, I notice Leo trying not to laugh. I mean, I know I *want* to make him laugh, but *with* me not *at* me! Then he leaps over and offers me a hand. I reach up and take it. Quickly, so he doesn't see mine shaking a bit.

Then Leo's actual hand is in mine. Or rather mine is in his. And time stops for a moment as cartoon deer and rabbits scamper around us and birds fly down from the trees and softly sing, 'You're the One That I Want,' before fireworks explode above us.

Stop it!

He pulls me to my feet much more easily than most other people, or for that matter industrial cranes, could.

99

'Well, this has been wonderful for me, I don't know about you,' I say as I brush myself down and avoid eye contact at all costs, as that might just make me fall down again.

He laughs. A short, sharp, chesty laugh that almost melts me.

Then he helps Noah up. 'Hey, little dude, that looks pretty bad. I can get you a plaster if you want.'

'No, no, that's OK!' I get in quick, but Noah's not going to pass up the chance of a free plaster that easily.

'YES! Plaster, plaster, plaster, plaster!' he chants.

'Well, sorry, y-yeah,' I stutter. 'If it's not too much trouble?'

'Totally fine. I'm Leo by the way,' he says, turning to walk back down the path into his house. 'Come on in.'

'*Leo*, you say? Nice to meet you!' I say, relieved that the phone thing earlier seems to have left no impression on him whatsoever. 'Actually, we're fine here!'

But Noah's already trotted off after him, the pain from his mortal wound now fading as the excitement of a new place and person takes over.

So, what else can I do? I follow them in. To Leo's house. Through his lovely front door. My heart is hopping around my chest like a bunny on a trampoline.

We head through his hall, past the living room and into the kitchen. It's a small terraced house about the same size as ours, except with much nicer stuff inside. The walls are painted white, not pukey peach or squitty-poo brown like ours, and they don't have cracks in them. Also, unlike ours, pictures are hanging on them rather than a few bad school photos of Noah and me Blu-Tacked up in their cardboard frames. Whereas our sofa and chairs are disgustingly old fashioned, his are retro chic. The kitchen is shiny and white and all the cupboard doors are still attached to the cupboards. Proper fancy.

'Take a seat,' he says, waving a hand at some really cool, brightly coloured plastic chairs surrounding a wooden kitchen table covered in papers, pens and notebooks.

Then, among the papers, I see my handwriting. The jokes I wrote for him are totally there, right in front of me! I concentrate hard on looking anywhere in the room but at those notes. If he knows I wrote them and then thinks I engineered this 'accidental' visit, he may well have me arrested for stalking.

I can imagine the trial even now, and for some reason in my imagination the prosecuting lawyer is played by Stephen Fry: 'And so I put it to you, Ms Swinton, that given that Exhibit A, your handwritten and, may I say, *deeply* unfunny notes, were found in the defendant's house, you did knowingly and with malicious intent commit the depraved and wicked act of throwing an infant on to a pavement merely for your own romantic gain . . .'

Oh, shut up, brain!

Noah sits down and the chair creaks under him, making me wonder what kind of noise it would make if I sat down on one.

'Nah, I'm good, thanks,' I say, as calmly as possible. I catch a glimpse of my reflection on the side of the cooker and see that my face has a big smear of mud down one side.

Thanks, Noah.

I frantically rub at it with the sleeve of my school jumper as Leo rummages around in a cupboard.

'I know they're in here somewhere. I'm always scraping my knees playing pirates or hopscotch – you know how it is – so Mum usually keeps us stocked up with plasters – Ah, here they are.'

I can't even tell if the hopscotch thing is a joke, my brain feels so scrambled.

Leo turns round sharply on his heel and sees me rubbing at my face before I have a chance to stop.

Oh, ball-bags.

'You want a cloth or something for that?' he says with a grin.

'Nah, I'm good, thanks. I think it suits me, contours my cheekbones, y'know . . . if I had any cheekbones.'

He laughs, which is heavenly, then hands me the plasters and an antiseptic wipe.

'Take a seat,' he says again.

And to be honest the idea of not having to try and stand coolly on my shaking legs is a good one, so I pull out a chair and throw myself down on it enthusiastically, but of course I've forgotten the creak Noah's made under him and the chair reacts to my parked butt cheeks with an almighty fart sound.

'Pig farted! Pig farted!' chants Noah with glee.

Noah usually calls me Hay or Haylah, so why, oh why has he chosen to go with that *name now?*

I feel myself burn nuclear-red. 'Just so you know, that was the chair,' I say.

Leo laughs and sits down opposite us, and his chair also farts.

Thank. God.

I start cleaning up Noah's knee in the awkward silence, punctuated only by Noah's giggles at the chair fart. In any other company, it would simply be classed as a normal pause, but here, with Leo in the room and my notes staring up at me from the table, it's as awkward a silence as there has ever been in the history of silence. It's the loudest silence I have ever heard.

What do I say? What do I say? Tell me! What do I say?

Then at last Leo breaks through the crushing dead air.

'We really should do something about these farting chairs,' he says calmly, as if he hadn't even noticed the decades-long pause. 'I think it's just the plastic moving against the metal legs or something. When my grandma sits on them, it's super cringey. Although at her age it's probably a good cover, y'know – "it wasn't me, it was the chair" kinda thing.'

'That could be a selling point,' I say, grabbing desperately at the funny that pops into my head and going with it. 'Perhaps you should suggest to the manufacturers that they rebrand them as "modesty chairs".' I dab at Noah's knee with the wipe.

'Great idea,' nods Leo. 'Especially if they also had a naturally farty smell about them.'

'Oooh, nice. The slogan could be "Modesty Chairs – we take the blame so you don't have to",' I say, thanking God for the silence-busting gift of humour and looking Leo in the eye for the first time.

'Yeah! Or "Chairs that have mastered the *fart* of misdirection",' he says with *that* smile that he does, the one that makes my knees go weak.

'Very strong, or how about "*They'll* never know when *you* let one go"?' I say, actually starting to enjoy the conversation.

'Nice!' he says.

'IT STINGS!' screeches Noah, and to be honest I had completely forgotten he was there.

'Sorry, Noah – all cleaned up now, just need to put the plaster on.'

'So you're Noah?' says Leo. 'Nice to meet you. I'm Leo.'

He holds out his hand to a beaming Noah, who grabs it with his left hand and shakes it wildly.

'I like your hands,' says Noah. 'The top and bottom are different colours. Like different kinds of chocolate.'

'NOAH! Sorry, Leo, he's, well, he's four . . .' I say as if that explains everything.

Why, oh why am I having to excuse my family's apparent racism on my first proper meeting with Leo?

But Leo laughs. Not in an embarrassed way. A proper belly laugh.

'Thanks, mate. I like your hands too. They're like white chocolate. My favourite,' Leo says, then he turns to me. 'And you're . . . Pig?'

'Ha ha ha ha! Right, yeah, well, no, I mean, my name's Haylah, but everyone calls me Pig, so yeah. It's Pig. Anyway!' I garble in approximately 1.5 seconds flat. 'You're all patched up now, Noah, and I think we ought to leave Leo to it, OK?'

'Aw, OK,' says Noah sadly.

'Yeah, I do have stuff to do actually,' says Leo, pointing at the notebook. And MY jokes next to it.

Oh God ... why did he point at them? He knows they're from me! No, he can't know. Can he?

But, even if he doesn't, what if Noah recognizes my handwriting? What if he says something about it with his big dopey blabbermouth? *Don't be silly! Noah can't write his name yet – he doesn't even know what handwriting is –* but still, what if Leo knows?

What if he asks me straight out if I wrote them? What will I say? How can I possibly explain posting random, anonymous jokes through his locker without sounding like the total freak I undoubtedly am?

Head him off! Attack first!

'So what stuff are you doing – homework?' I ask, my voice shaking a little. And here it comes. He's going to ask me about my notes. *Oh God.*

'Nah, I'm just trying to write some comedy stuff. I do a bit of stand-up, y'know. Can't sing or dance and I like being onstage so ... that's what I do.'

He doesn't know. Oh, thank God. After all, he can't know they're from me, can he? Relief rushes through me and I almost let out a yelp of glee.

'Oh, that's right,' I say as casually as possible, screwing up my nose and looking to the ceiling as if trying to recall a distant and unimportant memory. 'I *think* I saw you in assembly the other day?'

'Yeah, I noticed you in there actually,' he says.

What?

'You did?'

He did?

'Yeah – you didn't laugh. It's always the way when you're in front of an audience. You don't notice all the people who *do* laugh, you only notice the ones who don't.' He's looking at me carefully now, which is part amazing and part horrifying. 'And I thought maybe it was because you don't have a sense of humour or something but, well, today you've been making the funnies so . . . now I'm thinking, and I'm trying not to sound too desperate here, but . . .' He clasps his hands together and looks longingly at me with an exaggerated look of desperation. And it's just eye-meltingly cute. '*Why in the name of everything holy didn't you laugh?*'

This makes me giggle. A shameful girl-giggle I've never produced before. But, God, he's *right*: I didn't laugh the other day in assembly. I was too busy sitting on the edge of my seat, frozen stiff, staring at him, captivated by the way he owned the stage and made everyone feel that the joke he was telling was for their ears only. I thought he was hilarious, but I guess I only laughed *inside* my head.

Which isn't really what stand-up comedians are after.

'Oh. Balls. Sorry, no, actually I thought you were –' *careful, Pig, don't get too enthusiastic or he'll be on to you* – 'good. Really . . . good.'

'Good?'

'Yeah, you know, erm, funny.'

'Well, that's kinda what I was going for . . .'

'Hay likes funny!' says Noah, and my heart jumps into my throat fearing what he's going to say next. 'She's going to be a com–'

'Communist!' I interrupt desperately. 'I want to be a communist!'

'You do?' says Leo, looking confused.

'Yeah,' I say, grabbing Noah's hand and pulling him towards the front door before this gets any worse. 'I just love that whole everyone-sharing-property thing and those cute little red books you get.'

That's communism, right?

'Anyway,' I say, dragging Noah down the hall, 'it's been fun. Thanks for the, y'know, knee . . . thing.'

'Plaster?' Leo offers, following us down the hallway.

'Yep, and, erm, good luck with the comedy.' And then it strikes me I might never get this chance again, so I grab Noah's hand tight for support and go for it. 'I thought you were . . . brilliant actually. I loved it.'

'Thanks! Really? Thanks. And, hey, good luck with the communism,' he says, smiling, seemingly genuinely pleased. 'Oh, and I hope your phone stops being weird.'

Oh knickers. He does remember.

'Right! Yep. Noah, say thank you.'

Noah raises his hands in the air and screams, 'THANK YOU!' like a total nutcase.

'You're welcome, little dude. Hope the knee gets better. See you around, Haylah.'

'Yeah, I'm round!'

Round? Oh God, did I just say that? And Leo laughs and closes the door behind us.

Phew.

We survived. He doesn't know I wrote the notes. Which is brilliant, and also he looks like he might be using them to write his new set, which is totally super amazing. That the words that came out of *M Y* head might end up coming out of *his* mouth. Well, it makes me feel light-headed with excitement.

And even with the massively embarrassing falling over, the mud on face, the casual racism, the farting chairs and the admission of roundness, I can't stop moronically smiling all the way home.

TWELVE

But my good mood is busted the minute we get home and I discover Mum is there with the beige beardy weirdy Santa. Again. And they're sitting *way* too close to each other on the sofa for my liking.

'Ruben!' Noah hollers as he runs into the room and jumps up to sit in between them. I stand in the doorway with my arms folded.

'Hey, guys,' says the Beard, with a mouth disgustingly full of custard-cream biscuit. 'I just brought your mum home from her shift – thought I'd stay for a cuppa.'

'Stay for tea!' says Noah, and my heart sinks.

'Aw, thanks, Noah, but I probably ought to be getting off home soon,' he says.

'Yeah, Noah, he probably ought to be getting home soon,' I say, arms still crossed and tapping my foot on the floor like an old cartoon of a fuming housewife. Steam might shoot out of my ears soon.

'So, guys, how was school?' says Mum, hugging Noah and ignoring my tapping.

'I broke my leg,' Noah says, proudly showing them his knee. 'But we went to Leo's house and he fixed it.'

'Ow, that looks painful,' simpers the Beard. 'You must have been really brave!'

The patronizing, whiny fart.

I raise my eyebrows at him, at everyone, though apparently no one sees.

'Who's Leo?' Mum asks me. She raises her head at me with a *look* in her eyes. 'A *boyfriend*, Haylah?'

'Mum! No, he's no one,' I huff. She catches my eye-roll this time. 'I'm going to get changed.'

'Whoa, that's new, Haylah!' she says as I walk off. 'Changing out of school uniform before tea! Never thought I'd see the day.'

'Well. Sometimes things change without anyone being told anything – isn't that right?' I respond as I thump up the stairs.

'OK . . .' says Mum, clearly trying to hide the fact that she's getting pretty angry with me now. 'Was school all right, love?' she calls in a forced bright tone, but my bedroom door slams behind me and I don't reply.

I sit on my bed, grab my pillow and hug it over my stomach. I know I'm being an arse. I know I'm hurting Mum's feelings. But I can't help the way I feel.

Which is angry.

And hungry.

I should have taken some snacks from the kitchen before I stormed off. But if I went back down there now it would kind of spoil the drama of the whole door-slamming protest. It would be like Lady Gaga ending her show with a big firework explosion that fades to black, and then creeping back onstage with a torch, on her hands and knees, trying to find a lost contact lens.

Plus, I'd have to see them snuggled up on the sofa together again. I mean, I know Noah's sitting between them, but still. One sofa. Both of them on it. Eurgh.

All right, so I know he's just a guy and she's just a woman, staring into a beard, asking him to give her a lift home, but somehow the whole thing stinks. I mean, why didn't she tell me about him? This is *my* home too, right? And then she just brings this chin-jumper-wearing, bald-ankled cack-flump right into the centre of our lives with no questions asked. I mean, what if he's got a wife and five kids Mum doesn't know about? Or maybe she *does* know about them and they're having a proper affair – ugh! So gross. What if he's a serial killer? That beard has serial killer written all over it. Alongside the crumbs from the custard creams he just ate. *Our* custard creams.

Mum knocks on my door, and before I can tell her to go away she comes in and sits on the end of my bed. She puts a hand on my foot and squeezes it as she begins to talk.

'Hi, babe. Ruben's gone now . . . Look, we both know this is *difficult* for you . . .'

So it's 'we both' now, is it? I think furiously.

'. . . but all this slamming of doors and being outright rude to my . . . *friend* . . . well, it's just not like you.'

'But he's not a "friend" though, is he? He's a *boyfriend*, right?' I say.

Mum looks a mixture of pleased and cross. 'Well, maybe. Look, I told you, I don't *know* yet. We're going to take it slow and see what happens, OK?'

'Not really.'

Definitely swinging to cross. 'Haylah! I would say you're acting like a little kid, but even Noah's better than this. He's actually the one being cool about Ruben.'

'That's because he doesn't remember what it was like when Dad lived here!' I say before my brain has a chance to shut my mouth.

'What do you mean?' says Mum, her face flashing red with – what? Anger? Hurt? Embarrassment?

'I mean,' I say slowly, 'he doesn't remember the shouting, the yelling, the throwing of things, the sound as Dad closed the door for the last time.'

My voice goes all squeaky and I can't help it: I start to cry. *Stupid eyes.*

'Oh, love,' says Mum, and she moves closer to me for a hug, but I shrug her away.

'Look, Mum,' I say, shaking the tears off, 'I just don't know anything about him. I mean, do you? How do you know he's not a serial killer or . . . a Nazi, or a satanist, or a . . . trainspotter.'

She laughs a little.

'I'm serious!' I say.

'OK, OK. Look, I've known him at work for a year and a half. He's been divorced for five years, he doesn't have any kids, and with his job they'd have done a background and police check so I doubt very much he's a serial killer.

He was brought up Irish-Catholic, and though he doesn't go to church any more I doubt he's a satanist either. And, as far as I know, he's not into trainspotting, though if you must know he is a bit of a twitcher.'

'Oh my GOD, that's *disgusting*! What does that even mean?'

'It means birdwatcher, Hay, nothing sinister! And you know what, if you want to know anything else about him, just *ask* him. He's not Dad, Hay. He's a good guy. He's friendly and he's pretty funny too. You might actually *like* him, you never know.' She's fiddling with a loose thread on my duvet cover.

'Mmm-hmm,' I say, unconvinced.

Mum sighs. 'Look, I'll probably never love a guy again like I loved your dad. But he wasn't good for me, or for any of us, and he left. And . . . I'm sorry that happened, and I promise I won't get into another proper relationship unless I'm as sure as I can be that we won't get hurt again. But I've been on my own for a long time now, Hay, and I work my butt off and hardly have time to see my girlfriends any more and, well, at the moment it's just nice to be with someone. It's nice to have something more exciting to think about than topping up the rinse aid again, you know?'

I laugh a little. And I know she's right. I know she works crazy hard for us and that her social life's died a grisly death lately. But I mean, couldn't she just join a book club again or something, rather than hook up with this guy? I meet her eyes and they look soft and sad.

'Fine. It's just . . . I like it when it's just us.'

'I know, love. I do too. He's not moving in or anything like that! So it's still just us. We'll *always* be just us, but maybe it'll be just us plus another one *some* of the time. OK?'

This all sounds unreasonably reasonable. And I'm about to agree when I remember the other thing that's been bugging me.

'OK. But I want you to stay the same, and already you're changing . . . for him.'

Mum looks confused. 'How do you mean?'

'The make-up? The leg-shaving? I thought you were against doing that sort of stuff just because of what some bloke might think of you.'

She's back picking at that loose thread again. 'I am. I don't . . . Look, Ruben likes *me* for being *me*, and that's the important thing. I'm not under any pressure from him to do that . . . stuff. I guess I'm just doing it *because* I feel more confident, more attractive. Does that make sense?'

'No,' I say, though my heart's not in it.

She doesn't seem to hear anyway. 'And it's just a bit of lippy and a smooth set of shins – it's hardly like I'm getting extreme plastic surgery and breast enlargements.'

'Mum, if you got breast enlargements, we'd have to employ a scaffolder to construct your bras.'

Mum laughs so I go on. 'We'd have to inform NASA before they think they've discovered two new planets careering into ours.'

She laughs some more.

'There'd be panic in the streets as people flee from the unidentified orbs of destruction.'

'Yes, thank you, Hay,' she laughs. 'Can I get a hug now?' We hug.

'I love you, gorgeous girl,' she says.

'Love you too, Mum. Oh and . . .'

And I know this sounds bad, but as we pull away from the hug I figure it's a good time to ask about Friday night. So slowly and gently, with my head slightly to the side and my eyes as innocent and big as I can make them, I say, 'Can I go round to Chloe's on Friday night? I just think I need a little space. Is that OK? They'll bring me back by eleven or whatever.'

'Well, I'll have work, but . . . yeah, OK. I think you deserve a break.'

Yay! I think. *The spell worked!*

Then she ruins the moment by going on, 'Maybe Ruben can babysit Noah.'

Ugh! Why did she have to say that? Now I'm cross again.

'I see. So you'd just leave Noah alone with him?'

Mum sighs with frustration. 'Yes, I would. Noah likes Ruben – *they* get on really well together.'

'Yeah, but, Mum, Noah likes the Grumpy Old Troll from *Dora the Explorer* – it doesn't mean you should get *him* round to babysit, does it?'

'Haylah . . .'

And I know I'm breaking my own spell, but I just can't stop myself. 'I'm not saying Ruben's the Grumpy Old Troll! Although, now you mention it, there is a striking resemblance.'

'Haylah!' Mum is getting cross again too. 'Do you want to go round to Chloe's or not?'

I hate it when she slam-dunks me into submission. But she's won and she knows she has. Reluctantly, I relent.

'Sorry, yes, I do. It's fine – he can babysit. Thanks, Mum.' Though the 'thanks' is a bit sarcastic.

She sighs again. 'You need to do your homework, OK?'

'I am – look.' I wave my hands towards a pile of papers on my desk, hoping she won't look too closely. But she gets up and starts to examine them. I squirm.

'This isn't homework, it's jokes. You're writing *jokes*. Haylah, love, we've talked about this! I think it's great that you write, well, anything, but every parents' evening your teachers tell me that if you just knuckled down and concentrated on your schoolwork rather than always having your head in the clouds, thinking up stuff to put in all these *notebooks* of yours, you'd be getting straight As.'

'OK, fine, I'll do some homework. Happy now?' I say, grabbing my German workbook off the floor. '*Sieh zu, wie ich die dumme deutsche Hausaufgaben mache . . .*'

'Ecstatic,' she says with a clueless frown.

When she leaves, I chuck the German book across the room.

I know what's she's saying. I know she's trying to 'take it slow' with Ruben, but I can't shake off the feeling that she's going to get hurt. That we all are. That we're better off without anyone, and definitely without him. He's not right for her, for us – he's too much of a bearded weirdo. He's a *beardo*. And sooner or later he'll realize he doesn't want to deal with someone else's stroppy teenage daughter and nutso little son and he'll leave her. And she'll get depressed again, like after Dad left, and she didn't get out of bed for weeks.

Well, whatever. If it's what she wants, I guess.

I grab my notebook. Screw the German. I know how to ask, 'Wo ist die Jugendherberge?' and that their word for fart is pupsen. What else do you really need?

I clear my mind. And start writing down more jokes.

Sometimes I just write about funny stuff that happened that day, but sometimes I think of a punchline – maybe something people say a lot – and then I work backwards to make it into a joke like

I dislocated my shoulder the other day.
  I told the gym teacher I didn't want to play tennis.
  But he twisted my arm.

Or

Did you hear about the man who suddenly quit eating red meat?
  Yeah, he went cold turkey.

Or

I've got a big karate-chopping exam next week.
  So I ought to hit the books.

OK, so these might not be *great* jokes, but at least they take my mind off Mum and the Grumpy Old Troll.

*

Later we eat dinner and then play 'Guess Who' with Noah – it's his favourite game, but only when we play our own version: 'Facial Stereotypes' as we call it, or as Noah calls it, 'Faecal Stereotip! Faecal Stereotip!'

He doesn't really understand the game, but he thinks it's funny because we think it's funny.

Basically, as with the normal version, you have a load of cartoon faces in front of you and you have to narrow down which character the other team chose, but instead of asking, 'Is it a woman?' or 'Do they wear glasses?' and so on, you have to ask questions about their personality.

We stand up all our characters, Mum picks a card and me and Noah ask the questions.

'OK, so . . . do they throw big parties?'

'No,' says Mum.

'Right, Noah, so we have to put down all the party animals, like Andy, Kyle, Rebecca, Emily . . . Oooh, and Ashley. She's wearing a beret, definitely up for a party.'

'Do they have ADHD?'

'No,' says Mum, laughing.

We put down Jay and Brandon.

'Would they know how to spell "unnecessarily"?'

'Yes, definitely,' says Mum.

Down go all the stupid-looking faces.

'If someone dropped a ten-pound note in front of them, would they pick it up and keep it?'

'No.'

Down go all the shifty-looking faces.

'Do they get mostly swiped left on Tinder?'

'Quite possibly, yes.'

Down go all the good-looking people.

'Could they be a vicar in a local church?'

'Yes,' Mum laughs.

Down go anyone remaining who's slightly young and trendy.

'Do they have a weird collection of Star Trek figurines.'

'Erm . . . It wouldn't surprise me – yes!'

And we're down to two – Nick, an old, fat, balding guy with glasses and tufts of white hair above his ears, and David. Who has a beige beard.

And I really want to ask, 'Does this look like someone you'd trust to babysit your child?'

But before I do Noah comes in with, 'Does he look like someone who'd be fun to play with?'

'Yes, Noah, I think he does!' says Mum.

'It's David!' he shouts triumphantly, and Mum turns her card round to show beardy blimmin' David.

'Well, of course you chose the one with the beard,' I snipe.

'Indeed I did, Haylah. That OK with you?' says Mum with her jokey, 'sassy' look, which involves a raised eyebrow and pouty lips.

'I suppose,' I say, 'if you like that kind of thing.'

'I do like that sort of thing, yes,' Mum replies, but this time with a warning tone in her voice.

'I like beards! I WANT ONE!' says Noah.

And the evening feels spoiled again (THANKS, RUBEN) so I make my excuses and head back to my room.

Once there, my thoughts shoot back to Leo. I was in his house – actually in his house! *And* he thought I was funny, *and* I'm pretty sure he was using my jokes – MY JOKES – to write his set for Friday night! I should have just told him they were mine, but that would definitely have been super awkward and he would have seen me for the desperate stalker that I am. And then I – *Oh God, did I really tell him I was a communist?*

I'm not entirely sure what it is I've claimed to be, so I look up communism on my phone and it turns out it caused loads of deaths due to starvation and genocide, and that cute-sounding *Little Red Book* I'd heard of was actually a book used by a bad Chinese dude called Chairman Mao who killed, like, millions of people. *And for some reason I thought* THIS *sounded better than owning up to wanting to be a comedian?*

Before it gets cemented in his head that I'm a mental, communism-obsessed maniac, I should just tell him I wrote the jokes. Tell him I want to be a comedian too, and then he'll realize that we have loads in common, that out of all the kids at school it's just the two of us who share a pure love of the funny. So it kind of makes sense that we should totally hang out together.

And possibly curl up intertwined on a sofa, feeding each other grapes.

Lying on my bed, I start staging the conversation in my head. I imagine walking up to him on Friday night and saying, 'Yeah, so, funny thing is, I'm not *actually* a huge fan of occasionally genocidal political movements. I just find it hard to talk to people about wanting to be a comedian in case they laugh at me. Which . . . is kind of ironic because comedians should want to be laughed at. But the thing is, I don't want to be laughed *at*, I want to be laughed *with*. Which is why I said I was a communist, which I'm not really and . . .'

OH, FOR GOD'S SAKE! I CAN'T EVEN MAKE THIS CONVERSATION WORK IN MY HEAD! HOW AM I EVER GOING TO MAKE HIM THINK I'M ANYTHING OTHER THAN A LOSER IN REAL LIFE?

Breathe, Pig, just breathe. Write some more jokes. That's what you're good at. Stick to that. Post them quietly and anonymously through his locker for the next few days, and then go on Friday night, keep your mouth shut and just enjoy watching lovely Leo from a distance.

A safe distance. Where he can't hear any of the nonsense that comes out of your big, stupid, pig mouth.

THIRTEEN

Over the next week things stay frosty at home with Mum, which is horrible and completely the fault of that face-fungus-wearing twit who seems to be at our house every ruddy day – eating our biscuits, bellowing his festive laugh and making me heave with his naked ankles. There isn't so much an atmosphere in the house as a *twatmosphere*, if you will.

But confining myself to my room helps me concentrate on writing some new stuff that I think Leo would perform really well, and at school I post the jokes into his locker. I get quite good at slinking around the metal maze unseen, never revealing my secret identity. Like a comedy ninja.

I normally do it in the morning, while the lockers are reasonably quiet, on the way back from returning the register to the office. Which is almost worth it just for the look on Mrs Perkins's face every morning when I shoot my hand up first to offer to take it. She frowns at me, and you can almost see the cogs turning behind her eyes. She knows I'm up to something, but can't put her finger on what and it's driving her crazy. Chloe and Kas just think I'm using it as an excuse to get some extra snacks from the vending machine. I'm so desperate to hide my true motive I play up to this by eating extra KitKats in front of them. Which is obviously really tough, but it's the kind of sacrifice a true comedy ninja is willing to make for her art.

On Friday, I'm so super excited about seeing Leo perform again at the open-mic night that I lose my mind a little and, caught up in the excitement, underneath my latest joke I write, stupidly,

Feel free to use any of these tonight.

But as I walk away the doubt sets in. Maybe he doesn't want to use them at all. Maybe my notes are just annoying the crap out of him. They're probably not nearly as funny as anything he'd write and, now that I think about it, that last message telling him he can use this stuff tonight might sound really creepy so he's probably just binned them anyway.

The evening arrives, and with it a stomach filled with frantic, twitchy butterflies. *Oh, why have I put myself through this?* If he uses my jokes, I'm just going to explode with nerves, embarrassment and panic that no one will actually laugh at them. If he doesn't use them, I'll finally have proof of my complete loser status, knowing that the laughter I heard was not at the jokes themselves but at *me*, the idiot who wrote such drippy, bum-gravy material and posted it through his locker like a completely desperate twonk.

We get ready at Chloe's flat, and both Chloe and Kas look amazing. Chloe's in a black dress that clings to her like it's been painted on.

'Wow – your mum lets you wear that?' Kas asks her.

'Totally – she bought it for me. And she got me this padded bra. Look – I have boobs now!' she says, bouncing them around in the air like two juggling balls. If I did that, people would get injured.

'Well, you definitely have a very *pronounced* bosom today, my dear,' I say in a posh voice. 'Like BOOO-SOM,' I enunciate.

Kas and Chloe ignore me, and continue fussing over each other's outfits.

Kas's look is simple, but she looks great in it – tight jeans and a little stripy tank top. If I wore that, I wouldn't so much have a muffin top as a sack of muffins sitting on top of another sack of muffins.

I wear one of my man-sized checked shirts, trainers and some high-waisted jeans which come up almost to my boobs. When I do up the fly, it sounds like someone zipping up a tent.

'You look great, Pig!' says Chloe.

'Oh, shut up. I look like a cowgirl . . . who just ate a cow,' I say.

They laugh a little, but the truth is, standing next to them as we look in the mirror together, and knowing I'm going to see Leo later, I've never felt worse about my reflection. They look like beautiful women whereas I look like an overgrown, dumpy toddler. I don't want to look like them, or dress like them. I just don't want to look like this. Plain. Dull. Shapeless. It's a scientific wonder that someone as large as me could look so invisible.

But then that's what I've always aimed for with my clothes – to be invisible, to blend into my surroundings for fear that if I push myself to the foreground people will laugh *at* me, not with me. That they'll think, *Why's she wearing nice stuff? What the hell makes her think she's got a body worth highlighting with cool clothes?*

If you're fat and plain, you should at least have the dignity to dress like you *know* you're fat and plain, to stop others feeling the need to point it out, rather than attempting a look way out of your league. But on the other hand I wish I had the guts to, I don't know, wear a hat sometimes, or a big pair of boots, just something that makes me feel a little less drab and unimportant.

I do think my hair looks OK though. Chloe's done something to it with some hot roller things and drowned it in hairspray and now it falls in waves around my face. Just don't touch them – they look good, but feel like dried seaweed.

She coils my hair up round my cheeks a little more. 'There. You look great! Leo's bound to notice you tonight.'

I just roll my eyes and smile weakly at her.

I haven't told them about going into Leo's house the other day. Somehow I just wanted to keep that private, like a secret date that nobody knows about but me and Leo. Pathetic, I know.

'You would look great with a bob, you know – you really should think about getting your hair cut,' says Chloe, running her hands through her short blonde hair, which always looks amazing.

'No, she should totally keep the long hair – it flatters the face,' says Kas.

'Don't you mean my "pretty fat-girl face"?' I say, then quickly continue before they can look sad for me. 'But you're right. If I had a bob, my whole head would just look like a big bowling ball.'

We laugh.

We walk down the road with Chloe's sister Freya and her boyfriend Sulky Jake, a persistently moody car mechanic. I can never work out if he's genuinely depressed about something or if he's putting on the whole pouty, deep, surly thing to try to appear sexy. Which obviously worked for Freya, but I just don't get why anyone would want to go out with a guy who literally never smiles or laughs. I mean, I get that snogging's important (at least I can imagine it is) but, if you can't have a giggle or a full-on whole-body-shaking belly laugh with someone, what's the point? Who wants to snog a mouth that never smiles? You might as well date a trout.

At the end of the road is Jake's clapped-out old Ford Escort. It looks like it's held together with gaffer tape and prayers. He almost proudly, though still drearily, tells us he's 'doing it up in my dad's garage when I have spare time between other jobs'.

Which can't be very often, by the look of it.

Freya, tottering along the pavement in frighteningly high heels, insists she won't travel in the back of the car because 'I've got a modelling job next week, and sitting in the back of a car isn't good for ya skin – all the toxins and everything come through the vents at the front of the car and gather at the back in invisible toxic clouds that seep into your pores.'

It's the biggest load of ball-bags I've ever heard in my life and I'm about to tell her as much when I realize both my friends are nodding along, wide-eyed, trying to take in every word that comes out of Freya's perfectly pouty mouth.

'Wow, that's really interesting,' says Kas incorrectly as both she and Chloe link arms with Freya and strut down the road, with me clomping after them in my trainers, still mud-stained from the last time I took Noah to the park.

'I know,' says Freya, 'but you guys will be all right. I've got an amazing new home-made skin-peel that'll clean those toxins right out. You can all borrow some – it's made out of egg whites, yoghurt, sugar . . . Oh, what's the other ingredient . . .?'

'Desperation? The blood of an ugly virgin? Tears from the homeless?' I interject.

She frowns at me, trying to figure out what species I am cos it's definitely not the same as hers.

'Erm, no – oh yeah, that's it, vinegar, and of course a few other secret bits and bobs I can't possibly tell you about or the beauty police might arrest me!'

She giggles here, and Kas and Chloe both inexplicably laugh.

'I'll take some,' says Kas.

'Oh, me too. Thanks, sis,' says Chloe. She turns to me. 'You want some, Pig?'

'Nah, I'm good. I quite like my skin, y'know, *unpeeled* if possible. I'll take the eggs and sugar though – might bake myself up a toxin-fighting chocolate brownie!'

Freya stops as Jake carries on to his car, placing his guitar in the boot as gently as a new father puts his newborn into a pram. Freya whips her head round towards me and, in as serious a voice as I've ever heard her use, says, 'Don't joke about chocolate, babe. Did you know that stuff's got more toxins in it than a bottle of toilet cleaner?'

'No, I didn't know that. Yikes. Tastes a lot better though, right?'

I can hear Chloe stifling a giggle.

Seeing I'm a lost cause, Freya tuts and trots on towards the car, dragging her minions along with her, like a high-heeled giraffe sandwiched between two adoring gazelles.

Jake opens the back door, which almost falls off in his hands, points at me and says, 'You go in the middle, love.'

'Why's she got to go in the middle, babe?' says Freya.

But I noticed the car lurching to one side when the guitar went in the boot, so of course I already know why and just want us to skip past this next humiliation. As I clamber into the centre of the back seat, I say, through gritted teeth, 'No, it's fine. I don't mind the middle.' With each shuffle of my butt along the seat, the car sways from side to side like an old drunk relative at a wedding trying desperately not to keel over. Frankly, it'll be a miracle if this clapped-out heap gets us to the pub at all.

'I like the middle,' says Kas. 'Pig, you sure you don't want me to sit there? Doesn't look like you're fitting in all that well.'

Oh God, just get in and let this be over.

'No, really,' I say, almost hysterically, 'it's fine! I love the middle!'

'She has to sit there – suspension's busted and we have to keep the weight even. If she sits at the side, we might not make it round corners without rolling. In the middle there, she'll do a great job keeping us nice and stable, like the ballast tank of a ship.'

'Jake!' says Freya. 'Sorry, Pig.'

'Yeah, no, it's fine, makes total sense,' I hiss, hoping the red in my cheeks isn't showing too much.

Kas and Chloe get in on either side of me, and by the time we shut the doors we're squished together so much we're like one giant, hideous, three-headed, six-legged teenage-girl-freak. And when we get to the pub Kas and Chloe burst out of the doors like those joke snakes from a can, and I roll along the seat and fall out after them.

'This is so exciting! An evening out in a pub – I wonder who'll be here from school? All Leo's cool friends, I bet,' says Chloe as we walk in.

'Look, there's Leo – there's Leo! Look at him, Pig! LOOK!' whisper-shouts Kas to me.

Leo is leaning up against the bar, chatting to his mates from school – Jax, Mikey, that toothy girl Keesha who's always following him around, and about six others I recognize from Leo's year.

At the sight of him, my heart, which has already had one hell of a workout these last couple of weeks, somersaults into my throat. Just knowing he's onstage later, knowing he might use some of my jokes . . . or not . . . Either way lies probable total humiliation. The last thing I need on top of this is Chloe and Kas going on about how much I *luurve* him – I mean, what if he hears? I really want to tell them once and for all to just leave it, and that I do not '*like*' Leo like that, but somehow, seeing him here, the ability to find words and put them together has escaped me.

'Yeah, I see him. Look, I don't, there's nothing, he's not, I don't, so OK?' I splutter.

Kas and Chloe laugh and grab my hand as we follow Freya and Jake to a table, right in front of a small stage covered in a spaghetti-like mess of electronic leads leading to amplifiers, a mixing-desk thing covered in twiddly knobs, a microphone and a collection of guitars. Jake gently eases his guitar out of its case and writes his name on a whiteboard list next to the stage. At the top of the list it says, 'Poet? Musician? Comedian? Write your name below and perform here tonight!' There's about seven other names up there already, including Leo's. He's on sixth. I can't wait to see him, but I really wish I was hiding in a corner where he couldn't see me, not just a couple of metres away from the stage.

And why, oh WHY did I write that note saying I'd be here this evening? Oh God, he might work out that I'm the weird locker-note stalker! Idiot Pig.

Leo's dad, just about the coolest parent I've ever seen, with dreadlocks falling down over his leather waistcoat (which should look awful, but somehow really doesn't), comes over to our table and says 'Hey' to Jake, who's hovering behind us, clearly nervous about his set, although he'd never admit it. They fist-bump each other and then Leo's dad says, 'Brought some under-agers in this evening then, Jakey boy?'

Chloe, Kas and I squirm in our seats.

'Yeah, that's my girlfriend's little sister and her mates,' says Jake. 'What can I say – they're big fans.'

'I'm a big fan of Jake shutting the frick up, I'll give him that,' I whisper under my breath. Kas laughs and Chloe tells me to shush.

'All right, but no under-age drinking, OK?' says Leo's dad. 'And I've said the same to my boy and his mates. Don't wanna lose my licence, all right, girls?'

'Don't worry, Kingston. I'll keep an eye on them,' says Jake with a patronizing hand on Kas's shoulder. 'And don't talk when the acts are on, OK, kids?'

'Thanks, Jake, I don't think we could have worked that one out for ourselves,' I say. But unfortunately sarcasm seems to sail way over his head as he just nods and winks at me.

Jake gets us all Cokes, and pretty soon we actually start to have a good time. We used to have family pub lunches all the time when Dad was around, but I've never been in one with just my mates. It feels sophisticated somehow, fantastically grown up, which I know is a really dumb-nuts, non-grown-up thing to say, but there it is.

Me, Chloe and Kas gossip about the other kids from school in the pub, all older than us, and therefore a lot cooler than us.

'That's Slade Smith,' Kas whispers. 'He's dead cute!'

'Not as cute as Leo though – right, Pig?' says Chloe, too loudly.

'For the last time, I just like his stand-up, that's all, all right?' I hiss, determined not to look at him.

'Oooh – you should do a – what's it called – a set? He'd notice you then!' says Chloe brightly.

'*What?* Are you kidding – *what??*' I splutter. 'That's the Coke going straight to your head, Chlo, cos that idea's straight out of Crazyville,' I say, my face going red at the very thought of ever walking out on a stage, let alone in front of Leo.

'No, she's right! Why not? You're always thinking up funny stuff. You want to be a comedy . . . person?' says Kas.

'*Comedian.* Well, yes, but no, really, really, REALLY, really, no. No. Thank you. I'm just here to enjoy the –'

'Leo,' cuts in Kas with a widening of her eyes.

'Show!' I say.

They giggle. I scowl. The show begins.

The first act is a nauseating woman called Starlight who wears a floaty dress and feebly strums a guitar. She sings in a whiny, whingey voice and barely shuts her mouth between words or sounds so that everything is just a big vowelly nonsense.

Next up is a small guy with floppy blond hair who reads angry slam poetry from a small black notebook held up high in his outstretched hand. The names of all his poems have swear words in them.

After that, there's a couple of guitar-playing duos who are kind of OK, and a man who plays the bongos while rapping over them, which is just bewildering, although he manages to get the loudest applause at the end of his set just because everyone's relieved it's over.

Then ... *gulp* ... there's Leo. I can't help but stare at him as he walks up to the stage.

He passes, he turns towards me and, LITERALLY LIKE OUT OF MY DAYDREAM, his eye catches mine, and he says coolly, 'Oh, hi, Pig.'

Both Kas and Chloe's heads whip round and they stare at me, their necks extended, their mouths wide open, like an abandoned Hungry Hippos game.

'Wha–?' they start to say.

'Shh!' I say with a grin. 'You mustn't talk when the acts are on!'

Despite the worry of what Leo's going to say up there, I feel amazing. Like my insides are glowing. After the borderline disastrous meeting at his house, I totally thought he'd just ignore me if he saw me again, but he actually said hi to me! In front of Chloe and Kas!

I don't stop smiling as Leo's dad announces him. 'Well, for those of you who've been here before, there's no need to introduce this next act – he's handsome, charming, a real chip off the old block. It's my son, Leo Jackson!'

Whoops and cheers from his friends at the table behind ours.

Leo grabs the microphone off its stand and I try as hard as I can not to just stare at him like last time, especially now I know he'll notice whether I laugh or not. Not that I need to remind myself to laugh – he's just as funny as before, just as confident, and his timing is awesome. I make sure I laugh, but at the same time I realize he's halfway through his set and he hasn't used any of my jokes.

So that's it then. He thinks the jokes suck. He thinks the person who posted them through his locker sucks. It's over. It's done. Why was I kidding myself I knew how to write jokes? What do I know? I'm just a stupid, spherical simpleton posting unwanted nonsense through a door, like a junk-mail delivery clown.

I look down at my hands clutching the Coke glass as Leo gets more laughs and then . . .

And then . . .

My ears prick up as he starts talking about how hot it was the other day and – maybe, yes, oh my God, I can't believe it . . . yes! He's actually using one of my jokes! One of MY chuffin' jokes! And then, just as quick as it came, my elation is replaced by panic. *WHAT IF NOBODY LAUGHS??* I mean, there's an actual room here filled with actual people. Strangers, THE PUBLIC are here, listening to a joke that came from MY head, and if they reject that they reject me and *oh, good holy crap, why did I do this?*

But then . . . he hits the punchline.

'. . . you understand, right? Cos Waitrose sure didn't.'

Time stands still. Just for a moment. And I turn and I look around the pub to see people's faces lighting up with the biggest grins and then . . . laughing! Actually, properly belly-laughing. Partly because of me. And it feels like I've just been injected, straight into my brain, with pure total joy.

He's changed some of the wording so it fits his style better, but by the end of his set he's used all of them! ALL of MY jokes. And they ALL got laughs! He finishes up his set with the joke I gave him yesterday, and he doesn't change the wording to this one at all. Just says it exactly as I've written it:

'Yeah, that's my dad over there, so obviously I can't bad-mouth my parents too much tonight because, well, you know, *I value my life*. But isn't it weird how when you *are* merrily slagging off your parents, that's fine, but if one of your mates *joins in* with you that is NOT fine? *No one* can slag off *my* parents but *me*!

'It's like squeezing a zit on my own butt: it's fine for *me* to do it, but if your mate does it *for* you that's just plain *wrong*.'

A big laugh erupts and Leo pauses, then adds my final word:

'Apparently.'

This seals the deal, and now everyone is clapping and hollering with laughter. At *my* joke! And it feels frick-frackin' amazing. It doesn't even feel like he's getting the laughter and I'm not – it feels like we *both* are.

He smiles, thanks the audience, hangs up his microphone and swaggers off back to his mates, who all high-five him and pat him on the back.

'That was *so* funny!' says Kas.

And I laugh, still on a high from the whole intoxicating fog of this delicious feeling.

'So come on, Pig, quick, before the next act – how does he know your name?' says Chloe.

I shrug with a grin. After all, they always have boys passing them notes and getting their mates to ask them out. Why can't I have a little boy attention for once? Even if it is based on nothing more than my little brother falling over outside a boy's house.

'We've just seen each other around,' I say casually, unable to wipe the smirk from this bloody brilliant evening off my face.

'Ha ha! Pig, you dark horse, who knew?' says Kas, laughing.

On the other side of her though, Chloe looks pissy.

'Kept that a secret, didn't you?' she says.

'He only knows my name, Chloe – we're not engaged or anything!' I say, determined to enjoy every moment.

'Well, if you're not going to give us any more details, I'm off to the bog,' she says and saunters away.

'What's her problem?' I ask Kas.

'Oh, you know Chloe. She hates it when anyone else gets any attention from boys. Don't worry about it.'

And I'm not really. I'm mostly just thinking about the massive laughs me and Leo just got. Me *and* Leo. Together. Whether he knows it or not. Now that I know he likes the jokes, I really should just tell him I wrote them. But then that might ruin the whole thing – he probably thinks one of his mates wrote them, and if he finds out it's a dumpy girl two years younger than him he might freak out. So I'll keep it to myself – as my secret.

After all, I am sworn to never reveal my secret identity. For I am the comedy ninja. And my work here this evening is done.

By the time Chloe returns from the loo, Jake's playing his set. He plays slow love songs he's written himself, and though he's actually not bad on the guitar his lyrics are terrible, full of meaningless clichés, lines you wouldn't ever hear *anyone* say in real life, at least not without throwing up a bit. Stuff like, 'I'll always be true', 'your sweet caress' and 'my tender loving care'. He sings with a pained expression, his eyes closed, and at one point stops playing the guitar for a moment and clenches his fist in the air in a classic pulling-the-invisible-toilet-chain, boy-band move. Seriously.

When he starts his last song, Freya leans over to us and whispers excitedly, 'He wrote this one about me!' which makes me wonder why she's not worried if he openly wrote the other songs about some other girls. The song is called 'My Forever Passenger', and while the creepy love-song lyrics are still there he's bravely combined them with his love of fixing cars, at one point ambitiously rhyming 'heartache' with 'handbrake' and 'the way you felt' with 'fan belt'.

He walks offstage to the polite applause filling the room, and just nods as if to say, 'Yeah, I know, I'm amazing.'

And, while he's really, really not, it's cool. Why not let the guy have his moment? God knows, I'm having mine. I feel flip-out fantastic. And nothing's gonna spoil this feeling. Ever.

Argh (spoiler alert), who am I kidding?

FOURTEEN

Freya is all over Jake when he returns to the table, and we're also telling him what a great set it was, and talking about perhaps heading home soon, when Leo's dad announces, 'And next up we have . . . Pig. *Pig?* Can that be right? Erm, anyone called Pig around here?'

The colour and feeling drain from my whole body and I freeze.

Chloe leans over and says, 'Come on, Pig, they're waiting for you!'

'What? What's happening??' I manage to get out, wondering if this really is a daydream. Or a nightmare. 'No, no, I can't. Wait, what?'

Seeing the panic in my eyes, Kas puts an arm round me and whispers with a kind smile, 'Go on, Pig, you can do it – it's now or never!'

'Never! I choose never! Never's fine for me!' I say.

Then a voice behind me starts chanting, 'Pig! Pig! Pig! Pig!' and soon half the pub joins in and I realize there's no way out. The world is suddenly a blur.

'Take this, you'll need it,' says the same voice from behind me, and a glass of water is thrust into my unsteady hand. It occurs to me for a moment that the voice may have been Leo's, but there's no room in my head for that right now. There's only room for a swirling, sickening crapstorm of panic and dread.

I get up from my seat, but my knees have turned to jelly, and for a moment I think I may have actually forgotten how to walk. Somehow I manage to persuade my legs to move and I shuffle up to the stage. What else can I do?

The spotlights are blinding. Leo's dad covers the microphone and leans over to me. 'So you're Pig? Really?'

'Erm, yeah.'

'All right, well, what you doing, love?'

'Erm, I was told to come up here?'

'No, I mean singing? Poetry?'

'Right, erm . . . comedy?' I offer, although for a moment I think singing a hearty rendition of 'Summer of '69' might be the easier option; a quicker, simpler way to kill myself through humiliation rather than the torturous slow death I'm currently experiencing.

Leo's dad announces, 'And now, everyone, give it up for the comedy stylings of . . . Pig!'

He leaves the stage as a smattering of applause echoes around the otherwise now silent and expectant pub.

I move to the middle of the stage. Spotlight on me. Faces in the dark staring at me. My mind a complete blank. It's so close to an actual nightmare I suddenly panic that I'm not wearing all my clothes. Too late now if I'm not.

I glug down some water, though somehow my throat still feels like it's lined with sandpaper.

Who the hell *put my name up for this?*

Chloe. Must have been her. When she sloped off to the 'loo' after finding out about me knowing Leo.

How could she?

With a now violently convulsing hand, I put the glass down on a small table next to the microphone stand.

The microphone itself is way too high up for me. I struggle with it, trying to angle it down, but it won't budge. So, with hands still quivering like dying fish, I yank it out of its holster. There's a yelping feedback sound from the speakers behind me, and as they squeal my stomach turns and I consider just running offstage, out of the door and as far away as I can possibly get.

But no, I'm here. People are waiting for me to say something. Technically – *technically* – this is what I've always wanted. I *have* to do it now. But my mind is still blank.

Just say something. Anything!

'Hello. This is my, er, first stand-up.'

The words are barely recognizable as human sounds – it turns out it's very hard to talk when there's literally no moisture in your mouth. Lips are sticking together. Teeth are sticking to lips. Tongue has adhered to roof of mouth. I cough, reach down, take another gulp of water, put the glass back down.

The room is SO painfully silent. My brain is a hive of confusion and panic. I know I've written countless jokes in the past that are stored in there somewhere, but somehow none of them can break through. They're all mashed up, tangled in the furthest reaches of my idiot mind.

Deep breath.

I can do this.

Maybe.

'So, yeah, this is my first stand-up. I'm sure you'll be surprised to hear that.'

A tiny laugh echoes around the room. Tiny, but a laugh nonetheless. This makes me feel better.

'And, erm . . . yeah, get used to it because I *will* be this awkward for the whole routine.' This gets a proper laugh from the audience. A slightly nervous, pitying laugh, but a laugh all the same. Enough to spur me on. I scan my brain for something, *anything*, *any* of the jokes I've ever written, just something to say. And slowly the fog in my brain starts to clear, at least enough for a couple of possibly half-decent funny thoughts to break through.

'Man, this is scary. I mean, despite my dainty appearance, I don't scare easily. But *this*, whoa! I *am* scared of spiders though. I know it's a cliché, but there we go.'

I've relaxed a bit now, so I use a trick I've seen stand-ups use.

'Anyone else in here scared of spiders?'

A few people shout yes. Excellent!

With every word I speak, my confidence grows. 'Right, you people – *you're the enlightened.*'

A bigger laugh – the room is actually enjoying my joke. Maybe I can do this!

'And the rest of you, you *ignorant* lot, you just don't understand, do you? You just don't *get* that it's not that we don't *like* spiders, it's not that we think our *personalities* are incompatible. *We just know they are genuinely the work of the devil.* And seriously, if an eight-fingered disembodied hand with beady eyes and a sack of venom runs at you, who's the idiot? The dude who wants to pet it, or the dude who runs the hell away?'

It actually gets a proper laugh – the comedy gods are smiling down on me!

'So anyway, it wasn't my idea to come up here, it was actually my, er, "friends". I say "*friends*", but, erm, now it feels more like we're Hunger Games contestants: even if I survive this, I'm still going to have to kill at least one of them.'

Another proper laugh fills the room, giving me a high I've never experienced before.

'We love you, Pig!' shouts Kas.

I squint into the darkness behind the blinding spotlight to smile at Kas. *I'm starting to ruddy well enjoy this! It's everything I've always imagined it might be!*

And then I see that Leo, *my* Leo, is sitting next to Chloe, his arm resting on the back of the seat behind her, almost like his arm is *around* her. He whispers something to her and they both giggle.

My thoughts jumble up. *What? What is this? How could she . . .? Just what?*

Then I remember everyone's looking at me. I need to keep going.

'Umm, yeah, so everyone calls me Pig.' I look down at my big wobbly body, then up again. 'I think it's cos I'm just slightly more intelligent than a dog.'

People laugh.

'No, but I guess we should discuss the elephant in the room, but, erm . . . I forget what that is . . . which is weird because usually I never forget.'

It takes a moment for people to get this, but when they do there's another big laugh, which would have felt great if it wasn't for Leo and Chloe. *Why the hell is his arm still on the back of her chair?*

'No, but seriously, erm, I know that I'm on the big side, and healthy eating and obesity is a big important issue now and, well, I read just this week that apparently one in every three Americans has . . . eaten the other two.'

Another laugh.

'So at least I know I'm not alone and, well, I actually truly believe that inside every *thin* girl there's a *fat* girl trying to . . . eat her way out.'

A bigger laugh and a few claps too.

Leo laughs as well, and then Chloe whispers something to him, her mouth right next to his ear. Closer to him than I'll ever get. He carries on laughing, but he's looking right towards me, and it suddenly feels like they're laughing *at* me, not with me. Is this why she put my name down for this? Because she was jealous that Leo knew my name, not hers, and she wanted to get me away so she could move in on him?

My brain turns to mush. The fog sets in again. The room is staring at me and I'm saying nothing. I've got nothing. I'm done. I can't do this any more. I can't do this ever again.

'So that's it. Thank you, erm, yeah.'

With shaking hands, I put the microphone back in its stand as people applaud and a few even whoop. Out of sympathy, I'm guessing. Sympathy for the stupid fat girl who just made a complete arse of herself onstage.

They are clapping quite loudly though. Perhaps I wasn't so bad after all? I got *some* laughs. And if it hadn't been for – argh – Chloe and Leo, maybe it would have been half OK?

Leo's dad emerges from the shadows at the side of the stage. As I turn to walk off past him, he smiles at me, then suddenly reaches his arms out. So, without thinking, I move in for a much-needed hug.

Wow, what a nice guy.

Then when his arms, instead of reaching round me, reach behind me, I realize with a devastating thud in my insides that he was actually just trying to catch the microphone stand, which I'm knocking over with my butt as I turn round.

Time lapses into a painful slow motion, forcing me to fully absorb every humiliating millisecond as I stand onstage, in front of everyone, my arms round Leo's dad's waist as he lunges in vain to save the mic stand, a victim of the destructive power of my arse cheeks.

The stand crashes to the ground, sending the water in my cup flying and dispensing its contents over the electrical equipment behind me. There's a loud bang, and a flash lights up the gawping faces of the audience before all the electrics go out and the pub is plunged into darkness and, for a moment, a stunned silence.

Then, 'That'll do, Pig, that'll do,' says Leo's dad.

Everyone screeches with laughter and applauds wildly. And this time they definitely *are* all laughing *at* me.

'No need to worry, everyone!' shouts Leo's dad as I sheepishly unclamp my arms from around his waist. 'Leo – go and flip the switch in the fuse box, mate!'

People start to turn on the torches on their mobile phones, illuminating the pub enough for me to see the embarrassing mess I've made of the stage.

'I'm so sorry, what can I do?' I say, crouching down and trying to mop up the water on the floor with the sleeves of my shirt.

'Nothing, love. Accidents happen – don't worry about it. Just move back and let me deal with it, OK?' says Leo's dad.

'OK, yep, no problem,' I say, trying to hold myself together as Chloe and Kas gather round in the semi-darkness.

'You all right, Pig?' they say through great fits of giggles.

Their laughter *at* me, and knowing it was Chloe who put my name down for this torturous mess in the first place sends me over the edge, and I can feel the hot sting of tears behind my eyes. I get up and run past them, to the door and out of the pub, then up the street.

'Pig!' they call, coming after me. But I don't want to hear it.

I run to Jake's car and lean up against it. As it lurches under my weight, I put my head in my hands and the tears start to fall. And then the car alarm goes off, screeching and wailing into the night air.

Just my luck that the only thing that actually works on this car is the sodding alarm, which is in fine voice as it screams to the world to come and look at the idiot.

Kas and Chloe run up the road towards me.

'Bloody hell, Pig,' says Kas, giggling, 'it's not your night, is it?'

'I'll go and get Jake!' says Chloe, laughing.

Then Kas notices my tears and puts an arm round me. 'Seriously, don't worry about it, Pig. It's all fine. You were great in there!'

'I was *awful*. It was awful. Please, I don't want to talk about it,' I say, shrugging her off and turning away.

'But you totally nailed it – and did you see Leo watching you? He was loving it too.'

'Oh, I bet he was, loving having his arm round Chloe anyway,' I spit back.

'It wasn't like that, honest. He just came and sat next to Chloe – it's not her fault,' says Kas.

I turn to her, my blush of humiliation deepening. 'Whatever. And really I couldn't give a crap. Like you say, it's *fine*.' I look back up the road, wishing it would open up and swallow me.

We wait in silence until Jake and Freya come back with Chloe, then we all get in the car, with me in the middle, of course, doing what I'm best at, being a big lump of human ballast. I look down at my hands as I pick at my fingernails, my crispy hair falling down on either side of my face, forming a useful set of curtains between me and Chloe and Kas.

Chloe goes to say something to me – probably the same nonsense Kas said, that it was all 'fine', that I did 'great', that all my dreams of doing stand-up haven't just been dropped from a great height into a great steaming pile of turd burgers. But out of the corner of my eye I see Kas raising a hand up to Chloe and shaking her head, the universal symbol for 'Don't say anything now or she might go mental.'

This does not make me feel better.

'That was a good night, right, girls?' says Jake as he drives us home, blissfully clueless about the silent drama going on in the back seat.

'You played great, babe!' says Freya, reaching over and resting a hand on his thigh.

'Thanks, yeah, it felt good, like everyone was really feeling it, y'know?' he says. 'And, Pig, I gotta say that was the funniest thing I've ever seen – the end of your set when you grabbed Kingston and knocked the stand down and . . .' He can't finish the sentence because he's actually laughing so hard. Jake. A boy who NEVER laughs. Laughing. So he does have a sense of humour. It's just a mean one.

'Yeah,' I say, 'that was the big ending I was going for.'

'Well, you've definitely got the big end, love,' he says.

'Jake!' says Freya, clearly enjoying seeing her boyfriend actually jovial for once but, to her credit, trying not to laugh along with him for my sake.

'What? She *wants* to be funny, ain't that right, Pig?' says Jake.

'Yep,' I snap, 'that's exactly right. This is just what I want.'

'You know,' says Chloe, foolishly going against Kas's advice to shut the hell up, 'Leo said –'

'I don't want to know what Leo said,' I bark at her. 'I just wanna go home, OK?'

'Fine,' says Chloe in a huff. And then an awkward silence travels with us all the way back to my house.

FIFTEEN

After Jake's car has spewed me out on to the pavement, I ignore Kas's awkward lip-sucking smile as she gets back into the car, then I yell a short, sharp goodbye to them all, storm up to my front door and slam it behind me.

I go into the living room, and Beige Beardo is sitting on our sofa, watching our TV. I'd managed to avoid him earlier, and what with everything else had totally forgotten he was here.

Gee, thanks, universe, for chucking this dungball at me after tonight's already been a crock of crapola. Just what I need.

'Good night?' he asks, and I can't help it. I start crying again.

'Hey, whoa, what is it?' he asks, alarmed and turning off the TV.

'Nothing,' I blub, collapsing on to the armchair with my elbows on my knees and my head in my hands. I should just go up to my bedroom. The last thing I want to do is cry in front of this moron. But I can't seem to find the will to heave myself out of this chair now I'm in it.

The sofa over the other side of the room groans as Ruben shifts round awkwardly on it to face me. 'You OK? Do I need to call your mum?'

I take my hands away from my face, start to run my fingers through my hair, but of course Chloe's cemented it in place with all the ruddy hairspray, so I extract my fingers and throw myself against the back of the chair, trying as hard as hell to sniff away the tears. 'No, no, it's fine, really, it's nothing.'

'I think I should call her . . .' He starts patting down the sofa around him, looking for his phone.

'I said it's nothing!' I shriek, at a pitch that definitely betrays the insistence that it's 'nothing'.

'OK, OK.' Ruben raises his empty hands towards me. 'So . . . do you wanna – *talk* about it or anything?' His voice goes weirdly high on 'anything'. He clearly doesn't know how to deal with this, though watching him flounder about awkwardly, *trying* to deal with this, is actually taking my mind off the crappy evening. A bit.

'No,' I sniffle, dropping my head back against the armchair and staring at the ceiling.

'Well, do you wanna watch TV or . . . play cards or something to take your mind off the "nothing" that made you cry?'

I huff a sigh of frustration. Play cards? *What a spanner.*

'Look, I'm not a little kid on a hospital ward. You can't just get out the playdough and make everything go away, OK?' I snap.

Then I feel the tiniest bit bad about being pissy at him. I stick my head forward, and for a moment look over at him, and see only kind and hurt eyes looking back at me. I roll my eyes and let my head fall back again as I resume my ceiling-gazing. I know he's only trying to make me feel better. And there's something about him that's strangely comforting. Oh God, am I actually starting to like him now? This evening's going from bad to worse.

'Sorry,' I say.

'No, sure,' he says. Then I hear him tapping out a beat on his beige corduroy thighs, as if percussion would somehow diffuse the awkwardness in the air. He clears his throat. 'So, er, your mum tells me you want to be a comedian. Sometimes she tells some of your jokes at work. They're pretty funny,' he says, with a tentative chuckle. 'Like, erm, what was that one? Oh yeah – "Everyone's talking about infections these days. They've totally gone viral." '

He tells the joke all wrong, with the stress on the wrong words. But still, I don't know if it's because it's kind of sweet that he remembered one of my jokes or whether it's because the joke itself is a tiny bit funny, but either way I can't help cracking a small smile. 'Yeah, I remember that one. Mum always likes it when I give her a hospital-based joke.'

But then the idea of writing jokes shoots my thoughts right back to the nightmare of this evening and I shudder at the memory.

'But, no, I don't wanna be a … comedian. Not any more,' I say.

'Oh,' he says. 'Sorry to hear that.'

With every ounce of effort left in me, I sit forward and look at him, then I rest my elbow on the arm of the chair and let my head loll on to it. Truth is, I'm feeling so crappy my body's having trouble finding the will to hold itself properly upright. 'Look, if you must know, we went to an open-mic night in a pub tonight.'

'Did you?' Ruben beams. 'That's great!' And then he remembers my age. 'Hang on, a pub? Haylah, I'm pretty sure your mum wouldn't be cool with that. Also, weren't you meant to be at Chloe's?'

'Calm down, Chewbacca. I didn't drink or anything!' I snort, immediately regretting it as he aims those sad, understanding eyes in my direction again. This is all I need, a smattering of guilt on top of this evening's already unbearable crap-cocktail of humiliation and defeat. 'Please don't tell her, and, look, that's not the point. The point is, my so-called "friend" made me get up onstage tonight, totally unplanned, and I tried to do the comedian thing, but . . . it was all a big fat disaster. I totally humiliated myself. Onstage. In front of everyone. Including some older kids. I don't know how I'm going to show my face in school on Monday.'

Ruben looks genuinely sympathetic. 'Oh, Haylah, that's awful. I'm so sorry. But, hey, you know, I hear most comedians epic fail onstage the first few times, right?'

I try to sail past his trying to be down-with-the-kids talk, but frankly it serves as a stark reminder that I'm talking to a total twazzock. Yet still I carry on talking to him. Possibly because I'm too upset to think clearly. I stare down at the carpet. 'Maybe, but . . . this was different.

There was – there was a guy there that I like and . . . Oh God, it's awful . . .!' and I sob some more.

The sofa Ruben's on groans as he shifts his weight, and for a moment I'm slightly panicky that he's going to get up and come and give me a hug or something. I mean, surely we both know that the only way that gross-out scenario can end up is with him in the back of an ambulance, right?

Luckily, he thinks better of it. 'Oh, come on, don't cry! Erm, look, if he's a good guy, a *little* thing like this isn't gonna put him off, is it?'

'It's not a *little thing*, all right? If you haven't noticed, nothing about me is *little*,' I spit. Honestly, I'm trying not to, but it's like he wants me to go mental at him.

'No, no, I didn't mean *little*. I'm just trying to make you feel better. I'm sorry.' Ruben laughs. 'I really want us to be friends, Haylah – and I'm making a rubbish job of it.'

And then, like a lightning bolt, I suddenly see his gentle, calm voice and kind and understanding words for the manipulative mind games they are. Of course he wants me to like him. Because then I'll encourage Mum to like him, and then he'll wheedle himself and his pet beard into our lives for good, changing everything, taking Mum's love and attention away from us, until he abandons her and I have to clear up the mess he leaves behind.

And why am I even talking to this twit about stuff I haven't even said to my mum? And how dare he come in here and tell me my living nightmare this evening is just a 'little' thing – he knows nothing about me, about any of us.

The angry fire in my belly gives me a new energy, so I stand up, my hands on my hips. 'Didn't Mum say you could go when I get home?'

'Sure, but I don't wanna leave you upset. I know she wouldn't want that.'

And then, maybe because he's just being so annoyingly nice, when all I really want to do is hate him, I see red. I stand up and fire all the anger of this evening's humiliation and disaster right into his furry face.

I gesticulate wildly, one finger pointing and the other firmly anchored to my hip. It's an imitation of a well-worn stance of Mum's when she's angry, but it seems to work. He actually flinches as I hiss at him.

'Well, how the *hell* do you know what she wants and doesn't want? You don't *know* her, you don't *know* us, you don't know what we went through with . . . Dad, with anything! OK, Noah seems to like you. Well, NEWSFLASH! Noah also likes jamming crayons up his nose – doesn't mean it's good for him! And the longer you stay around, the harder it will be on him when you leave, so – so why don't you just move on to the next bored and lonely middle-aged single mum and leave us alone, yeah?'

My rant over, Ruben slumps forward, his elbows on his knees, looking down at the floor. He rubs his thumb against the back of his other hand and seems to be building up to something, and for a moment I think he might stand up and slap me, which would be *great* because then I'd really have a reason to hate him. But instead he sighs, looks up at me, a sadness growing behind his eyes and red cheeks glowing behind his beard, and says, 'Because I love her, OK?'

'What?' I say, my hands dropping from their strong Mum position down to my sides. I wasn't expecting this. And part of me is thinking, *How DARE he? He doesn't know her, not like we do – he can't love her the same*, and another part is thinking, *Oh God, they really are going to get married. Everything's going to change. It's going to be Dad all over again. This just stinks.*

He takes another deep sigh.

'It's true. I love your mum. Look, she doesn't know it, so please don't tell her, but . . . I've loved her for years. She's funny and warm and clever and –'

'Yeah, all right, you're actually making me heave a little bit now.'

'OK, OK. We've been friends at work for a long time . . . But I didn't ask her out because I knew what she'd been through, what you'd all been through, with your dad leaving and everything, but now seemed like a good time, and I don't know if she feels the same yet but –'

'She doesn't. OK?' I gabble.

What? Where did that come from?

Ruben looks bewildered, and actually seems to deflate in front of me, like a punctured Ewok blimp. I feel a bit bad and also a bit panicky about what I'm going to say next as the words rise in me like a belch that can't be swallowed down.

'She told me the other day that she just thinks you're a friend and it's all a bit awkward because she knows you like her more than that and she'd never love anyone else like she loved Dad, so . . .' I trail off.

I've gone too far and I know it. Ruben will see through this, see through the desperate yammering of someone who's had a cack-pot of an evening. He'll tell Mum what I said and then, oh God, then I'll really be in trouble . . .

But instead he just says, 'Right,' and looks back down at the floor. 'Understood,' he says, nodding slowly.

'Sorry,' I say, still angry, but getting a small flash forward to the guilt I'm going to feel later. I push it away and look at the floor too.

'OK, so I'd better leave now,' he says, getting up from the sofa, grabbing his coat and avoiding eye contact with me as he passes.

Possibly because he's crying.

'Yeah. I think you should leave. It'll be best. For all of us,' I say softly.

He nods. And leaves.

I sit back down in the armchair. In silence. I can feel the itchiness of tears drying on my cheeks. I try to rally my emotions, keep them strong, keep them onside. I've done a *good* thing here. I mean, how *dare* he try and be my friend? How *dare* he fall in love with my mother? Come here and throw his *niceness* around and expect to be made a part of the *family*?

I seethe.

I grit my teeth.

I cool down.

And then I feel terrible.

But I mean, I'm right, aren't I? Better he leaves now than later? I'm just thinking of Mum, and Noah. We're better off staying as we are. No point in bringing in some new relationship that might just break us all again. After tonight, I don't really think there's any point in trying anything new.

It only ever ends in humiliation and disaster.

SIXTEEN

The next morning I wake up late, but it only takes a second before the memories of the horrible night before start jabbing at my brain like skewers. I don't want to come out from under my duvet. Possibly ever. Then – as usual – Noah bursts through my door and starts jumping on me.

'Haylah, Haylah!' he hollers.

'Ow! Noah, what is it?' I say, my arms flailing around in the air, trying to stop him or push him off.

'Ruben's here!'

'Again? What? Why?' I say, prising my eyelids open.

I feel bad about dumping all that stuff on Ruben last night, and I know I shouldn't have taken it out on him, but I still think telling him it was going nowhere with Mum was the right thing to do. For her sake. For our sakes.

But he's back here again already, so I guess he just ignored me. And probably told Mum what a cow I was.

'I think maybe we had so much fun last night Ruben's come back to play with me again!' screeches Noah. I manage to push him off me and he jumps down to the floor, though unfortunately it doesn't stop him from enthusiastically banging on about Ruben and embellishing his speech with energetic actions. 'We played knights and dragons! He was a big dragon, and then he was a princess and I had to save him from a castle!'

'A big bearded princess. Wow, I bet all the other knights were jealous,' I say, pulling the duvet back up to my ears.

'And we played "Spoon Balloon"!'

I roll on to my belly, burying my head in my pillow. 'That's not even a thing, Noah.'

'It is! You get a balloon – we got one out of the birfday box – you know, the one with all the candles and buntyling and –'

'Yeah, I know the birthday box . . .'

'And you hold a spoon and *hit* the balloon in the air.'

He hits me hard on the bum to illustrate his point.

'Ow. Sounds like quite a sport. I'm surprised they haven't put that in the Olympics yet,' I say.

He climbs up on me again, sitting on my back, facing my feet. The weight makes breathing slightly challenging, but the pressure digging me further down into the mattress is strangely comforting. 'Yeah, so he's here again and Mum's making tea and says she wants me and you to go to the corner shop so we can buy a treat like a cake or a gingeybread man or a biscuit or a sausage.'

'I doubt she wants me to buy a sausage to have with tea, Noah, but biscuits actually sound good. Ugh. All right, I'll get up.'

'I like sausages! Especially with Smash,' he says before raising his little fists into the air, thumping them down on my bum and yelling, 'Hulk Smash!'

'Brilliant,' I wheeze. 'Right, bog off so I can get dressed.'

And he jumps down and prances out of my room, singing, 'Sausage time, sausage time, sausage time!' as he goes.

I pull on some comfort clothes – anything I can unearth from the piles of debris on the floor that's soft and baggy, which ends up being jogging bottoms that'll never realistically be used to jog in and a smock-like T-shirt of Mum's. I emerge from my room, my curled and hairsprayed hair from last night now clumped together and stuck to my cheeks, looking like a big brown octopus clinging to a pumpkin.

Ruben is sitting at the dining table, picking at his fingernails, while Mum makes a pot of tea.

I brace myself. I bet he's at least told her about me going to a pub last night to get back at me for what I said to him and I'm about to get a right rollocking.

'Oh, hi, love!' Mum says brightly. 'Good night at Chloe's?'

'Erm . . . yeah,' I say, shooting a questioning look at Ruben, but he doesn't look up from his fingernails.

'Could you just pop to the shops with Noah, darlin', and get some biscuits or something?'

'Yep, OK. Come on, Noah,' I say.

We walk up the road and round the corner to the local mini supermarket and pick up some flapjacks and biscuits and a chocolate bar to keep us going on the way home – a sort of pre-snack snack. Noah insists on doing the self-service checkout, which takes forever as he turns each item round in his chubby little hands first before finding the barcode and gently presenting it to the scanner, as if it might bite him if he doesn't keep his palms flat and fingers together. An angry queue builds up behind us.

'You're not feeding a goat, Noah – if you just wave the thing in front of the scanner, it finds it for you!' I hiss through gritted teeth.

'I just like to help it out,' he says, resting his other hand on the carrier bag until the machine panics and tells everyone that there's an 'unexpected item in the bagging area'.

Walking back to the house, chomping on our chocolate bars, even the chocolatey goodness fails to remove the memories of last night. Flashbacks of me trying to cuddle Leo's dad while my arse destroys the stage in front of a howling audience, including Leo with his arms round Chloe, haunt me with every step.

'We're back!' I holler as we get in.

'Somebody's here to see you, Haylah!' shouts Mum in a slightly giggly voice I don't really recognize.

'Who's here? Who's here? Who's here?' chants Noah as I take his shoes off.

Oh God, I think, *it's Chloe wanting to talk about last night and how she's now in love with Leo and he with her.*

I walk into the sitting room and see . . . Leo.

Leo Jackson.

Actually Leo.

Leo Jackson.

Sitting in our armchair and sipping from a cup of tea.

I stand, frozen, not knowing what to say.

'LEO!' says Noah.

'It's *Leo*,' says Mum, trying to jolt me into action.

'Right. Yeah. Hi, erm . . .'

'Hey, Haylah,' he says.

Mum saunters up to me with a giggly grin on her face, then says, 'Me and Ruben actually have some stuff to talk about, babe, so if you could take Leo and Noah into your room for a bit that would be great.'

'Right. Noah and, erm . . .'

'Leo,' says Leo with a grin.

'Yes, Leo, of course!' I say, slightly hysterically.

'Follow me, Leo!' shouts Noah as he leads LEO up the stairs and *into* MY room.

'No funny business – leave the door open, Hay!' Mum yells after me, making my cheeks burn with embarrassment.

Oh God. Oh God. Oh God. I bet he's here to tell me how much I owe his dad for all the equipment I exploded last night onstage. *And* my room looks like a church jumble sale. *And* my huge knickers are on the floor. *And* I'm wearing clothes that make me look like the 'before' photo in an advert for the local gym. *And* my hair looks like someone threw a poo at a melon. *Oh God. Oh God. Oh God.*

Noah immediately starts jumping on the bed. Leo follows him in and stands in the middle of my room, his hands in his pockets, grinning at me and seemingly enjoying the chaos he's causing. I rush past him and grab at the huge pile of clothes, books and food wrappers on my desk chair and throw them into a corner.

'You can sit there, if you want. And sorry about the, you know, mess. It's normally much more tidy.'

'No it's not!' says Noah.

'That's cool,' Leo says. 'You should see my room.'

'Hmm,' I manage to get out as my cheeks go redder still at the very thought that I might ever, for any reason, be in Leo's bedroom.

He sits on the chair and I on the bed, next to Noah, who's still jumping up and down.

'Leo, can we play "Faecal Stereotip" or "Guess the Smell" or "Spoon Balloon"?'

'I don't actually know what any of those things are, but yeah, I mean, "Spoon Balloon" sounds pretty awesome.'

'It's really not,' I say.

'Well, it sounds like the better of the three,' whispers Leo.

'Actually, "Guess the Smell" isn't as bad as it sounds,' I say.

'Really?'

'No, actually, it is,' I say, fishing around on the floor for Mum's ancient iPad. 'Look, Noah, play on this for a bit, yeah?'

'*Ohhhhh*. OK then. But will you watch me?'

'Sorry, Leo, just, er, give me a minute?' I say.

'Sure,' he says, leaning back and swivelling from side to side on my desk chair.

I get Noah playing some Lego Batman game on the iPad and pretend to show an interest for a few minutes:

'You're so good at this, Noah! See if you can get to the next level, without asking for any help at all, yeah?' etc., etc.

Eventually, when he's engrossed in the game and the biscuit he's chomping down on, and my heart rate has calmed to a mere hammering and my face has returned to a near-human colour, I turn back to Leo.

'He's a cute kid,' he says.

'Oh sure, he looks cute now, but you just try to take that biscuit away from him and you'll witness his true identity – as the devil's child.'

'I'm not Nevil's child!' says Noah.

Leo laughs, and then continues leaning back in my chair and staring at me. And I suddenly feel painfully self-conscious. I sit down on the bed, leaning against the wall behind me, grabbing one of my pillows and hugging it over my stomach.

'Anyhoo,' I say stupidly, 'so, erm, it's nice to, but, well, why are you here? And come to think of it,' I add, 'how did you know where I live?'

'Your friend – Chloe, is it? She told me last night.'

'Uh-huh,' I say.

'She's pretty cool actually,' he says.

'Yep. She's the best,' I say, trying and failing not to sound sarcastic.

Maybe that's why he's here. Maybe he wants to ask her out. That's normally why boys speak to me.

'You liked my set last night then?' he says.

'Yeah, I loved it! I laughed this time – you saw that I laughed?'

'Yes,' he says with a smirk. 'So I guess you like your own jokes more than mine?'

'What? No, my set was awful. Didn't you see it? I had nothing to say and then I molested your dad before destroying the building.'

164

'Ha, yes, I saw. And you did pretty good actually, for a first time, but I didn't mean that. I meant the jokes you wrote for me. The jokes in my locker.'

'Oh –' The colour drains from my face. I lean forward and bury my head in the pillow. 'God. You know about that then?'

'I figured it out,' he says cheerfully.

I sit back up, though I still can't bring myself to look him in the eye. 'Right. Right. Right. When?'

'Well, I had a pretty good idea when you were skulking around the lockers, pretending to take phone calls. My advice to you if you ever wanna be a spy is, don't. Then, when we met at my house, you were funny, proper funny, naturally funny, like you could say anything, and it just, well, it sounds funny. I wish I had that.'

I look up at him as he spins all the way round on my chair, grinning. 'I do? You do?' I say, trying hard to cover up just how ecstatically happy I feel right now.

'And, total shocker, I didn't *really* buy the whole "communist" thing.'

'Oh no, that's completely true. I mean, if the comedy career falls through, it's good to have a backup plan, right? And the world can never have enough communist dictators,' I say.

He laughs. And it sends tingles up my spine.

'True,' he says, and he's stopped spinning round now and is leaning towards me, his elbows resting on his knees and his hands loosely interlinked. 'Anyway, I knew for sure when I saw you a bunch of times hanging around my locker again at the end of school – you know, when you were *pretending* to tie your lace-less shoes, or give a Year Seven who wasn't even talking to you directions –'

I feel the familiar hot glow spreading over my cheeks again.

'Yeah, yeah, OK, so I'm not really built for stealth,' I say, clinging tightly to the pillow on my lap. 'Look, I'm sorry. You probably think I'm a complete freak, and you probably wouldn't be wrong in thinking that either. I just love comedy and I like writing jokes and, I don't know, I saw you do your set in assembly and it, well, I guess it *inspired* me, or something that sounds less tragic . . . you know, just to see someone only a bit older than me do a kick-ass comedy set. Then, well, I kind of overheard you saying you didn't have any new material for the pub gig and –'

'Overheard when you were stalking me, you mean,' he says with a smile.

'Well, you know, "stalking" is such a *strong* word . . .' Then I cover my face with my right hand and look at him pleadingly through my fingers. 'Look, I'm sorry. I'm embarrassed. I promise I'll leave you alone now, I won't write secret jokes for you again or anything else weird, and we can just forget about this whole sorry tale, OK?'

'No, not OK,' he says, spinning round on my chair again.

I look down at the pillow and gulp. 'Right, no, of course. Let me know how much I owe your dad for the equipment and I'll, I don't know, pay him back in instalments out of my pocket money or something.'

He stops spinning again and, with his head on one side, nose screwed up and upturned hands, gives me an exaggerated 'you're nuts!' look. 'It's a *pub*, Haylah, drinks get spilled all the time. It's fine – it's all fixed! What I mean is, it's *not* OK to stop writing jokes for me.'

Relief floods through me as I stare at him with my mouth open. 'Wait, what? Really?'

'Look, I'm here because you're funny, and you write really good material and . . .' He pauses, like he's choosing what he says next carefully. 'Well, there's this big competition, the London Young Comic of the Year, coming up in a couple of weeks. And I know it's kind of stupid, but last year I was a runner-up, and I really want to win this year, and I think, if you're up for it, maybe if *you* helped me write my set, I might stand a chance. The prize is a thousand pounds, so, if I win, we could share it. What do you think?'

'You want *me* to write your jokes?'

'Well, no. I thought we'd write them together. I mean, I *would* write them myself, but I've got all these exams this year, and coursework, and argh! It's a nightmare just getting that done, and obviously I *can* write kick-ass funny stuff . . .'

'Obviously,' I say.

'But it takes me forever to come up with it. With your help, I think it would happen a lot quicker cos, well, funny stuff just seems to spill out of you like . . .'

'Vomit?' I suggest.

'Ha, er, *exactly*, but, you know, funny vomit,' he says, smiling. 'Go on, we'll have a laugh, and we might get five hundred pounds each. What d'you reckon?'

He says this like I need persuading.

'Hmm,' I say, pretending to think about it for about two seconds. 'Yeah, OK.'

'Sweet!' he says, spinning round triumphantly with his legs and arms outstretched, making Noah look up from the iPad and laugh.

Battling to keep my outside looking cool and calm while my brain sings songs of joy, I agree to meet him at his place (*his* place!) on Monday after school. I'll have Noah with me, but Leo says he has a PlayStation to keep him busy so it's all good.

'It's a date!' he says as we both stand up to leave.

'It is?' I say before my brain has a chance to stop my mouth from utter muppetry.

'Yeah! I just mean it's an *appointment*, in the diary, yeah? Why?' He lowers his voice to an almost-whisper and leans down towards me. 'What did *you* mean?' And then he actually winks at me, then laughs as I turn away to hide my blushing grin.

'Right, little guy, I've gotta shoot. High-five me, Noah!' Noah dutifully high-fives him.

We walk to the front door past Mum, who's now sitting on her own in the living room, staring into her cup of tea. I didn't know Ruben had left, but hey, I'm not complaining.

'Bye, Mrs Swinton, nice to have met you,' says Leo, but instead of being impressed with this gorgeous and beautifully polite guy I've brought into our home, she just keeps staring into the mug.

'Sorry,' I whisper to him as we reach the front door. 'Don't know what's going on there.'

'No worries. See you Monday, yeah?' he says, and then he leaves.

I lean up against the door after it closes and bite my bottom lip to stop myself screeching with delight before skipping back into the living room.

'Well?' I say to Mum. 'What do you think of Leo?'

'Who? Oh yeah, love, he's great,' she says, but her voice is flat and lifeless.

'You OK, Mum?'

'Yeah, just ... Well, just so you know, Ruben's not going to be coming round any more ...'

'Oh,' I say, realizing that he did actually listen to what I said last night. Well then, that's good. I guess.

I sit down next to her and put my hand on her knee.

'How come?' I say, trying to sound clueless about the whole thing.

And she tells me that Ruben's basically dumped her, and she doesn't understand why. He told her he didn't want to put any relationship 'pressure' on her blah-blah-blah, so he's backing off, going to swap his working hours around so they don't bump into each other so much, and he's taking a few weeks off, going to stay with his brother in London to get some 'perspective' on it all.

'Maybe he's just realized he doesn't actually like me that much. Oh well, never mind,' she says with a heavy sigh.

'I'm sorry,' I say, feeling the heavy weight of guilt on my chest, but clinging to the fact that I know this is the right thing in the long run. 'But, you know, maybe it's for the best, Mum. I mean, Noah was starting to get attached to him, and the longer he stayed the more it would hurt Noah, and you, if he left later, so ... maybe it's good that he went now?'

'Thanks for trying to make me feel better, Hay. Come and give me a big old hug.'

As we hug, she sniffs and I'm afraid she's about to cry and I HATE it when Mum cries, especially as this is kind of my fault, so I say to her, 'Plus, he didn't wear any socks. I mean, the man wore literally NO socks. Like, what is that about? You don't need that kind of madness in your life. He can take his obscene ankles elsewhere, am I right!'

She stops the sniffing, but she doesn't laugh. Instead, she pulls away from our hug and says flatly, 'Yeah. You're probably right.'

Then she sighs and quickly shakes her head, her hair flying around her face and, as if she's shaken off the sad mask she was wearing, she emerges with a smile at the end. Even if it does seem a little forced.

Her voice back to its normal bouncy self, she says, 'Now, go get me some ice cream and let's watch a crappy Disney movie together while you tell me about lovely Leo!'

'Yay!' I say, skipping off to the freezer.

And I know she's totally going to be OK. The bearded troll is gone. Leo's my new best comedy friend. We're having ice cream.

Best. Day. Ever.

SEVENTEEN

On Monday morning, Noah refuses to put his uniform on as he's convinced he's now 'allergic to jumpers' (he's not actually allergic to anything but he hears other kids talking about their conditions at school and he wants a part of the action. The other day he insisted he couldn't wipe his bum any more because he was 'dyslexic'). Then he insists on walking to school backwards for most of the journey because he's 'bored of forward walking'. So inevitably I get to school late. Again.

I walk down the corridor, and to be honest I'm not really looking forward to seeing Chloe as I'm still annoyed with her about Friday night. She sent me a few messages asking if I was OK over the weekend, but I was pretty short with my responses.

On the other hand, my head is merrily filled with the song 'I'm going round to Leo's after school, do-dah, do-dah! Because he thinks that I'm so cool, do-dah do-dah-day!' Which leaves little room for annoyance. So I decide not to mention anything to Chloe about Friday night, or about Leo, as I don't want anything to ruin this feeling. But of course this is ridiculously optimistic.

When I walk into the classroom, I can sense that something is not quite right. The air in the room tenses up as I enter, and the roar of thirty-three students all bellowing and shrieking at each other deadens to a purr. All eyes in the room fix on me; some stifle their giggles, others let them loose, and a few hands are cupped round clueless nearby ears as whispers are exchanged.

My cheeks burn red as I run my hands down the buttons of my shirt, checking to see that I've remembered to dress myself correctly and that one of my boobs hasn't flopped out without me noticing. Then my brain catches up with the rest of the class as I realize what they must be laughing at.

Oh, please, no.

'Late again, Haylah?' says Mrs Perkins.

'Yeah, sorry, miss,' I mumble.

'Too busy trying to snog other people's dads!' says a voice from a group of boys at the side of the class.

That confirms it. *Everyone* knows about Friday night. About my disastrous attempt at being a comedian ending in me groping Leo's dad and my butt cheeks laying waste to the stage like two fleshy steamrollers.

'What was that, Greg?' says Mrs Perkins.

'Nothing, miss,' says class bully and massive twonknut Greg before he carries on sniggering with the rest of the room.

I raise my head high. I won't let them get the better of me.

'Well, obviously not *your* dad, Greg,' I blurt, 'who, if he's anything like you, is so ugly that when he looks in a mirror it slaps him.'

'Ha ha! Roasted!' yells Dylan, slapping his mate Greg hard on the back.

Greg slumps down into his chair as the rest of the class laugh, but this time at least it's *with* me. Then they swiftly return to their morning gossip and general arsing about. I make my way over to Chloe and Kas at the back of the class, trying to keep up the appearance of someone unaffected by the laughter and sneers when inside I want to die a little.

'How the hell does everyone know about Friday night?' I hiss as I chuck my bag on the table.

'I don't know. I guess some of Leo's friends spread it around school?' says Kas.

'Don't worry about it, Pig. By lunchtime, everyone will have forgotten,' says Chloe.

And suddenly lunchtime seems as far away as the sun.

We chat a little, but the atmosphere between the three of us is frosty. The last time I saw them on Friday night I snapped at Chloe, then stormed off slamming the door behind me. Chloe probably thinks I need to apologize. But frankly I think she needs to apologize to me for flirting with Leo, putting me forward for a gig I didn't want to do and laughing at the disastrous consequences. I think about saying something to her, but she's better at arguing than me and I know she'd win. So I just keep my mouth shut.

The room falls silent for a moment as Jules and Destiny, a couple of fellow Frick House girls from the year above who sometimes sit with us in whole house sports days and assemblies, but consider themselves too cool to do so at any other time, sashay into the room.

'Can I help you, girls?' booms Mrs Perkins.

'Just got some Frick House business with the girls at the back, miss.'

'Fine, but be quick about it,' tuts Mrs Perkins before returning her attention to her newspaper.

They strut towards us as the rest of the room loses interest and returns to their general twitting about.

They both perch on our table and Destiny leans towards me. 'So, Pig – I've gotta know if it's true. I heard you threw a pint of beer in Leo Jackson's dad's face when he wouldn't snog you, is that right?'

'No! What? And I DON'T want to talk about it but NO, that definitely did NOT happen! Why, is that what's going around?' I exclaim.

'All right, all right, calm yourself down, woman, it's just what we heard!' says Destiny, her hands raised to me, indicating that they're backing away from the wounded beast in case she lashes out at them again. I rest my head in my hands, willing the world to go away.

'Chloe,' says Jules, 'your nails. Look. A. Mazing. Where did you get them done?'

Jules always talks with a lot of full stops. As if everything she says is. Of. HUGE. Importance.

Chloe's face lights up like someone's just given her an Oscar.

'My sister did them,' she says proudly. 'She's training to be a beautician.'

'Wow! They. Are. SO. Awesome. Would she do mine?' says Jules.

I look at Chloe's nails as she fans them out on the table in front of us. Each is decorated in a different colour and pattern: spots, swirls, hearts and zigzags with a glossy, glittery finish. They look like the nail equivalent of an explosion in a Care Bears factory and it makes my eyes twitch just to look at them.

'Subtle,' I say sarcastically. But everyone ignores me.

'Yeah, I'll ask her,' says Chloe, still beaming at Jules and Destiny's attention. 'Maybe if you come round on Saturday she can set up a nail bar in our house!'

'That. Would be. Super. Awesome,' says Jules before turning back to me. 'So. You're saying. It's *not* true then, Pig, right? So? What *did* happen?'

'NOTHING! Nothing happened, all right? Can you just leave it, PLEASE?' I bark, and put my head in my hands again.

'Oooh, all right,' sings Destiny. 'Keep your knickers on. Come on, Jules. We know when we're not wanted.'

Kas and Chloe try to apologize on my behalf, but Destiny and Jules are done and, thankfully, prance away.

'This is terrible!' I say, repeatedly banging my head on the table.

'Don't worry, Pig. They're coming to the nail bar so I'm sure it'll all be cool with them if you apologize there.'

'Not *that*! I couldn't give a monkey's bumhole about a stupid nail bar or being forgiven for sticking up for myself to the twit-tits twins! I'm talking about the Leo's dad thing!'

Seriously! How do they not get that this is a huge deal?

'Oh, that,' says Kas sheepishly.

'Yes, that!' I say.

'Well, I think a nail bar's a great idea,' mumbles Chloe.

Then they both take it in turns to tell me not to worry about it and persuade me not to give up the comedy career, reminding me that things often go wrong the first time you try them, 'like when Freya first dyed Chloe's hair and it went orange'.

'Yeah, but she didn't knock over the sink with her butt and then try to get off with the shower, did she?' I say.

'Well, no,' admits Chloe. 'That's true.'

Her lack of sympathy when she was the cause of the whole thing is really starting to get on my nerves.

I try to focus back on the 'I'm going round to Leo's house after school' ditty in my head, but it's faded and been replaced by an angry chant of 'You're a big tit and they know you are, do-dah do-dah . . . Leo's gonna think you're such a loser, do-dah do-dah-day'. Which is depressing and doesn't even rhyme as well as the first one.

Stupid brain.

'You *were* really good though, Pig, on Friday night,' says Kas, 'until the, y'know, end.'

'Thanks,' I say.

'Wasn't Jake amazing though!' says Chloe.

'Well, yes,' says Kas, sensing my annoyance with Chloe, but trying (as always) to keep the peace. 'But Pig was amazing too, wasn't she, Chlo?'

'Yeah, of course,' she says.

'Look, can we change the subject,' I say, 'to *anything* else at all?'

'OK, OK,' says Kas. 'So Stevie keeps looking over at you again, Chloe. Have you noticed?'

'Yeah, totally. Do you think he likes me?'

'You should so ask him out,' says Kas.

'Do you think he'll say yes?' says Chloe.

This torturous car crash of a conversation drones on for what feels like a lifetime until I eventually slam my hand down on the table and explode.

'Oh, for God's sake, Chloe! You're, like, the prettiest girl in the year and Stevie's a scrawny little spiky-haired twit-flump. You *know* you could have any boy you want! But, hey, if that's your kind of thing, go for it – he's not going to say *no*, is he?'

I stop myself before I say anything more. I *really* don't want to have an argument with Chloe. She'd totally win and take Kas with her, abandoning me all day to face the sniggers and gossip alone. I brace myself for her to come back at me, but instead her Hollywood-grade smile spreads over her face. It seems she's only really heard the words 'prettiest' and 'any boy you want' and she thinks I'm paying her a compliment.

'God, you're *right*, Pig. I should just go for it, yeah?' she says excitedly.

'Erm . . . yeah?' I say.
Phew.

I get through the rest of the morning, ignoring the jibes from a few kids in the corridors and concentrating instead on thinking about what to say to Leo after school. I need to make sure I've got something good to offer – otherwise he might not ask me back again. To *his* house. Just me and him. Argh! Well, technically and Noah, but still basically just me and him.

Me and Leo.

I still don't tell Kas or Chloe about it. I don't want the questions. I don't want the giggling and laughing at the very hopeless idea of me and Leo. This is *my* special thing and I want to keep it that way.

At lunch, Chloe gets me to ask Stevie out for her. After the look of panic on his face fades as he realizes it's not *me* asking him out, of course he says yes. Then me and Kas have to spend the rest of the lunch break lurking near them as they stand in a corner, awkwardly holding hands, and, though they don't say much to each other, whenever Stevie whispers something to Chloe she laughs with what me and Kas know full well is her hysterical fake laugh. Then at the end of lunch they awkwardly snog while his friends whoop.

'Don't we look great together?' Chloe says when she finally breaks away from him and returns to us.

They don't. Stevie's quite cute, I guess, if you're into the little-runty-guy-in-the-boy-band kind of look. But he's also incredibly nervous and Chloe's about a foot taller than him, so with his spiky hair they have the look of an RSPCA worker trying to save a lost hedgehog.

Of course we agree though, and tell her they look fabulous together.

'Just like a celebrity couple,' Kas adds, to Chloe's delight.

I didn't know Pixie Lott was dating the Wimpy Kid, I think.

And yes, OK, I'm well aware that I'm basically jealous. Of the snogging and the boyfriend and the being wanted by a guy. Though I don't want to be wanted by just any guy, of course. Just the one whose house I'm actually going to today after school. Eek!

EIGHTEEN

At the end of the day, relieved to be leaving school yet full of nerves about seeing Leo, I pick up Noah and we walk to Leo's house, the now familiar Leo-induced frantic heartbeat pounding around my body.

He answers the door, already changed into his hoodie and jeans, and, giving a big friendly 'Hey, Pig', he waves us inside. We go into his living room, so unlike ours, so stylish, so clean. He starts up the PlayStation and gets Noah playing some age-inappropriate driving game where the idea seems to be to hit as many pedestrians as possible. Noah seems to like it.

Leaving him there we head back to the kitchen and Leo gets us a lemonade. Not supermarket-own bubbly piss water like we have, but proper branded stuff that actually tastes like lemons. He asks me how school was and I say, 'Oh, y'know, fine.'

And he seems to accept that answer, which makes me think he's not aware that everyone knows about Friday night. Because the last thing I want to bring up with Leo is *that* again.

He sits at the table, in front of his laptop, and pats the chair next to him.

'Well, are you gonna sit down or what?' he says.

'Yeah, OK,' I say, bracing myself for the fart noise his chairs make and praying the thing doesn't collapse as I sit on it.

'Excuse me,' I say as it resounds with a hearty *frrrt*. 'Must be all those vegetables I eat.'

He laughs a little, then says, 'Oh sorry, did you want something to eat? I should have offered. I think we have some Jaffa Cakes somewhere.'

'No, no, I'm fine, thanks,' I say, swallowing down the saliva that the mention of Jaffa Cakes produces in my mouth. The truth is, I could quite happily inhale a whole packet now in one breath, but I don't want to eat in front of Leo. It's bad enough that he can *see* that I'm fat, that overeating isn't one of those bad habits you can hide from others like taking drugs, picking your nose or watching reality television. So, sure, he *knows* I'm big – the image of me as a big person is unavoidably lodged in his head – but I really don't want to implant the image of me stuffing my big piggy face with food in there as well.

'Right,' I say, trying to get a handle on the situation, while feeling a little light-headed when I realize that our knees are almost touching under the table. 'So, how do you want to do this? Have you got any, er, ideas already that we can go with first?'

He stares at his laptop screen, opening a new Word page. 'Nope, nothin'. To be honest, I was kinda hoping you would.'

He smirks at me, his eyebrows raised, his soft brown eyes melting my soul.

GET A GRIP, GIRL!

I clear my throat, reach down to my bag and retrieve a pad of paper and a pen. Just so I've got something to hold and look at. *Oh God, we're sitting so damned close.* 'OK. Well, I haven't got anything yet, but maybe we can come up with some stuff together?'

'Notebook and pen,' he says as I slap them on the table in front of me. 'I like that you do things old-school.'

'Right,' I say, not wanting to tell him it's actually because we can't afford a laptop.

'Anyway, I mean, the stuff you wrote for me last time was great, probably better than most of the stuff I write. So, how did you do that?'

'Oh, you know,' I say, twiddling the pen a little too manically in my hand. 'I just thought about what would sound funny coming from *you*. You get the best laughs when you're being *you*, right? I mean, you've got this great onstage laddish, teenage persona working for you, so I just went with that.'

'Well, you must get me pretty good if you managed to write me so well.' He gently elbows my arm and I feel my cheeks burning. I laugh a little through my nose in response and look down at my notepad and scribble with the pen, trying to get it to work. He's sitting right next to me though, and can clearly see that it is working.

Stop it, woman!

'So what's *your* onstage character then?' he asks.

'Oh no, I'm never getting up there again, believe me.'

'Come on! OK, so you're not ready just yet, but you will be. You do wanna be a stand-up, right – that's your aim with all this joke-writing?'

'Well, yeah, one day, sure. It's all I've ever wanted to do, but . . .' I trail off.

'OK, so, when you do, what'll be your onstage *thing*?'

'I don't know.' I sit back in the chair. 'I guess my size. I mean, that's the obvious one, right? Stuff like, "I'm not fat because obesity runs in my family, I'm fat because *no one* runs in my family." '

He laughs and the laughter starts to calm my nerves. 'That's a good joke. But I don't think that's your onstage persona sorted cos you're *not* fat.'

I'm not sure what to do with this. I can't quite work out if he's saying it to be nice, as a statement of fact (false fact), or if he's just messing with me.

I *think* he's trying to be nice, but it's just making me feel strange and awkward. So I shrug it off and say, 'This isn't about me anyway, it's about you. So, as I said, you've got that whole teenage, laddish, cool and, well, erm, good-looking vibe going on in your stage persona, so I think we should just play about with that some more. We should write down what your character is expected to say and then sometimes go against it, like the opposite of what's expected of you. You do that really well – like when you talk about getting a mate to squeeze a zit on your butt or shoving frozen food down your trousers.'

'OK. Tell me more about my good-looking vibe though,' he says, resting his head on his palm and pulling his best model-like pout.

'Tart,' I say with a smile, and I foolishly glance at him and lose myself for a moment in his dreaminess ... 'So anyway,' I say, steering my eyes back down to the notepad as my cheeks start to burn again, 'we should write more bits like that. But then you know all this stuff already, being a runner-up in the London Young Comic of the Year and everything.'

Leo shrugs. 'Actually, I don't really know this stuff, or maybe I do, but I don't really analyse it. I just write what I think is funny, and sometimes it works and sometimes it doesn't, but, well, it'd be kinda nice if more stuff worked, so a few lessons is great! How do you know all this?'

'I'm a comedy genius,' I deadpan.

'Well, obviously.'

'Actually, I'm a comedy geek who watches a lot of stand-up and soaks up just about any video, podcast or book I can find about how to write jokes and do comedy. So I've picked up a few tips and tricks along the way.'

'Got it. So, genius, where do we start? I've gotta say, my mind's a blank at the moment. I mean, I've got all this coursework and exams and ...' He pauses and frowns. 'Well, my mum and dad are putting all this pressure on because they want me to go to Cambridge University.'

'Cambridge? Wow, I didn't know you were that clever.'

'Thanks.'

I look up at him and nervously chew on the end of my pen. 'No, I just mean, I don't know. That's, like, for the *super* clever.'

'Yeah, I guess that doesn't go with the whole *good-looking*, cool, teenage, *good-looking*, laddish, *good-looking* persona I've got, right?'

I laugh. 'I guess! So Cambridge – wow! That's exciting.'

He shuffles around a little in his chair, and for the first time looks ever so slightly awkward. 'I don't know. I mean, I've gotta get straight As and go for an interview and stuff, so I might not get in. If I win the competition, that would actually help as they like that kind of extra-curricular stuff. Anyway, I do really wanna go, though not for the reasons my mum and dad want me to. They want me to go so I can have this bright future and glittering career as God knows what, but, well, I really just wanna go for . . .'

'The Footlights!' I yell, a little too energetically.

'Yeah, great way to get onstage and make a name for yourself. So you know about them?'

'Of course! The Cambridge Footlights – an amazing comedy sketch group. God, that'd be awesome! You lucky thing.'

'No reason why you couldn't come in a few years' time. You're clever, right?'

'Nah, I mean, urgh, everyone says if I worked harder I'd get top marks, but that means actually working harder. Plus, what if I do put in the work only for everyone to find out I'm not that clever after all? Better for people to think you're clever and lazy than a hard worker and a dumb-ass, right?'

'Screw what everyone else thinks. It's possible that if you work harder you might get into the Cambridge Footlights, so that's worth potentially looking like a dumb-ass.'

'Huh. Maybe. It would be cool. I mean, that's where loads of brilliant comedians started out: David Mitchell, Robert Webb, Stephen Fry, Richard Ayoade, Sandy Toksvig, Monty Python, Mel and Sue . . .'

'Wow, you really know your comedians,' he says, impressed.

'I told you, I'm a comedy geek.'

This is great! I think. *I'm actually relaxing into a conversation with him and not sounding like a total idiot!*

'Well, I think it's cool. And kinda sexy,' he says, making me choke on my lemonade, spitting quite a lot of it out on to the table and my notebook. I try to dry it with the cuff of my school jumper.

Yep, very sexy.

'Oh God, I'm so sorry!' I splutter. 'But "cool and sexy"? I can assure you no one else thinks that!'

He leans back in his chair. 'Balls. Everyone finds funny people attractive.'

'No, I think you'll find that everyone finds funny *men* attractive. Funny women are just seen as gobby and strange. Fun maybe, but still not fanciable, just peculiar. Funny works for boys, but us teenage girls aren't expected to be funny – we should be more interested in our nails or hair or clothes.'

'That's *so* not true. Who told you that?' he says.

'The world told me that,' I say, staring down at the table. I turn to him. 'Look, truth is, I don't get boyfriends and stuff, and I know it's probably because I'm . . . big . . . but I also think it's because I'm funny, or at least I try to be.'

'Don't be stupid,' he says, putting his hands in the front pocket of his hoodie. 'Everyone always puts "sense of humour" on their list of what they want in a girlfriend or boyfriend.'

'Yes, but to a girl "sense of humour" means someone who'll make them laugh. To a guy that means someone who'll *laugh at their jokes*.'

He laughs. 'Well, I find girls who make me laugh super sexy.'

I cough again and, not knowing where to look or what to do, I pull my hair over my cheeks, which I can feel are glowing like lava bubbles.

'Well, whatever,' I say, my voice coming out screechy and weird. 'We'd better get some work done. Where to start? So, erm –' I tap the pen on my notebook – 'comedy. If you want to win the competition this time, you – *we* – need to up our game. We need your routine to be unique, memorable. To proper laugh at something you need to be caught off guard. So we know we're going with your teenage, laddish persona, but we don't want to pick the obvious stuff, so first we need to start with a list of that, then discard it.'

'A list! Now that's definitely sexy.'

I'm actually getting used to his random little *flirtations* I guess you'd call them, so I manage to reply pretty quickly. 'I know, right. List-makers are super hot.'

So we spend time coming up with the obvious stuff, and by the end of it we've got a really good list. Gaming, hating shopping blah-blah-blah.

'You're sure this is stuff we *shouldn't* use, right?' says Leo, looking at the list.

'Yep. Or at least, if we do, we should put a new twist on it.'

'OK, so what *can* we write jokes about?'

'Something that sounds a bit more real. I mean, in what ways *aren't* you a stereotypical teenage boy? Maybe we could kick off there?'

And then we start talking, really talking, about him, his life, about what he's into, what he's not into, and I learn that while he ticks a few of the usual teenage-boy boxes – gaming, social media and an obsession with trainers being a few of them – he's also a stickler for proper spelling and punctuation in messaging, he can't skateboard to save his life (he gets the bus everywhere), he likes reading P. G. Wodehouse books (*I know, right, just adorable!*), he's scared of drugs and he hates dystopian films. Plus, of course, the fact that he's trying to get into Cambridge.

Every time either of us laughs, it's like my insides go all shiny and tingly and I don't ever want the feeling to end. It's like we've got a genuine spark, a connection. When he eventually says he ought to get on with his homework and I realize I have to go, my heart deflates a little.

'So we'll both try to think of some jokes based around this stuff before we next meet, yeah?' I say, desperately hoping he actually wants to get together again as already I can't wait.

'Sounds good. I'm free on Thursday after school. Why don't I come to yours this time?' he says, leaning in and adding in a whisper, 'I'll promise your mum we'll keep your bedroom door open.'

My face goes bright red. 'Right, yeah, that would be, that would be, that would be cool,' I say, trying so hard to sound casual and in no way utterly, utterly desperate for this whole thing to *never* end, *ever*. 'My mum will be there, probably asleep after a night shift though.'

'OK, I'll try not to make you laugh too loudly with all the amazing new ideas I'm gonna have by then.' He grabs the empty lemonade glasses from the table and takes them to the sink. 'So, will your dad be there too?'

'What?'

'Your dad? The bearded guy?'

'OH! No, no. The bearded troll is *not* my dad, and no, he won't be there, thank God. He and my mum had a little *thing – eurgh* – but it was nothing, and now it's all over so you don't have to worry about him.'

'Shame, I liked him.'

'You did?' I say, frowning.

'Yeah, he was cool, and funny, cracked a couple of jokes, made me laugh.'

'He did?' I say.

'Yeah, and your mum was laughing too. It was kinda cute – they looked really happy together. Anyway, seems a shame they've split up is all.'

I start packing away my notebook and pen into my bag. 'I don't know, I thought he was a bit of a tit.'

'Oh.' He nods and rubs his chin. 'I get it. You don't want your mum to be with someone else cos they'll never be as good as your real dad, right?'

'No! Believe me, a squashed slug on the pavement would be as good as my dad.'

'Wow, harsh,' he says, hands in the air in surrender.

I get up and sling my bag over my shoulder to the soundtrack of a relieved chair loudly farting.

He wafts his hand in front of his nose and pretends to gag. 'Seriously, girl, you wanna see a doctor about that.'

'Oh no, if I actually farted, believe me you'd know about it. So would everyone in the streets. In Moscow.'

He laughs, then says in his most sarcastic voice, 'Yeah, you're right – it's a *mystery* why you haven't got a boy-friend yet.'

'I know, right? I'm *all* woman.'

This is chuffin' brilliant. I've never flirted with a guy before, but it kinda feels like that's what we're doing now.

Then Leo gets serious again. 'But, you know, just to quickly go back to what we were talking about before you farted so explosively ... my mum and dad split up too. Mum left Dad for Pete – this is Pete's house. Anyway, I didn't like him much at first either. I mean, for one thing he's *white*! When it's just me and him walking around town, I think people think he's my parole officer.'

I laugh.

'Oooh, that's good,' he says. 'I should write that down, right?'

'Actually, I don't know,' I say. 'There was a moment when I thought, if I laugh, is that racist?'

He smirks. 'Yeah, but that's not my problem.'

'True, and if it's funny, and you're only offending yourself, anything goes, right?'

'Totally. But look, the point is, I got to like Pete because he makes my mum happy and Dad didn't. And when Mum's happy I'm happy, because before she used to get mad at me before I even woke up. But now, well, it's at least teatime before she starts throwing dishes at my head.'

'Bit clichéd,' I say with a laugh. 'Don't write that one down. Well, my mum *is* happy – she's cool with it being just us.'

'OK, I hear you. I'll butt out. Anyway,' he says, and as he walks past me he raises an eyebrow, 'speaking of dads and butts –'

So he *does* know I'm the talk of the school. I cringe and cover my face with my hands and look at him through the gaps between my fingers. 'Urgh – I can't believe I did something that made those two words exist in the same sentence!'

'Don't worry about it – no one will even remember it tomorrow. Oh, but my dad wants to know when you're free for your second date.'

'Eurgh! Shut up!' I say, elbowing him in the ribs in a desperate and pathetic attempt at more body contact with him, however violent and jumper-clad.

I gather up Noah and his stuff and we step out of the front door.

Just before we go, Leo suddenly says: 'Oh, Haylah, if it's OK with you, I think it's best if people don't know I'm getting help with the comedy-writing thing. There'll be quite a few mates coming to the competition gig and, I don't know, they might not laugh so much if they think it's not all coming from me, yeah?'

'Yeah, erm, OK, makes sense,' I say. And I *guess* it does.

'Thanks. You're awesome.' he says, 'And, y'know, pretty funny. For a girl.'

Then he actually winks at me.

'Shut up!' I say with a nauseatingly flirtatious voice I've never used before. I will my cheeks not to respond to his wink, but they ignore me and glow hotter than the surface of the sun. I turn away from him and grab Noah's hand.

'Say goodbye, Noah.'

'Bye, Leo!' he says. Then, looking at me, says very loudly, 'Your face looks weird, Hay. All hot and smiley.'

NINETEEN

Back at home, Mum's sitting on the sofa, munching her way through a tube of Pringles and staring at a TV that isn't even on. This can't be good.

Noah runs in and jumps up next to her.

'Hey, Mum, how was work?' I ask, trying to keep things chipper.

She takes a moment to answer. 'Oh, you know, fine. How was school, both of you?'

'I painted a dinosaur and called him Jeff,' says Noah proudly, his mouth already stuffed with crisps.

'That sounds great. And you, Hay?'

'Pretty much the same. Dinosaur, yep, Jeff, yep, same stuff. And you got my message about us going round to Leo's after school, right?'

'Yeah . . . oh, is it not three thirty then?'

'No, Mum, it's half five,' I say, collapsing down into the armchair.

'Oh. I guess I didn't notice the time go. So how was Leo? Are you and him –?'

'No! No, we're just friends. I'm helping him out with a school project, that's all. I mean, I like him, but I don't think he likes me, not like that. I think. He might though. I'm not sure.' I sigh, staring up at the celling before snapping out of my trance and saying, 'Anyway, can he come over on Thursday after school?'

'Yeah, sure, love, that's fine,' she says in a small voice.

'He's going to Cambridge, you know. The university. When he finishes school. Gonna join the Footlights and everything.'

'Cambridge. Wow. That's nice,' she says, stroking Noah's hair.

'Is Ruben coming round again soon?' says Noah.

Mum winces. 'No, love. No, he's not.'

'I miss him!' says Noah before I distract him and my guilt by putting on the TV.

After a couple of episodes of *Hey Duggee*, I get up to go to my room, touching Mum's arm as I pass her and Noah – they're lying on the sofa together.

'Are you OK, Mum?' I ask.

'What?' She looks up at me. 'Yeah, of course. I'll get some tea in a bit, OK? Some pasta or something.'

'That would be great, if you're not too tired.'

'No, I'm fine, babe. I'm fine.'

She'll be OK, I think, *in a day or so*. I grab a snack, then head to my bedroom. I pull off my school shirt and 'sturdy fit' school trousers, dig around in my wardrobe among the mountain of baggy jeans, check shirts and hoodies, and pull on something slightly more comfortable, though just as dull.

After changing, I lie back on my bed, replaying my conversations with Leo from this afternoon in my mind. I think maybe he likes me, not just as a mate but *likes* me likes me. I smile as I think of us sitting at his kitchen table next to each other, our arms resting on the table, almost touching. Then I think of his smile. His laugh. And his eyes. And the way he'd looked at me like no boy has ever looked at me before. Like I was a girl. A girl worth looking at.

I get up and go over to my full-length mirror, trying to see in myself what he might have. Some womanly, attractive quality that's crept into my being without me noticing. Some sign that I might be changing from the chubby child-caterpillar I was into the beautiful, graceful butterfly I might become.

But no.

Staring back at me is the same brown-haired dumpling of a girl I've always been, the only difference between me now and me as a toddler being the large bosoms that have sprouted from my chest, and the fact that adults no longer look at me and say things like, 'Oooh, she's just so squidgy – I could eat her right up!' It's an unavoidable truth that what's seen as endearing in a toddler – a round tummy, food around their mouth, snot bubbles coming out of their nose, that look of intense concentration as they fill their nappy – does not remain endearing in a teenager.

I sigh as I attempt to change the reflection in front of me. I fold my hair up, trying to imagine what I'd look like if I did cut it into a bob, but a pink balloon wearing a helmet stares back at me. Then I pull down the bottom of my jumper as far as it will go and hold it taut at the back to imagine what a dress like Chloe and Kas are always telling me to wear would look like.

But I just look like someone stuffed a pug into a sock.

I've never wanted to wear dresses anyway. Dresses are too girlie for me. And I'm not girlie. I don't even *want* to be girlie. But I am a girl. And I do like being a girl. Just not the kind everyone else seems to want to see.

We all know it's proper *girlie girls* that people want, and we all know what girlie girls *should* look like. And act like. We see it on the TV. In magazines. In films. They should be sexy yet innocent, gossipy yet sensitive, flirty and giggly, and always pretty and happy, with faultless, fatless skin and pouty lips. Any girl who is different is considered inferior, so, if she's brash or plain or tough or strong or loud or ambitious or clumsy or bossy or sarcastic or big or funny, she is less than girlie, making her less than a girl.

Boys, on the other hand, come in all shapes and sizes and personality types, and they'll still fit the idea of what a boy should be. There just seem to be more ways to be considered attractive for them. Just look at Stevie. Tiny, quiet, shy, stupid – nothing traditionally 'boyish' there – yet still, according to Chloe (your classic, pretty girlie girl), a complete hotty.

But there's only one kind of girl that boys want and I'm not it. And there's nothing I can do about that. So surely Leo *can't* like me, not like *that*. After all, what's to like?

But then he *did* say I wasn't fat. And he *sort of* said that I was sexy. Which of course doesn't mean I'm thin or that I actually *am* sexy, but still. It's the nicest thing a boy's ever said to me. Apart from when Noah once told me he loved me more than ice cream.

I lie back on my bed again. Close my eyes and think about Leo. And imagine him kissing me.

Which is actually a really girlie thing to do.

TWENTY

Over the next few days at school, I look out for Leo, but I don't see him. However, at least my reputation as a dad-snatcher with destructive buttocks begins to fade. There's the odd giggle or comment, but now that the worst of the humiliation has faded I laugh along with them, giving it the whole, 'Yeah, I agree, I *am* an idiot, aren't I!' act, and pretty soon people lose interest.

The atmosphere between me, Chloe and Kas stays super awkward though. We've been best friends for years and sometimes, like all good friends, we fall out (though not Kas really; she always takes the sensible middle ground). We argue. We make up. It's all fine, part of being friends, right? But recently we've been falling out more and it feels different somehow. And it scares me that we might be growing apart. As if the differences between us, which started off as tiny insignificant cracks, are widening as we grow up and will soon become huge chasms too wide to cross.

Our friendship used to be simple. It was all about laughing, playing, being silly together. Now sometimes it feels like it's all boyfriends, fashion, moisturizer and nail routines. I can't keep up with it, and I'm not sure I want to. But I can't imagine a world without these two. We need each other and we know each other better than anyone.

But perhaps they don't know me all that well any more – perhaps that's the problem. I don't let them in as much as I did. I don't tell them stuff. I don't tell them I don't want to wear the clothes they're wearing, not because I think I'll look bad in them (though this is true), but because they're just not *me*. I don't tell them I don't want to be thought of as 'hot' – I just want to be thought of as funny. I don't tell them I like a boy, not because I think me and him would look good together but because he makes me laugh. I don't tell them because I'm afraid they'll realize I'm just too different from them and they won't want me around any more.

But all this is making me think that maybe I *should* tell them about Leo. I should let them in, otherwise I might lose them forever. And anyway it's nice to have some 'girlie' news to share for once.

So, when we're sitting outside on the grass at break time, I take a deep breath and go for it. I tell them everything – how I secretly wrote the jokes for Leo, how he came round to my house and asked me to write his set with him. I tell them I went to his house. I tell them about the farting chairs, about how cool he is with Noah, how I made him laugh, how he made me laugh, how he told me I *wasn't* fat. I tell them I think he might like me. I tell them I *know* I like him.

And it's great – they lap it all up, getting excited and giggling in all the right places, and it feels amazing. I should have told them from the start – it was crazy not to. They're my friends – my *best* friends. What was I thinking not telling them about the best thing that's ever happened to me?

Their mouths are open for much of the story, and when I'm done Kas giggles and says, 'Well, O.M.Geeesus that's aMAzing, Pig! You and Leo!'

'Why didn't you tell us before?' says Chloe, actually sounding a bit hurt. 'I mean, we all knew you fancied Leo – why didn't you just own up?'

'I know, I'm sorry. I just, I don't know, I thought you'd think it was hopeless, or stupid, or something. Plus, at the open-mic night, it kinda looked like *you* were into Leo.'

Uh-oh, I shouldn't have said that. Chloe's puppy-dog hurt look changes to she-beast in a split second.

'What? No it didn't! It's not *my* fault he came and sat next to me, is it?'

'Whatever. It doesn't matter now, does it?' says Kas brightly, trying, as always, to keep the peace.

'I guess not,' says Chloe. Then her eyes light up. 'I can't believe you've been in Leo Jackson's house. That's SO FRICKIN' cool.'

Phew. The she-beast's back in her cave.

'I know, right?' I say, my heart glowing at their excitement.

Then, on our way to a history lesson, the three of us still on a high about my news, Chloe suddenly slaps me in the stomach with the back of her hand.

'Ow! What?' I say.

'Shh – look. It's LEO, over there!'

My insides flip out. He's at the end of the corridor, walking towards us with a bunch of his mates, including that tall girl, Keesha, right beside him as always, a shaft of sunlight through the window lighting up her teeth braces and making her resemble a harmonica-playing stick insect.

I back up against the wall, not sure what to do. Chloe and Kas gather round.

'Well, go on then – go and say hi. I mean, he's your mate now, right?' says Kas excitedly.

Oh God. If I don't say hi to him, Chloe and Kas will think I'm lying about the whole thing, but if I do say hi to him in front of his mates, he might not like it and then the whole thing will be off. But then why shouldn't he like it? I mean, we are mates now, right? Mildly flirtatious mates at that.

But what if he cringes with embarrassment at me? I'm not saying he would . . . I mean, he probably wouldn't, but what if he does? I'm not sure I could take that. And it's probably not fair to put him on the spot like that. Best to just let him walk on by.

'Nah, not now,' I say as casually as possible. 'Actually, do you know what? I think I need a wee. Let's go back to the loos over there.' I point pathetically in the opposite direction to Leo, who's now almost in front of us.

'Don't be a knob – go on!' says Chloe, nudging me out from the safety of the wall with her elbow.

I try to catch his eye as he walks past to see what he'll do, but he doesn't spot me. Or perhaps he pretends not to. No, no, I'm sure it's just that he *doesn't* see me.

And then, just as he's past us, Chloe, with one hand on her hip, yells in her most flirty voice, 'Hi, Leo!'

'Shh!' I whisper-shout to her.

'What?' she hisses back. 'You're *friends* with him now, right?'

He turns. I look at him hopefully. His eyes flick to mine and then immediately away, settling instead on Chloe as he casually says, 'Hi, girls,' before carrying on down the corridor.

His mates laugh as they walk away, one of them slapping him on the back and saying, 'That your fan club?'

He laughs. 'Yeah, you know it!'

Great. That's just bloody great.

Once he's disappeared out of sight, the disappointment and embarrassment that he didn't say anything to me, coupled with annoyance at myself for not having the guts just to say hi, and the nerve of my so-called 'best friend' giving him the full-on flirty treatment, get the better of me. My heart starts pumping fast as I explode at Chloe.

'Why did you have to be all flirty with him? Why can't you just let *me* have a boy to myself for once?'

'What? I wasn't being flirty! I was just being *friendly*. And anyway I thought the whole point was that you're mates with him now. I mean, you're writing his comedy stuff, so the least he can do is say hi to you in school, right?'

I sigh a 'gah' of frustration at her. 'Look, he doesn't want everyone to know I'm helping him, so we agreed I wouldn't talk to him at school or anything, OK?'

'Well, that's hardly fair of him, is it?' says Chloe indignantly.

'It doesn't bother me, so why should it bother you?' I fire back.

'Just seems like he's using you, that's all. I mean, he wasn't too embarrassed to talk to *me* the other night.'

Argh! She's so full of herself sometimes, it drives me crazy.

'Oh, so now you're saying he's just too embarrassed to talk to *me*, is that it?' I say.

'No! Don't be stupid, Pig. I didn't mean that at all!' says Chloe.

Oh, she totally *did mean that.*

'Well, what *did* you mean then?' I say. 'Because I'm clearly too "stupid" to work it out.'

'Calm down, Pig. No one's saying anything, all right?' says Kas.

Argh! Grow a pair, Kas! I swear, if another country dropped a nuclear bomb on ours, she'd probably say, 'I'm sure they didn't *mean* to – they just let it go by accident. Let's give them another chance, yeah?'

'Look,' says Chloe, facing me squarely now, her arms folded tightly over her chest, 'I'm just saying that if a boy has you round to his house, doing his homework –'

'Comedy set actually.'

'Whatever. If he does that and then doesn't even *look* at you when he's with his mates, let alone talk to you, that's messed up, OK?'

'But if I'm OK with it it's not messed up, is it? What me and Leo have is special. We've spoken more to each other than you ever have with *Stevie* or any of your supposed *"boyfriends"*.'

And that's it: now I've pushed her well and truly over the edge and the she-beast is fully out to play now, fangs bared.

'Well, at least they're proud to be seen with me,' she says.

Oh my God, can you believe *this girl? I mean, this is bang out of order, right?*

I move towards her, an angry frown plastered across my face as my hands gesticulate wildly to make my point. 'Well, *maybe* what I've got with Leo is about more than just looks. Maybe, Chloe, just *maybe*, the *world* is about more than just looking *"hot"* and having *slaggy* nails, but of course, like most things, *you* wouldn't understand that, *would you*?'

I'm breathing loudly through my nose now, possibly sounding a little bit like an actual pig, and after a second I step back from her.

Oh crapballs. I've gone way too far. But she did push me. I mean, what did she expect?

Chloe unfolds her arms and scowls at me, and for a moment I'm not sure if she's about to cry or throw a punch at me. I brace myself.

'Well, if that's what you think of me,' she fumes, 'why the *hell* are we friends at all, Pig?'

'Sometimes I have NO IDEA,' I hiss back.

I immediately regret it. But it's too late. It's out there now.

'Erm, I think what Chloe's *trying* to say is that she's concerned about you, Pig, in case he's just using you, you know?' says Kas pathetically.

'He's NOT using me. You guys just can't imagine that there might be a boy out there who actually *likes* me. *Me*, not you two for once. I knew I shouldn't have told you.'

Now I'm really fuming. So much for them understanding.

'Well, maybe if you had told us earlier, we could have actually helped, given you some advice, you know, talked it through. I mean, best friends are supposed to tell each other *everything*,' spits Chloe, refolding her arms across her chest like a barricade against me.

'Well, maybe I didn't want your advice, and maybe I don't want to tell you guys *everything* because I know you'll only laugh at me and tell me I stand no chance with *any* guy *ever*.'

'We wouldn't say that!' says Kas.

'Shut up!' both me and Chloe say to her at the same time.

'When have we *ever* said anything like that to you? It's all in your head, Pig. And that's not our fault,' says Chloe.

Then there's an awkward silence as I try to fold my arms over my chest like Chloe. But my arms either have to go above my boobs, making me look like I'm doing one of those Russian Cossack dances, or below them, so I look like I'm doing the actions to 'Miss Polly Had a Dolly'. I unfurl them and carry on steamrolling.

'Oh, come on, admit it, you don't think I stand a chance with someone like Leo because I'm not *thin* and *beautiful* and *preened* and *plucked* and painted up like a trashy fairy on top of a pound-store Christmas tree.'

'Hey!' says Kas.

'You're just *jealous* because me and Kas *care* about what we look like – I mean, you could too! If you wanted to be thinner, you *could* lose weight, you know. Isn't that right, Kas?'

Oh, I cannot believe she's played the fat card.

Chloe looks at Kas with an expression that says, 'If you don't agree with me I will boil your family alive.'

'Erm . . .' says Kas, looking confused and terrified, like a child who's just been told to choose between her deranged mum and her violent dad in a divorce.

Chloe rolls her eyes at her and tuts as I boil over with so much anger, it's a wonder I'm not breathing fire.

'I don't *want* to lose weight! Doesn't it cross your tiny mind that I'm happy with the way I am and maybe Leo is too? And that perhaps it's a real shame that my so-called "*friends*" don't feel the same way,' I blaze.

'We're not the ones who go on about how "fat" you are, Pig – *you* are. So, if you're really happy about your weight, STOP BANGING ON ABOUT IT!' says Chloe.

Kas, meanwhile, has her hands on her cheeks and the expression of someone who's watching the gross bits from a horror film she really doesn't wanna see, but can't quite turn away from.

'Do y'know what? Maybe *you're* the jealous one,' I hit back at Chloe. 'You couldn't stand that Leo knew *me* on

Friday night, which is why you were all over him like cheap perfume instead of watching your friend onstage.'

'Jealous? Of you? Hardly!' yells Chloe, looking me up and down. 'I *don't* think so. Anyway, I've got Stevie, an *actual* boyfriend, not just some bloke who uses then ignores me.'

'Stevie is an upturned toilet brush with about as much personality as a *flannel*! I'm sure you'll both be very happy together!' I yell back.

'We *are* actually, thank you, and Kas is going out with Stevie's best friend Isaac now, so you might have to find someone else to hang around with at lunchtime. Maybe Leo? Oh no, hang on a minute – he doesn't even want to be SEEN with you.'

I scowl at Kas. 'You are?'

She shrugs and says sheepishly, 'Well, yeah, I think so. He got Stevie to give me a ruler, and on it he'd written "u + me =" and then he'd drawn a heart with a smiley face on it. At least I think it was a heart . . . it may have been a bum.'

'Wow, that's romantic,' I scoff.

'Oh, don't be like that, Pig,' says Kas.

'No, that's fine. You guys go off and be your little love quartet – don't worry about me.' I knew this would happen. They think I'm holding them back and were just waiting for a chance to get rid of me. Well, fine.

'Right. I've had enough of this. C'mon, Kas,' says Chloe, turning on her heel, linking her arm through Kas's and dragging her down the corridor. Kas turns back to me and shrugs as they leave.

'FINE!' I yell after them before storming off in the opposite direction.

I keep walking until I get to the girls' toilet. There's no one else here. They're all in their lessons. Still absolutely furious, I thump my hands down next to the sink, then go into a cubicle and sit on the closed lid of the toilet.

And, as the adrenalin-fuelled anger fades, the tears come. Thick and fast.

TWENTY-ONE

At lunch, Kas tries to smile at me, but Chloe elbows her in the ribs, making it clear that's not acceptable, and then carries on pretending I'm invisible.

I don't want to sit with them anyway. Right now it makes me angry just knowing they're in the same room as me. And they're wrong about Leo using me.

Just. Plain. Wrong.

So I look around the room and see Grace, Poppy and Fajah, a group of girls I've barely spoken to before, who always seem friendly enough. Who needs Chloe and Kas? It might be nice to hang with a different group for once and these girls look all right. If you squint. They're flashing their phone screens at each other and giggling as I sit down next to them.

'Oh, hey, Pig!' says Fajah.

'Hiya. Do you mind if I sit with you guys?' I say.

'No, that would be fab!' she says.

Dylan is at the next table, and he leans back in his chair and says, 'Admit it, Pig, you just want to sit closer to me, right?'

Why is he always on my case?

'Shut up, Dylan,' I say, and thankfully he does.

Grace puffs on her inhaler and giggles, and Poppy carries on biting her nails. 'So what are you guys chuckling about?' I ask.

As they start showing me the latest 'hilarious' memes of pets falling off tables, I get an unwelcome insight into what a slow death might feel like.

Then they talk about their latest crafting adventures, showing each other their recent creations on Instagram: Grace has knitted some butterflies, Poppy's made candles in old yoghurt pots and Fajah's recently painted some pebbles to look like the members of some boy band called Boy Zinc. When I ask why, they all look at me as if I've just punched a puppy in the face.

Truth is, I don't get the point of humourless, light conversation. I only want conversation that's meaningful or funny. Not the stuff in between. I can't do small talk. I can't talk about the weather or TV or what you did at the weekend. I don't give a toss and I'm only interested in talking about those things if they're a vehicle for the funny. I might look like I'm listening, but I'm just thinking about turning whatever you've just said into a joke. Which, now I come to think of it, must be quite annoying. I guess Kas and Chloe put up with a lot. Anyway, aim for the laugh or aim for the interesting. Anything in between is just point-less arse-drivel.

After lunch, with nowhere else to go and trying to avoid Chloe and Kas as they stand in the corner of the field, silently holding Stevie and Isaac's quivering hands, I find myself hanging with the cat-meme trio again. They sit cross-legged on the steps of the science block, wittering on about their favourite TV shows from last week – soap operas and reality shows I've never seen before because I'm too busy watching comedy shows and stand-up routines. True, Kas and Chloe watch these shows too, but when they discuss them it's with the full expectation that I'll be sarcastic about them and make us all laugh. These guys, however, don't seem to understand sarcasm. Or wit. Or possibly even fun.

'Yeah,' says Fajah as she froths with excitement over last night's dramas, which they've already been blabbering on about for a full twenty minutes, 'and did you see when Craig came in and found Ruth snogging Lisa? I was like. Oh. My. Giddy. Gosh.'

'Right! And neither of them know about the baby he's just had with Neesha!' adds Poppy, her freckly cheeks glowing red with anger at the unfortunate 'Craig'.

Grace says nothing, just continues to grin while staring at the ground and sucking one of her plaits, which she's evidently just dunked in her yoghurt. On purpose.

'And there he was last week having a go at Duncan for his affair!' says Fajah.

'Well,' says Poppy, 'as my mum always says, "People in glass houses shouldn't throw –"'

'Nude parties?' I offer, trying to inject a bit of humour into this rotting corpse of a conversation.

They all look at me with bewildered expressions on their faces.

'No, I think it's "stones", Pig.'

'Oh, right,' I say, the will to live draining from my body. 'Of course.'

The school day drags on until it eventually claws its way across the finish line that is the final school bell. I gather up my things and leave quickly so I can avoid Chloe and Kas and also get home before Leo arrives. At my house. Yay!

I take Noah home and find that Mum's still asleep in her room after her night shift, so I quietly fix us a snack, tidy up by piling the crap everywhere into large teetering crap mountains and get changed before he arrives.

Then I just stand in the hall, facing the front door, waiting for his knock. Like a complete saddo. My heart pounding.

Leo's actually going to be *here*, walking through that door, *my* door, any minute now!

Maybe I should message him? No, don't message him, you desperate freak!

Any minute now . . .

Really soon . . .

Twenty minutes later and half my brain is shouting at the other half that of course he's not coming. I embarrassed him in the corridor earlier – well, *Chloe* did – and now he doesn't want anything more to do with me. But the other half of my brain is convinced he'll be here because obviously he's falling in love with me. Because that half of my brain is stupid and blindly optimistic, like a cow packing a picnic for a lovely day out at the abattoir.

Noah comes and stands next to me, shovelling Cheesy Puffs into his mouth.

'Whatcha doin'?' he asks.

'Just waiting for Leo. He's coming round. Should be here any minute.'

'Leo, Leo! I love Leo!' says Noah as if he's reading my mind.

'Just be cool, Noah!' I hiss as I check my reflection in the hall mirror yet again. Not to see how good I look, just to reassure myself I don't have eye bogeys or a Jaffa Cake stuck between my teeth.

I face the door again. Willing its frosted-glass panel to be filled with the blurry shape of Leo.

We stand in silence, apart from the crunch of Noah's little teeth chomping on the crisps and his hands rummaging around the packet for the next one. When it's empty, he casually chucks it on the floor.

'Why's he not here yet?' he asks, spraying the hall with bright orange crumbs. 'I don't think he's coming.'

'He'll be here all right, Noah!' I crouch down to his level like Mum says we should when we have to tell him off. 'Pick the packet up and put it in the bin, don't talk with your mouth full, and go and clean your hands before he gets here. I can't tell what's Cheesy Puffs and what's your fingers any more.'

Then Leo knocks on the door. And my internal organs somersault into each other.

'Yay!' Noah squeals with delight, clasping his orange fingers round my face and squeezing. 'He's here!'

'Argh, Noah!' I spring to my feet and look in the mirror again. An angry Oompa Loompa stares back at me.

'I'll get it!' chirps Noah as he waddles towards the door.

'Wait! Noah, no!' I say, desperately scrubbing at my cheeks with my sleeve, and only managing to spread the disaster zone further.

But of course Noah ignores me and opens the door.

'Hey,' says Leo as casually as ever.

'Hello!' I say, hoping his eyes haven't yet adjusted to the dim light in our hall, but of course they have.

'Wow, you trying out a new tan? It's very ... erm, Trumpesque,' he says.

'Thanks, yeah, I'm going to run over a guinea pig and wear it as a wig tomorrow just to complete the look.'

He laughs and my embarrassment fades just a bit.

'Do you mind if I just go and . . .' I mime wiping my face.

'No, sure – you do what you gotta do.'

I run to the kitchen and violently scrub at my cheeks with a scourer.

'Hey, little dude,' I hear Leo say to Noah as they walk into the living room. 'Wow, you're strong. Like a little Hulk. So how're you doing?' From the slow thudding scrape of Leo's footsteps I conclude that Noah has clamped himself round one of his legs for a ride, like a maniac.

'Sorry about him!' I call back to Leo.

'I'm jolly today!' squeals Noah. 'My jolly knows NO END!'

'Good to know,' says Leo.

'I've drawn a picture of you – you wanna see?' says Noah.

'You have?' I say suspiciously, emerging from the kitchen with the slight improvement of bright red cheeks rather than bright orange ones.

Noah pounds his way up the stairs to retrieve his drawing as Leo slumps down on to our embarrassment of a sofa.

'Shh, Noah! Remember Mum's sleeping, yeah?' I whisper-shout after him.

'Oh, sorry,' Leo whispers back, his arm outstretched along the back of the sofa, looking super relaxed, as I stand by the hall doorway, not sure what to do with my hands. 'How's she doing with the whole break-up and everything?'

'What? Oh, that – no, it was nothing. She's fine. You want a drink?'

I get us both a Coke as I hear Noah trundle back down the stairs and thrust his drawing into Leo's hands.

'Wow!' says Leo, laughing. 'That's so cool, bro. And that's me, right?'

'Yep,' says Noah.

'And that's Haylah, right?'

'Yep.'

'And what are we doing?' asks Leo.

'You're getting married and here's all your brown babies.'

Oh. Holy. Bumcracks.

I drop the Coke bottle and it pours all over the worktop as I rush out of the kitchen and grab the bit of paper out of Leo's hands.

'Noah!' I shout.

'Shh!' Noah says, his little podgy finger up to his mouth. 'Mum's sleeping!'

'Leo, I'm so sorry, I had no idea he'd drawn this!'

'What?' says Leo, still laughing. 'I like it – I think he's really captured you.'

I look at the drawing. For Leo, he's drawn a recognizable head, torso and stick arms and legs, and coloured everything brown. And for me he's just drawn a massive pink circle with lopsided eyes and an angry-looking mouth.

'Wow, thanks, Noah.'

'You're welcome!' He beams. 'You can keep it if you want, Leo.'

'No, I'm sure Leo doesn't want –'

'Yeah, I do!' says Leo, and he yanks the drawing back from me with a smirk, folds it up carefully and puts it in his pocket. 'Thanks, little dude.'

After getting Noah settled in front of some trippy cartoon about robot police bears, we go into the kitchen to sit at the dining table.

'Sorry, you have to add your own fart noises to our chairs,' I say.

Leo makes a huge authentic fart noise with his lips as he sits down and both of us laugh.

'The truth is that nothing any comedian ever wrote, or says, is ever as funny as a fart noise,' I say.

'True. We may as well give up now,' he agrees. 'Sorry I'm late by the way.'

'You are? I hadn't noticed – doesn't matter.' I OOZE calm and cool.

'Just had some stuff to do.'

'Right,' I say, and for an annoyed moment I think about bringing up the whole 'and why didn't you even look at me at school earlier?' thing, but I think better of it. He's here now, and that's what matters.

I grab my pen and notebook as Leo gets his laptop out of his bag and opens up the notes we made the other day.

'OK, we've got our list of teenage-bloke topics to use only if we twist or, as you Cambridge boys would have it, "*subvert*" them, and so ... is there anywhere you want to start, any more specifically Leo-esque ideas you've had?'

'I dunno, but I was on the bus the other day with my mates, and I kinda thought there might be funny stuff there.'

'Oooh, I love it,' I say. 'I mean, God, yeah. I have to get the bus everywhere too. And they've got to be a comedy goldmine. I mean, they stink and they're dangerous. There's no seat belts, no airbags ... and yet parents encourage us to go on these things.'

Leo laughs. 'I know, right? And there's always one dodgy weirdo on a bus, even at 9 a.m.'

'Yep, that's standard issue on every bus I've ever been on, and, hey, if there's never been a dodgy weirdo on your bus, guess what? *You're* the weirdo.'

'Right!' He laughs again. 'And then it's just rows of teenagers and old people, ordinarily natural enemies, thrown together through circumstance,' he says. And I laugh.

We keep going like this, writing good stuff, making each other laugh, and it's bliss. Then we start weaving what we have into something resembling a comedy routine, putting in as many punchlines as we can, saying the lines out loud to get the rhythm right. By the time Mum comes downstairs, we have a pretty strong comedy 'bit' to kick off his set.

'Right, that's a good little opener,' I say. 'Now you need to practise it in front of an audience.'

'What, here? Now?' Leo protests, looking just slightly less than his normal confident and chilled self.

'Yeah, why not?' I say. 'Mum! Noah!'

'Wait, Haylah, no. I'm not ready!'

Good God, it's so cute that he's actually nervous about this.

'It'll be fine. You can just read it off your laptop for now, but it'll help us make sure it all works.'

So me, Mum and Noah sit on the sofa together with Leo standing in front of us.

'Oh, a bit of comedy's just what I need!' says Mum, nestling her bum further down into the sofa.

'OK, Noah,' I say, 'you introduce him.'

'Live from our living room, it's Leo . . .! Wait, what's your second name?' he whispers.

'Jackson,' says Leo.

'Leo Duck-son!'

'Brilliant,' I say and the three of us clap and whoop.

And Leo begins. 'So, everyone always wonders why teenagers are so grumpy. You know, you hear adults banging on about it. All the time. Well, you wanna know why we're grumpy? BECAUSE YOU MAKE US GET THE BUS EVERYWHERE!'

Mum gives an appreciative laugh and Leo relaxes a bit.

'Yeah, that's right. And you know what? It's the same reason *old people* are grumpy.'

'Oooh, yeah, leave a pause there, that works well,' I whisper.

'Shh!' says Mum.

Leo takes a deep breath and gets back into it.

'That's right, rickety old buses up and down the country are rammed full of old people and teenagers. Two groups of people who should *not* be in the same space. Natural enemies pushed together by the shared experience of *nobody* wanting to spend time in a car with us.

'So we're stuck together. Only we teenagers have it worse than the old folk because it takes a lifetime to learn the bus timetables, so at least *they* know where they're going.

'Then, of course, there's the standard-issue bus weirdo. You know the guy. There's one on every route. The guy who shuffles on, slurping from a can of beer, even at 9 a.m., angrily muttering to himself. The guy who the bus driver *knows by name*. "All right, Norman," he says sternly to him as he gets on, as if to say, "I've got my eye on you, Norman, so don't attack too many kids today."

'But, y'know, the worst thing is, our *parents* are in on this. My mum's like, "No, I can't take you, darlin' – just get the bus!" And I'm like, "Just a few short years ago you wouldn't let me sit in our car unless I was bound and shackled in a safety seat three times the size of me!"

'I mean, I know I'm not the cute toddler I once was, but *seriously*, woman, has your love for me gone downhill so quickly that you've changed from "Nothing's gonna harm MY angel!" to "Yeah, boy, you go sit in that giant metal deathtrap with the unhinged stranger. You'll *probably* be fine."

'And you wonder why we're a bit grumpy.'

By this point, Mum's beside herself with laughter, as am I, even though I just wrote the stuff down. Leo performs it so well, putting stresses on all the right words, leaving pauses in all the right places, and his high-pitched mum impression is just hilarious. Noah, who hasn't got a clue why he's laughing, giggles along too as he just thinks it's funny when we laugh.

Leo slumps down into the armchair. 'So it's good, right?' he asks us.

Mum wipes her eyes. 'It's brilliant! You guys wrote that?'

'Well, Haylah wrote most of it really.'

'No I didn't,' I say, embarrassed. 'We wrote it together and, well, you nailed it.'

He smiles at us.

'You're so going to win that competition, Leo,' I say.

'What competition?' Mum asks.

Leo stays for tea and we tell her all about the competition next Saturday, and she immediately whips her phone out at the dinner table and buys us all tickets to see it.

'You should do a set as well, Haylah. Don't you think, Leo?' says Mum with a mouthful of food. Meanwhile, I'm trying to eat as slowly and daintily as I can, which is not easy with a meat-feast pizza.

'Yeah, I do,' he says, though he doesn't sound convinced. I'm certain it's because he knows I'm not ready to get up onstage again after the last disaster.

'No, no way. I'm not even nearly there yet,' I say.

'Hmm, you're probably right. Well, maybe in a couple of years, sweetheart?' says Mum.

'Yeah, maybe,' I say.

I see Leo out after tea, even though everything inside me wants him to stay, possibly forever. We agree to meet up at his house on Monday, and then maybe two more times next week before the gig. And I can't wait. Before he leaves, he leans in and gives me a kiss on the cheek.

'Your family's amazing,' he says, 'and so are you.'

'Thank you,' I say, blushing red from the kiss.

Leo's kiss. On my actual cheek!

But again I want to ask him why, if he thinks I'm so 'awesome', he didn't say hi to me at school. But I don't want to ruin the moment, so instead I just say, 'See ya Monday then, yeah?'

'Yep, see ya, Haylah.'

I go back into the living room, a big smug grin on my face.

'Come here, love,' says Mum and I slump down into her arms. 'You're so clever, writing all that stuff.'

'Thanks, Mum.'

'You sure you're happy for him to perform it though? I mean, he gets all the credit when you did the hard work,' she says, stroking my hair.

'What? No, it's not like that – we're a team. Me and Leo. Lots of comedians write together.'

'OK, OK. Just make sure you're doing what *you* want to do, not what some guy wants you to do for him.'

I sit up, moving my head away from her hand. 'He's not "some guy", Mum, he's *Leo*.'

'They're all just some guy eventually, love,' she says, staring into the distance, her mind elsewhere.

'I thought you liked him!'

'I do, I do,' she says, snapping her thoughts back into the room. 'I just think he probably knows how much *you* like him and I don't want you to get used.'

'HE'S NOT USING ME! Why does everyone think that?!' I explode, getting up from the sofa.

Ugh, that was a mistake.

'Who else thinks that, love?' She narrows her eyes.

'No one, nothing. It's all fine. In fact, it's all great. He doesn't know I *like* him like that, and who said I did anyway? Look, we're just friends doing something cool together. He's not *using* me – he just thinks I'm good.'

'OK, babe, if you're sure,' she says, sounding totally unsure that I'm sure.

'I am,' I say as I walk off to my room. 'Totally.'

TWENTY-TWO

The next week at school is super crappy and I live for the times I'll be meeting up with Leo again. I continue to avoid Chloe and Kas as much as possible, and they me. If they walk past me in the corridor, I immediately pretend to be best friends with the trio I've latched on to, laughing heartily as if one of them has just told the best joke I've ever heard, when the truth is, I don't think they'd know actual humour if it dressed up as a court jester and slapped them round the head with a rubber chicken. And, whenever she passes, Chloe throws her chin up high as if she's balancing something of great importance on the end of it, and Kas tries to smile sheepishly at me, but I refuse to smile back.

Kas occasionally sends me messages, saying things like, 'We miss you, Pig,' and 'Please don't be mad at me, I'm not taking sides with Chloe, it's just, well, you know what she's like,' and, 'Chloe's sorry, please come back!'

Sitting on my bed, I read through them on my phone again. I'm about to reply to Kas when I think, *No! Chloe's the one who needs to say sorry, not Kas on her behalf. They're just jealous of me and Leo. Don't play them at their own game. They're being childish and pathetic. I'm not like that – I'm mature. I'm sophisticated.* I think this as I bite into my third doughnut, the jam spilling down my chin and on to my onesie pyjamas.

What gets me through the week are my afternoons with Leo. Which are crazy awesome. We talk, we laugh, we write. We come up with two other 'bits' for his stand-up, one centring round his insistence on proper punctuation ('because knowing the difference between "Let's eat, Baby" and "Let's eat baby" can save a relationship, and possibly the life of an infant'). In the other he took the piss out of dystopian films (which he 'wouldn't watch even if they were the last films on earth'). How he didn't need to go to the cinema to watch confused, weary teenagers with dull clothing and bad nutrition squinting in the hazy sunlight, as that was what he faced at school every Monday morning.

Before we know it, it's Thursday and we have the whole required five-minute set finished, and every time I hear Leo practise it (which gives me a great excuse to just stare at him) it still makes me laugh. Before I leave, he performs it one more time as I sit on his sofa and watch him. Noah's not with us today as Mum had a rare day off and picked him up from school. So, for the first time ever, me and Leo are alone together. *For the first and last time,* I think. After all, when Saturday's over, there's no reason for us to spend time together again, at least not from his point of view.

'Well, I guess that's it then,' I say when he's finished. I bite my lip.

'But you're coming on Saturday, right?' he asks, flopping down on the sofa next to me.

Oh God, our legs are just millimetres apart.

'Of course. Wouldn't be anywhere else, right?' I say, drumming my fingers on my knees.

'I've got a load of my mates coming along so it should be a really good night. Why don't you bring your mates too? The more people on my side laughing loudly, the funnier the judges will think I am!'

'Hmm, maybe, but I'm in a new group of "friends" now, and to be honest they seem to have had their sense of humour surgically removed and replaced with a meme of a kitten in a top hat.'

'Why you hanging around with them then? What happened to what are their names? – Chloe and Kas?'

I haven't told Leo about our falling out; too much of it was to do with Chloe-Leo jealousy and Chloe's belief that I'm too fat and too ungirlie to ever attract a guy who isn't just using me for some other purpose. Neither of these seemed like things I wanted to talk to Leo about. On the other hand, we're about to say goodbye, probably never to be alone together again.

So I blurt out, 'Chloe and Kas think I'm making a tit of myself hanging around with you because you'll never be interested in me like I'm interested in you . . . because why would anyone be interested in *me* like that, right? I'm just fat and ungirlie and an embarrassment.'

I stare at the floor, my heart thumping in my chest like it's trying to get out and run away from the horrendous truth-bomb I've just dropped. But Leo doesn't flinch and his breathing remains calm. Probably because girls say this kind of stuff to him all the time.

Who am I kidding? Of course he already knows I fancy him. Everyone *fancies him.*

He takes a deep breath. 'Well, I don't think you're fat or ungirlie – and what was the other thing?'

'An embarrassment,' I murmur, still looking at the floor.

'Or an embarrassment. They're idiots if they think that.'

I glance up at him. 'Then why didn't you say hi to me in the corridor at school last week?'

'What? When?' he says, actually squirming in his seat a little and trying not to meet my gaze.

Now I turn and look right at Leo, and I see in his eyes that he knows exactly what I'm talking about. And I know in that instant what Chloe and Kas tried to tell me, and what I had suspected all along: that him ignoring me at school was no accident.

'You do know, Leo – when you were with Keesha and the rest of the cool brigade, and ignored me until Chloe said hi and fluttered her boobs in your direction, and then you were like, "Oooh, hi, girls," to them before telling your mates we were just your "fan club".'

'Oh, then,' he says, sounding a little ashamed, rubbing his chin.

'Yeah, *then*,' I say, feeling awkward at just how awkward I am making him feel, but also a little pissed off and a little brave, like I've got nothing to lose here. So I continue. 'And, for that matter, any other time you could have said hi at school or, God forbid, made conversation with me. And don't give me that "oooh, I don't want other people to know I'm not writing this on my own" crap because you didn't have to tell them *that* to say hi, did you? I mean, it could just be that we know each other, right? That's not *so* ridiculous, is it?'

Our eyes meet, and for once Leo's not smiling. Not even a little bit. Oh God, I've pissed him off. And I don't want it all to end like this.

Should have kept my big fat mouth shut.

'I'm sorry,' he says. 'I-I should have said hi. I should have talked to you. You're right, OK? I just, I don't know, I've worked hard to get where I am at school, to get good grades and still stay, I don't know, *popular*, I guess . . .'

'Oh, you poor thing! Good grades AND popularity – wow, that must be tough,' I say sharply.

He gets up and starts pacing around the room. 'Yeah, all right. I know it sounds rubbish. I just figured if I was seen hanging around with a girl two years younger it might not do me any favours, OK? If that makes me a bad person, then I'm sorry.'

'Uh-huh, but you were quite happy sliding your arm round my friend Chloe the other night at the open mic.'

Probably shouldn't have said that.

'What? No, I didn't! I sat next to her, sure, but you know what we talked about? *You* – how amazing you were up there. I said you had "a natural comic voice". "Yeah, she's so talented," she said, except then you went all mental, lost your train of thought and started sexually harassing my dad.'

'That was *because* of you and Chloe!'

Leo stops pacing for a moment and looks at me. 'It was? Well, didn't she tell you what we were talking about afterwards?'

'No,' I say, 'she didn't. Though I probably didn't give her the chance. She really said that about me?'

'Yeah, she did.'

Hmm.

'I was just so hacked off with her – for, well, for flirting with you and for putting my name down when I hadn't asked her –'

'No, *I* did that,' he says, with a guilty smile.

'What? ARGH! No! Why did you do that?' I yell, throwing my hands up in the air.

'Because by then I'd figured out you'd written me those cute notes with the jokes, and I thought you should give it a go.' He's leaning on the fireplace beaming at me.

'Brilliant. Thanks,' I say, trying to remain pissed off, but his use of the word 'cute' has made that difficult to sustain.

'Well, I didn't know it would end up like it did, did I? You're not ready for it yet, but your mum's right – you will be in a couple of years. You'll be a huge comedy star, you wait.'

'Thanks. Well, anyway, I'd better go,' I say, still pissed off. 'Don't want to cramp your style any longer, not when that impressive popularity of yours could be snatched away any minute if someone were to – gasp! – see us talking together.'

'Look,' he says, walking back over to the sofa and sitting next to me, even closer this time. He leans forward, resting his forearms on his knees. 'I'm going to be really honest now. You don't know what it's like – to be the, well, the "only black in the village".'

'It's a town.'

'You know what I mean.'

'Yeah. I know what you mean. I guess it is pretty bland and vanilla around here.'

'Yeah, so brown faces kinda stand out, and not in a good way. People don't automatically look at me and think, *Clever, funny, bright future*, so I have to work twice as hard as anyone else to get people thinking that.'

'Yeah, OK, I get it, and look, I do know how that feels, at least a little bit. I'm a plain, short, daughter-of-a-poor-single-mum fat girl. People hardly look at me and think, *Clever, funny, bright future*.'

'I do,' he says, then turns to face me. 'And you're NOT fat – why do you always say that about yourself? It's like you want to get in there and say it before someone else does.'

'So, what's wrong with that?' I look down at the cuff of my jumper, which I've pulled down over my hand and am now scratching at with my thumb.

'Well, maybe no one else *is* going to say it, or think it. You're a curvy, funny, beautiful girl, Haylah. Other people can see it, so maybe you should start seeing it too and stop assuming the world's out to get you.' There's a short silence before he says softly, 'So why didn't you want Chloe to flirt with me?'

He keeps his eyes on me. His words 'curvy', 'funny', 'beautiful' and 'girl' still dancing around my head, making me dizzy.

I take a deep breath and, like diving out of an aeroplane with only a questionable parachute into a horrific but exhilarating free fall, I just go for it.

I look up and lean over to kiss him.

And, for a moment, I think he's going to back away, but he cups one hand round my cheek as he slowly leans towards me, and when our lips meet fireworks explode in my head.

We kiss.

Proper kiss.

And it's heaven.

I don't know who pulls away first, maybe him, maybe me, and then we stare into each other's eyes for a moment as he holds my face in both his hands.

Then his eyes flick away from mine to the clock on the wall behind me. 'Argh, I'm sorry. That was amazing but, I'm sorry, I've gotta be somewhere in a bit,' he says, a little breathless.

'Yeah, of course. I'd better be going anyway,' I say with a smile that might never fade.

And we hold each other's hands to the front door.

'You do have a bright future, you know,' he says. 'You could be anything, do anything, if you really want it.'

'You too,' I say.

'See you on Saturday, yeah?' he says.

'Saturday,' I agree, still pulsing with a delicious electricity as he watches me walk away.

TWENTY-THREE

I walk home, standing tall, holding my head high and feeling like I just won the lottery, *Strictly Come Dancing* and the Nobel Peace Prize all in the same day.

A favourite song of Mum's, 'This Kiss', plays over and over in my head as I walk. I can't remember the words though, and I'm pretty sure they're not 'This kiss, this kiss! Unploppable. This kiss, this kiss! Abdominal . . .' But it's working for me, and when I cross the road I actually skip a little bit.

At home, me, Mum and Noah watch *The Lion King*, curled up on the sofa together, and though of course I tune in when Timon and Pumbaa are onscreen, I mostly just close my eyes and replay the kiss over and over in my head. Leo's hands on my face, his lips on mine. *Hakuna my matatas*, I wish I could freeze that moment and stay in it forever.

'Are you OK, love?' Mum asks flatly when the film's done. 'You look like you've got your head in the clouds as always.'

'Me? Yeah, I'm amazing. I'm great.'

'Things going well with Leo then?' she says.

For a second, I consider telling her about the kiss, but I'm not sure she'd approve. Oh sure, she'd love it if I actually had a boyfriend, in a six-year-olds-holding-hands kind of way, but probably not in a random-snog-with-an-older-guy-that-might-not-actually-be-part-of-any-kind-of-boyfriendy-relationship way.

Oh God, it might not actually be a boyfriendy relationship. It didn't feel like that though. I mean, we have got a relationship, right? We make each other laugh, love spending time together, talk about proper stuff, write comedy together, like (still can't believe it) *kissing* each other. Just because we haven't talked of boyfriend-girlfriend titles doesn't mean we're not pretty much there, right? Which is frickin' daydream-becoming-a-reality awesome beyond words!

I spend the rest of the evening constructing new daydreams where me and Leo become the king and queen of comedy, topping the bill at Live at the Apollo, hosting TV comedy panel shows together, starring in our own sitcom and getting our disgustingly lavish wedding photos in *Hello!* magazine. As I drift off to sleep, Stephen Fry is asking for our autographs at the end of an awards show where we've just won everything.

The next day at school, I see Kas and Chloe sitting at the back of our form room as always and I desperately want to talk to them. I want to tell them what happened. I want them to gasp and ask me questions and tell me how amazing it all is. But Chloe thrusts her nose in the air and turns away as I approach them, so I go over and sit with the crafting dorks in the other corner. And I have no intention of telling them anything about Leo and me.

I know now that Chloe wasn't flirting with Leo at the pub; she was actually just talking to him about me. And I know it wasn't her who put my name down for the open-mic list. But I'm still angry with her about everything else. And with Kas for going along with her.

They still think Leo's just using me because they can't imagine a boy might like me for me. And I also know they wouldn't understand why he doesn't talk to me at school – how could they ever get what it's like to have to work doubly hard because you're black, or fat, or poor or whatever, when fate gave them flat stomachs, beautiful faces, perfect hair and all the free gifts life showers on you when you have those things?

AND Chloe told me I should lose weight. I haven't forgotten that. I mean, I know she might be right, but friends aren't supposed to point out your faults. They're supposed to make you feel better about them. After all, I don't point out she's an airheaded tart. (OK, so I may have pointed that out a *little* bit in our argument, but I kind of think it's a trait she's proud of anyway.) Well, sod her. She can keep Kas and little hedgehog-headed Stevie.

I have Leo. I don't need them.

And that thought keeps me going for the rest of the day. Apart from when Dylan notices me eating lunch on the grass on my own, watching something (comedy of course) on my phone and can't resist being a jerk.

'Whatcha watching, Pig? Is it "Sexy Suzy in Her See-through Nightie"? Can I come and watch it with you?'

He walks towards me as his friends laugh.

'No, go away,' I say in a tired voice.

He nudges my shoe with his. 'Aww, you know you love me really.'

His friends laugh again.

'Just piss off, Dylan,' I hiss.

He raises his hands as he walks away. 'All right, all right, I was only being friendly.'

At the end of the day, reimagining for the sixty-thousandth time my kiss with Leo, I walk through my front door and hear Noah crying like I've never heard him before. The sound tears at my insides. I mean, sure, he cries all the time – he cries when he falls down, even if it's a slow fall on to soft grass. He cries when I tell him he can't have a third packet of crisps; he cries when I won't let him play with my box of tampons; he cries when we point out a tractor we're driving past that, by the time he looks up, is gone; he cries when I tell him soup isn't finger food – I mean, the boy can *cry* like a pro.

But this is different. He's really sobbing, quietly but desperately. I rush into the living room and over to where he's curled up in Mum's arms and kiss his wet face.

'What happened?' I ask Mum.

I look up at her and see that her cheeks are smeared wet with her own tears. I hate seeing Mum cry.

'Oh God, who's died?' I ask, suddenly really panicked.

Please don't say it's Granny Mo. Let it be creepy old Uncle Terry. He barely moves or says anything anyway so it wouldn't be all that much of a change for him.

'No one, love, it's fine. I'll talk to you in a minute. Just help me calm him down first.'

'Of course,' I say.

And together we talk softly to him, fix him snacks, give him cuddles and play a bit of I-spy to get his mind off whatever was bothering him. Eventually, we settle him with Mum's iPad and an episode of *Dora*, and then Mum leads me out into the kitchen. We sit next to each other at the table and I hold her hand.

Again, I ask her what happened.

'Your dad called.' She gulps hard and, through gritted teeth, says, 'To wish Noah a happy birthday.'

That fart-brained bag of bull crap – how dare he!

'What? That's two weeks from now, and when has he ever done that in recent years anyway?' I say, my insides burning with rage.

Mum tells me that she was in the loo when he called, and so Noah picked up the phone. By the time she came out of the toilet, Noah was sobbing down the phone and asking Dad when he was coming home and promising he'd never be naughty again if he did.

Noah can't even remember living with Dad – he left when he was so little. But he hears his friends talk about their dads, and I think it's just the idea of a dad he wants to come home, rather than actual Dad.

But of course he's never coming home. Which is good. But Noah doesn't understand that. So now he's pissed off with Mum, who grabbed the phone and told Dad where to stick it.

'Noah asked me why we never talk about Dad and why I'm mean to him when he phones,' says Mum. 'Argh, I've tried really hard not to bad-mouth him in front of you guys, but I guess he's picked up on it anyway. I dunno, maybe I've gone about the whole thing all wrong.'

She rests her head in her hands as the tears start rolling down her cheeks again. The only thing worse than seeing Mum cry is seeing Mum cry because of Dad.

'Oh, Mum, I'm so sorry. I'll talk to Noah, OK? He'll understand. I mean, not fully – the boy doesn't even understand that clowns aren't an actual race of people – but . . .'

She laughs a little, but not much, and my heart aches for her. It's so not her fault Dad's a complete family-wrecking scumhole.

'Thanks, Hay.' She goes back to sniffling, and then says something I haven't heard in a very long time. 'I just wish it could have been different for us, you know? Maybe if I'd been different, been a better wife, he wouldn't have . . .'

I always hated it when she blamed herself for Dad's twattishness.

'That's rubbish, Mum, and you know it. You did *nothing* wrong. Dad's a complete fanny-fart, and he didn't deserve you.'

'Oh, Hay, don't hate him. It wasn't all bad when he was around, you know. I mean, he used to make you laugh so much. You remember that, don't you?'

I think about it for a moment. 'Yeah,' I say softly, 'I remember.'

Memories of him reading bedtime stories to me, doing all the voices and prancing around my bedroom, making me giggle so much my belly hurt, rush into my head. Memories I usually block out.

'He does love you guys. He just, I dunno, he couldn't settle, always wanted more – more than me.'

'I don't know what to say, Mum. I'm sorry.'

'You don't have to say anything, babe. I shouldn't be putting all this on you, Hay. You're too young for this stuff. I'm sorry.'

But the truth is, I'm glad she's talking to me, *really* talking to me for once. We bottle up all this crap in our heads – it's good to pour it out once in a while.

'Don't be. I like it. I mean, I don't like what happened with Noah, but I like that we're talking, about Dad and everything.'

She gives a small smile. Then throws her hands up in the air. 'Ugh, but I'm hardly sending out the strong feminist vibes I want you to have! I mean, you know our worth shouldn't be defined by what guys think of us, right?'

I roll my eyes just a tiny bit. 'Yeah, I know, Mum. Girl power and all that.'

'I'm serious, Hay – don't ever let a guy get between you and happiness. Being with someone, well, it should only ever make everything else in your life better. It's just the icing on top of the cake. The cake itself is the important bit to get right. If the icing tastes crap, you can always strip it away and start again.'

'Dude, you're just making me hungry now.'

She laughs, but I know what she's saying. And I squirm a little in my chair as I think about falling out with Kas and Chloe just because of Leo. They're definitely major ingredients in my life cake. Problem is, Leo's just such a delicious icing. With sprinkles and everything. God, I wanna eat a cake right now.

Mum sighs, lost in her own thoughts. 'Your dad, well, by the end he made life taste really bad. But I dunno, I really thought Ruben was different . . .'

'Ruben?' The tiniest of alarm bells begins to go off in my head.

'Yeah. I mean, I know it was early days, but I thought we had something that might last. And that he just seemed to want to make my life better, and that he liked me the way I am, which . . . God, it felt good. It boosted my confidence so much. And yeah, Hay, I know this stuff makes you wanna vom, but I actually felt attractive for once, which I know I always tell you is not the important thing in life . . . but dang, it feels nice, not to be attractive to the world but just to one person, you know?' She buries her head in her hands again. 'Huh. Show's what I know though, right? I mean, maybe I'm just not the kind of woman who makes blokes want to stick around.'

'You are, Mum. Of course you are,' I say, starting to understand that maybe Ruben was actually good for her and also feeling the weight of guilt begin to crush down on my shoulders.

Bloody conscience.

'Then why did he leave me, Hay? Didn't even give a proper reason, just said it wasn't really working out. I guess maybe he didn't think he could ever love me. Oh, I'm so sorry, Hay. I don't know what I'm doing any more.' Her voice goes all squeaky and high.

'Oh, Mum, don't cry . . .'

But she does anyway, making my heart sink down to my toes. The only thing worse than seeing Mum cry because of Dad is seeing her cry because of me.

It's possible I've really screwed up here. I thought she'd just forget about Ruben when he left. I mean, he seems utterly forgettable, doesn't he? But I guess Mum might actually (eurgh) love him.

And now he's gone. Possibly partly – well, almost definitely – because of me.

And now she's depressed and heartbroken and really snotty and high-pitched, and it's all my fault. Mountain-man beard and lack of socks aside, I guess Ruben wasn't all that bad, not really. He was actually even kind of sweet. Gentle, even funny, I suppose, for a bearded guy, and great with Noah . . . and, well, yeah, he made Mum happy. And I scared him away. To be fair, I'd had a really crap night, *and* all I was trying to do was protect Mum and us from getting hurt (again) by an idiot guy (again). But I guess I'd tried to stop something from happening by trampling on it first.

Which is kind of dumb.

I should tell her it was all my fault. What's the worst that could happen? She slaps me? Never. Bans me from the house? She needs me for Noah's childcare. Hates me? Ugh. Possibly. But then she might appreciate my honesty, hug me, say I did the right thing, just glad she knows now. Who am I kidding? But frankly anything she does to me can't be as bad as my conscience, which now has my brain in an armlock and is pummelling it with slaps of shame. I take a deep breath.

'He does love you, Mum,' I whisper.

She turns to me, hers eyes wide open in surprise. 'What?' she says.

'That night he babysat Noah and I was at Chloe's . . . I came back and we talked and . . . he told me he loved you and stuff, but, well, I told him you . . .'

Mum shoots me a jagged look and her voice goes all growly. 'You told him what?'

Oh God. Maybe she will actually slap me.

She's drumming her fingernails on the table as I look anywhere but at her.

'I told him you didn't think of him like that, that he was, erm, nothing to you and it, well . . . I said it would be better for everyone if he just . . . left us alone.'

Admittedly, when I say it out loud like that, what I told him does sound *pretty* bad. But at least Mum's stopped crying now.

I glance at her, and her face has gone from broken-hearted kitten to ferocious lion. She sits bolt upright in her chair, glaring at me. '*You said what?*'

'I'm sorry, Mum!' I say, trying to buy myself some time while I eye up the best escape route. 'I didn't know you liked him that much. I thought it was just a little thing, y'know?'

'No, I don't know! And what the HELL gives you the right to mess around with my love life?'

'Ugh, your "love life" – don't make me heave!'

Shut up, mouth!

'HAYLAH!' she bellows as she stands up and looks down on me. In so many ways.

'I'm sorry, I'm sorry,' I say, standing up and edging away from her. 'I screwed up, OK? Why don't you just phone him, tell him it was my fault and get him back?'

'Because it's done, OK – it's over. I already tried ringing him to talk about everything and he won't take my phone calls, for God's sake!'

'I'm sorry, Mum. I – I just didn't want Noah getting hurt, or you for that matter. Look how upset you guys got after just one phone call from Dad – do you really want to put yourself and us through that again?'

'Haylah, I was taking things slow so that didn't happen! And if you were so worried about that, then why didn't you *talk* to me about it, instead of going behind my back, and getting rid of the only person who has brought me any happiness over the last few years?'

Ouch. Can you believe she just said that?

'So me and Noah aren't enough for you then?' I spit. And I know that really I'm angry with myself. But frankly it's easier to be angry with her.

'That's not what I meant and you know it.' She runs her fingers through her hair, looking utterly exasperated with me as I slowly back away towards the door. 'But it's not easy, you know, bringing up children on your own.'

And then I really snap. Because I was only trying to help her out here with Noah and everything, like I *always* help her out with Noah and everything, and sometimes – just sometimes – it would be nice to get a little appreciation.

So I take a step towards her. Possibly a step too far.

'Yeah, well, I *do* know actually. I mean, it's not just *you* bringing up Noah – in case you hadn't noticed, I'm basically his second parent while you're off at work or sleeping upstairs!'

Yep, definitely a step too far. I can almost see flames behind her eyes.

'I work *night shifts*, Haylah. I have to sleep sometime! Do you really think I *want* to work as much as I do? Don't you think I'd much rather be here with you and Noah? Do you really think this is how I planned my family life to be – always out, always exhausted, always on my own . . .? I didn't *choose* this for us, OK, it just happened. I'm sorry if that makes you hate me so much you don't *ever* want to see me happy again!'

'I *do* want to see you happy again!' I shout. 'And I DON'T HATE YOU!' I yell even louder.

'Well, you've got a funny way of showing it!' she shouts back.

'Stop shouting!' yells Noah from the doorway, and we both turn to him.

His face is shiny with tears and he screws up his nose before they start again. Mum runs over to him and scoops him up in her arms.

'Oh, Noah, I'm sorry, sweetie. It's all OK. We were just acting out something we saw on the TV yesterday.' She turns and scowls at me. '*Weren't we, Haylah?*' she says through gritted teeth.

'Yes. That's right. It was a scene from a horror film called *Mother from Hell*,' I say, before storming out into the hallway and screeching, 'I'm going out!'

And I figure, as I'm playing the role of a dramatic teenager here more than I ever have before, I may as well see it through, so I slam the door hard behind me. And it actually feels pretty good.

As I walk to I-don't-know-where, the burning anger slowly fades inside me and turns into a grey sludge of misery. I hardly ever argue with Mum, but when we do I'm normally safe in the knowledge that I'm completely in the right and she's completely in the wrong (obviously). But not this time. This time it's pretty much my fault. The whole Ruben thing – well, I kind of know that I've been a selfish git about it all.

I've tried so hard to ignore Dad leaving us I guess this is the resulting numptiness. I just wanted to keep Mum to ourselves, keep things the way they always are: safe, risk free. Hurt free. But nothing stays the same. I should know that by now. And if you hold something too close you only end up strangling it. I'm like that guy in the novel we're being forced to read in English, just a big brainless oaf squeezing the life out of a mouse with my big dumb hands.

Then I realize that somehow, without thinking, I've made my way on to Leo's road. I just want to feel like I did yesterday, when he kissed me and everything was right with the world and nothing bad could ever happen again.

I'll knock on his door, he'll give me *that* grin, invite me in and say wise, calming things to me, and we'll laugh and kiss and make the gloom disappear. I start to walk taller as I get near his house – but then his door opens and someone emerges.

It's Keesha, that harmonica-playing stick insect who's always hanging around him like a bad smell. Honestly, it's like she's stalking him or something. I hide behind a wheelie bin and peer round the corner at Leo as he appears behind her. She turns, the braces on her teeth glinting in the sunlight.

Then.

Oh God.

He kisses her.

And my heart drops out of my body and splats on to the pavement.

Everything in me wants to look away, but my eyes are fixed on them. It's a long drawn-out kiss, just like the one *we* shared yesterday. Only less awkward, arms casually slung around each other, like this is the most natural thing in the world – like they've done it hundreds of times before.

Finally, they part and he flashes *her* that grin, the same warm smile which yesterday made me feel like anything was possible, but which now makes me feel sick. My hands are shaking a bit as I remain hidden round the back of the bin (which I'm tempted to get into, waiting until it's collected and I'm taken away to a better place) until she leaves in the opposite direction and Leo closes the door.

I scrunch my eyes tight shut, trying to fight the tears as my head swims with darkness.

I've made a mess of *everything*.

Mum's furious with me.

Leo *was* using me after all.

And my friends . . . my friends . . . I've lost them too, and all over some stupid, stupid boy. Oh God, I've been such an idiot.

I get up and walk away on shaky legs. Then, with nowhere else to go, I head to Chloe's house. I plan what I'll say to her – I'll explain that I didn't know she was talking to Leo about me that night and that she was right about him all along, and I know she didn't really mean what she said about me, she was just angry, and I didn't mean all that stuff I said about her looking trashy and . . .

Oh God, she's so going to slap me.

I knock on the door. Chloe opens it, and instead of saying all that stuff I just start sobbing and she steps towards me, her eyes also filling with tears, and flings her arms round me.

'I'm so sorry,' I sob.

'I'm sorry too,' she sobs back.

'I didn't mean anything I said, and you were right all along,' I whimper.

'Well, I didn't mean anything I said. I was just being a massive tit head,' she blubs.

Kas runs through from the kitchen and joins the blubbering hugfest. Then we just stand there, a big ball of whimpering patheticness, occasionally splurging out between great gasps of teary sobs, 'I'm sorry!' 'I know, I'm sorry too!' 'I missed you guys!' 'I know – we missed you too.'

TWENTY-FOUR

Lounging back on Chloe's massive bed, surrounded by a sea of cushions, I stare up at her ceiling, still covered in the glow-in-the-dark stars I remember giving her for her eighth birthday. I tell them everything – all about the thing with Mum, and the thing with Leo. They gasp and make sympathetic awwing noises in all the right places.

'I can't believe you kissed him!' says Kas in awe.

'You've got guts, girl – it's incredible,' says Chloe. 'But that's really crappy about Keesha. I know they've been like an on-off thing for years, but I just thought they were off at the moment. I mean, you did know about their history, right?'

'No! Nobody told me!' I say, sniffing away the last of my tears. 'He never said *anything* to me about her. And she's not even *pretty* – I mean, I'm better-looking than her, right?'

And, yes, I know full well this isn't true and I know it goes against the whole sisterhood thing, but frankly sometimes you just wanna hear pretty little lies, OK?

'Oh God, yeah, babe!' says Kas.

'And funnier? Please say I'm funnier than her!' I splutter.

'SO much funnier,' says Chloe, reaching over and stroking my hair.

'So . . .' says Kas, lying on her belly, her chin resting on her hands, 'do you love him?'

'No! Well, I don't know, maybe . . . I mean, this hurts like hell on a jetski . . . so . . . I don't know.' My voice gets quieter as I realize something. 'Maybe I just love the way he made me feel.'

'How do you mean?' says Chloe.

'I guess it was just nice to not feel like the stupid dumpy one who'll never get a boyfriend, for once. I mean, that's what everyone else thinks of me.'

'Don't be silly, Pig. Nobody thinks of you like that!' says Kas.

'Yes they do. And even you do,' I say to Chloe. 'I mean, you pretty much said as much.'

Chloe sighs sadly. 'I was angry,' she says, lying on her back and cycling her long legs in the air. 'And . . . well, the truth is, I'm a bit jealous of you, OK?'

Wow. I never thought I'd hear Chloe say that in a bajillion years.

'Of *me*? What the hell for?'

Chloe stops and turns to me, propping her head on her palm. 'Because you're funny and clever and interesting, and that Friday night Leo – this cool, popular older guy, who, let's be honest, we all fancy – wouldn't stop talking about how amazing he thought you were.'

'Not "amazing" enough to stop him being embarrassed to be seen with me and snogging other people though, I guess.'

Ugh, saying it out loud makes it even more humiliating.

'I know, and I'm sorry he's done this to you,' says Chloe. 'But, I mean, *you've* got all that going on for you, and then on top of that *Kas* is a bloody genius.'

'Don't you mean a geek?' says Kas. 'That's what everyone thinks when you're in the top sets, right? And I have to work so hard to be in them. And before you say it, Pig, I know it's not all about guys and all that, but come on, who wants to date a know-it-all, bookish geek? I actually lied to Isaac and told him the reason I wasn't in his maths class was because I was in the remedial class below, just so I wouldn't seem so clever. I know, I know!' she says as I begin to splutter in fake outrage. 'It's bad and I feel terrible about it. But I just didn't want him to think I was weird.'

'I don't know – better to be a geek than an airhead,' says Chloe. 'Guys don't want to date me for my great conversation skills; they just wanna see how far they'll get with me so they can tell their mates.'

'So, Stevie and Isaac, they're not working out?' I say, wiping my nose on my sleeve.

'No, we totally dumped those two. You were right: they were complete plums who didn't actually wanna know us. Plus, they had the combined personality of a mackerel,' says Kas.

'Wow,' I say. 'I'm sorry.'

'I think Stevie simply didn't want to know me because, well, what's to know? I just wish I was more interesting, I guess.' Chloe sighs. 'And I wish I had bigger jugs.' She gives an exaggerated longing look at my giant rack, and with a sheepish smile I softly jiggle them from side to side, which makes her smile.

'I wish I wasn't such a nerd,' says Kas. 'And that my forehead wasn't so freakishly big.'

'Well, I wish I was more girlie,' I say. I don't usually, but at this moment I kinda do. Surely it'd be easier? 'Though physically, obviously, I'm perfection itself.'

We all laugh a little, then sigh.

'I just wish I was more normal,' we all say together.

We lie in silence, our hands behind our heads, staring up at the ceiling.

Until it dawns on me that *actually* the only problem with any of us is that right now we're being mega-morons.

'What the *hell* are we doing?' I say, sitting up. 'This is *crazy*, right?'

'What do you mean?' asks Kas.

'Well, listen to us! Firstly, who the hell wants to be "normal" anyway? And what is normal? If there is such a thing, it's probably super boring. And, secondly, look at us: we're sitting around complaining, but we're *all* clever, funny, brilliant –'

'Beautiful,' Chloe adds, sitting up and throwing her arms out to the side.

'Interesting!' says Kas, getting up on to her knees and taking a bow.

'Hell, yeah! We're all clever, funny, brilliant, beautiful, interesting, totally awesome girls, and any boy would be a lucky son-of-a-biscuit to have us, just the way we are. Why are we trying to be something else, something duller, just to please them?' I say.

'Because we fancy them?' says Chloe, embracing a purple velvet cushion like it's Harry Styles' face.

'Yeah, but I bet you anything *boys* don't think for one minute *they* need to change to get a girl,' I say. 'They might start playing the guitar or something because they think it makes them look cool or sexy, but they don't try to hide how clever they are, or change their personality or what they're into, or give up their mates or any of that crap just to please girls.'

'True,' admits Chloe.

'Then why do we do it? Why should we try and be something else?' I say.

'Well, when you put it like that . . .' says Chloe.

'Hell, yeah, we shouldn't change for anyone!' says Kas, throwing a cushion up in the air and catching it. 'If *boys* don't have to, *we* don't have to either!'

'God, I love feminism,' I say.

'Hmm, I don't know. Isn't it all about not wearing make-up and hating men?' says Chloe with a knowing smirk.

And we both throw cushions at her head.

'I'm sorry I lost the plot a bit. Lost track of you guys and myself and what really matters. Guess I was just blinded by Leo-ey good looks and charm. Whatever it cost me. But I'm well and truly back on the feminist train now. Both engines at full steam,' I say, grabbing my boobs and making us all laugh. 'Sorry I've been a total numpty.'

'We all have,' says Chloe.

'Numpty Dumpty,' says Kas, pointing at her own chest.

'Twat on a wall,' says Chloe, with a hand over her own heart.

'Agreed. Especially as, even though I didn't know about Keesha, I think deep down I did know you were right about Leo using me.'

'But he does really like you though, Pig. I mean, the way he was talking about you at the pub . . .' says Chloe.

'Yeah, and he wouldn't have kissed you if he didn't,' says Kas.

'I guess. But if a guy doesn't like you enough to talk to you in front of his mates, then it doesn't really count for much, does it? No matter what he says the excuse is. I knew he just wanted me to write his set for that frickin' competition and I just went along with it, even though it meant losing you guys and my self-respect. Well, it won't happen again – I'm not changing for anyone, especially not just to get a guy. Any changing I do will be for me, and IF I ever have a boy interested in me again –'

'You SO will, Pig,' says Chloe.

'Oh God, I hope so cos kissing's awesome,' I say.

We all briefly sigh in agreement.

'Anyway! If I do, it won't be because of what he wants me to be or do for him.'

'Yay! Go, Pig!' squeals Kas in excitement. 'You're right. We're *all* better off without these guys. There'll be better ones. Guys who like us for us. But . . . where are these good guys?'

'Yeah, how long do we have to wait for one to come along?' says Chloe.

And my thoughts shoot to my mum. And how long she's waited for the right guy, and how Ruben might just be that person. And how I messed things up for her.

'You know, there *are* good guys out there and . . . I think Ruben might be one,' I say. 'You know – the beardy guy. And I completely screwed it up for my mum. Made him dump her and run off to London, probably to get away from me as much as anything. And, argh, I don't know what to do to put it right.'

'So you like Beardy after all?' says Kas.

'I think I do. The sock thing's still super gross, but . . . well, he was cool that night after the pub, and he's really easy to talk to, and the main thing is, he makes Mum happy. But I blew it.'

'I'm sorry, Pig,' sympathizes Kas.

'Yeah, that's crappy. So is she still going to the comedy thing tomorrow night?' asks Chloe.

Oh crikey, the London Young Comic of the Year thing is TOMORROW. I'd completely forgotten about it. You know, what with all the trauma and heartbreak and first-class muppetry.

'Well, she was, but I hardly want to go now! I just don't think I can face Leo again.'

'Rubbish! Don't you dare let him get the better of you, Pig! *You* wrote that stuff and *you* deserve to see it performed onstage.'

'You really think I should go?' I say.

'Yes! We'll get tickets too. Loads of people from school are going, y'know, cos Leo's so popular and everything,' says Kas.

'Yes, dude, thanks, I'm aware of that,' I say.

'You know, for a clever person, Kas, you really are quite thick sometimes. But, yeah, come on – you've gotta go, Pig. At the very least, it's an excuse to get out of this scuzzy town and take a trip to London!' says Chloe.

And they're right. I might not love Leo but I still love comedy. I might have made a mess of things, but I shouldn't make decisions based on what a guy says or does. I wanna go to this thing and I wanna see my stuff performed, even if it is by him. I won't let him take my funny away from me!

'All right, screw it. I'm not gonna let him spoil my fun.'

'Yay! I love you guys,' says Kas, reaching out for a group hug.

'Ya big soppy geek,' I say, and she laughs as me and Chloe bury her in cushions and jump on her.

TWENTY-FIVE

On the way home, I think about Chloe and Kas, about how I hated being apart from them, about how we need each other, about how different we all are and about how great that is. I know that one day our lives might naturally split off on different paths – maybe I'll be president of the Cambridge Footlights, Kas will be the world's youngest prime minister and Chloe will be presenting *Love Island* – but for now I could no more remove myself from them than you can remove an egg from a cake after it's been baked. All you'd end up with is a crumbly mess.

When I get home, Mum's still angry. She's hiding in the kitchen, crashing around, sounding less like she's tidying it and more like she's angrily demolishing a shed full of china dolls. And I don't blame her, but all I want right now is a hug and it's not gonna happen. I could say sorry, but what difference would that make? I still drove away the guy she loves.

I go in and kiss Noah goodnight, impressed that he's somehow managing to sleep through Mum's racket, even though the gentlest raindrop on his window can wake him up, and then I disappear into my bedroom.

And in the quiet of my room the glow of my reunion with the girls fades, and I can't stop the memory of Leo kissing Keesha from replaying over and over again. The hope of us being together shot to bits in an instant, the sudden realization that I'd been a complete idiot, the humiliation of the whole thing ... it burns through my insides with each replay. I hug my pillow tight and curl up on my bed.

Ten minutes later, even though I haven't told her I'm back, my door opens and in walks Mum. Then, her psychic abilities as sharp as ever, she comes over to my bed, lies next to me and holds me tight as the tears break through.

'Oh, darling, what happened?' she whispers.

'He ... kissed ... me and then ... I saw him ... kissing ... someone else!' I sob.

She sighs and strokes my hair. 'Oh, sweetie. I'm so sorry.'

I cry some more and sniff some more and probably get snot all over her. And then, when I'm calmer, we sit up next to each other and lean back against the wall.

'I'm really, really sorry about Ruben, Mum . . .' I whimper.

And I know she's still angry with me about that, but somehow she's been able to divide her anger up and box some of it away, knowing I need a non-angry Mum right now. She's amazing.

'Shh, love, don't worry about that now. I just wanna make sure you're OK.'

'Why didn't you warn me I was heading into a stink-storm of love, Mum? I mean, it never ends well, does it?'

She sighs. 'Oh, don't say that, Hay. It *can* do, and I'm sure it will for you. But, I don't know, I guess you have to experience that first horrible heartbreak for yourself. It's like you can't teach kids that fire's really hot cos, whatever you say, until they feel the heat themselves, they're just gonna think it's really pretty and wanna dive right in. You have to learn through experience; you have to feel the heat – that's the only way.'

I think about that for a while, then say, 'Mum, that's like the crappest analogy ever.'

'Really? I thought it was pretty good! I mean, I'm thinking on my feet here, Hay!'

'Yeah, it's a nice idea and everything, but surely kids learn about fire being hot because most parents DO tell them it is and DO stop them from making a painful fool of themselves and sticking their hand in the flames? Otherwise A & E units the world over would be filled with hordes of screaming toddlers with third-degree burns.'

'I did try to warn you, a bit.'

'I know,' I say. 'Thanks. And I don't even think I, like, *love-loved* him or anything. But it still burns like hell. Well, perhaps not quite as hot as hell, but definitely like a really hot barbecue. He barbecued my heart, Mum.'

I mentally file away 'barbecued my heart' for my comedy notebook later. Every tragedy is an opportunity after all.

'I know he did, sweetie.' She puts her arm round my shoulders. 'And I know it hurts. Just because you didn't *fall* in love doesn't mean you didn't trip over it and hurt yourself pretty badly.'

And another one!

'Oooh, now that's good, Mum! Can I write that down?'

'Yeah,' she says, smiling. 'You can have that one for free.'
Then she kisses me on the cheek and gets up to leave.

And I can still see the hurt in her eyes about Ruben and what I did. Hurt that she's holding back because she knows I just need her to love me right now, and I love her all the more for it.

'You still want to go to the show tomorrow?' she asks. 'And you still want me and Noah to be there? Maybe we could set Noah loose on Leo.'

I laugh a little. 'Yeah. The girls think I should go and, well, it is still my stuff he's performing. Plus, you know, train's booked, tickets are bought . . . there'll be other people to see. It'll still be really good for me to go. I'm not gonna let him spoil our day, right?'

She smiles at me. 'Right. If you're sure. Love you, Hay.'

'Love you, Mum.'

And she leaves.

I lie back on my bed, wishing I could make everything right with Mum again by somehow fixing it with Ruben.

Then, like some telepathic fairy godmother in an A-cup, Chloe phones me with her idea for doing just that.

'So, Hay, if make-up has taught me one thing it's that *nothing is unfixable*,' she says. 'Has your mum still got Ruben's number in her phone?'

'I don't know. Probably. Why?'

'So I've been thinking. Your mum's coming to the competition, right?'

'Yeah, she is.'

'And Ruben's staying in London, yes? So you can solve your mum's problem by inviting Ruben along too!' says Chloe triumphantly.

'O.M.Geenius – that is good!' I say.

'Yeah! Pretend the invite's coming from your mum, and then when he shows up let *luurve* do the talking!' says Chloe.

'Eurgh, steady. Some of us have only recently eaten,' I say.

'Pig, when have you ever *not* recently eaten?' says Chloe.

I laugh. She tells me to just send the text and that I'm not allowed to wimp out of coming tomorrow and we say goodbye.

And, although I do know I should still go tomorrow, the thought of seeing Leo, of talking to him, knowing that his *girlfriend* will be there, knowing that he kissed me – and it meant *everything* to me, but *nothing* to him – fills me with dread, and makes me want to curl up into a ball, shrivel up and disappear.

But then why should I? What have *I* done wrong? I didn't know he was with someone else. All I've done is help him write a kick-ass set while he swans around with his girlfriend, ignoring me at school and snogging me when no one's looking. It was probably a charity kiss – he sees me as so pathetic no one else would ever want to kiss me so he might as well, just as a sign of gratitude for writing his set. Sending a thank-you card would have involved a whole lot less heartache.

Well, I'm done feeling sad and heartbroken. Now I'm just bloody angry.

He totally used me. It's all been about him – making *him* look better, keeping *his* cool-kid reputation intact, letting *him* win while I run around after him like a puppy dog begging for the odd smoochy treat he might throw my way.

I want *him* to look at *me* for a change. I want to show him that I'm not a loser who lies down and takes crap from anyone. I want to show him, and the school, and (might as well admit it) Dad, and the world that this is me: strong, funny, independent, confident, gobby me, and I won't be used, trodden on, ignored and sneered at any more.

But how do I do that?

The idea hits me like a thunderbolt. I'm gonna hit Leo where it hurts. Right in the funnies.

I am going to beat Leo at the competition tomorrow night.

As I sit in my room, fuming, the idea takes hold of me and sweeps me up in a whirl of excitement. I *am* funny. I know I am. The set at the pub, before it . . . well, before it all went buttocks up . . . wasn't *that* bad. It got laughs, and that was with nothing planned. I've got this evening and all of tomorrow before the gig to think of a proper set – that's a lot more than the thirty seconds of panic I had before that gig! And I've got loads of stuff already. I'll look through my notebooks and pluck out the best bits, combine them with some new stuff, then learn it, get up there, nail it, and *boom* – goodbye, heartbreak and humiliation, hello, confidence and comedic fame.

Then I look up the London Young Comic of the Year website and see that I've missed the application deadline by about two weeks.

Balls.

But this is the new me! Undeterred, I write a begging email to them on my phone, including a short video that I make of myself performing a few ideas I already had (just stuff I read out from old notebooks, to be honest with you), and I press send.

Then I send a message to Kas and Chloe asking them to meet me in town at ten tomorrow morning, saying I need their help with something.

I grab a pen and fresh notebook, and write and write pages of new material, this time for *me*, for my *own* stand-up routine, stuff *I* want to say, in my *own voice*.

And at two in the morning, drunk on tiredness and the E-numbers from the tub of Haribo sweets I've devoured, I am convinced, without a shadow of a doubt, that I can do this.

For I am the Queen of the Quips, the Princess of Puns, the Mistress of Mischief (no, wait, that sounds wrong).

But, oh, I can *SO* do this.

TWENTY-SIX

Saturday morning I wake up, bleary-eyed, to 'La Cucaracha' blasting out of my phone and only one thought rings through my head.

I so cannot *do this.*

I press snooze and slip back into a half-asleep daydream of me onstage, remembering none of my lines and getting no laughs whatsoever until I trip over a set of false teeth with gleaming braces still attached that someone has thrown at my feet. As I fall, to thunderous, cackling laughter, I see Keesha's gummy, toothless smile in the audience before Leo clamps his mouth over hers and they kiss to applause while people throw rotten eggs and vegetables at me.

When I finally surface from the nightmare, or possible premonition of this evening, it's 9. And I'm due in town with Chloe and Kas at 10.

I can't do this, I think again.

It's going to take all the courage I have to actually *go* to this thing and see Leo up there, knowing what he really thinks of me – an embarrassment that he kissed me out of nothing but sympathy and pity. I can't get up onstage and make more of a fool of myself on top of all that. *What was I thinking?*

Hopefully, my begging email to the competition didn't work. But, just in case, I grab my phone, intending to send another message telling them to ignore the last one as it was all just a terrible mistake.

But, ARGH, they've already replied!

To: Haylah Swinton <pig8008@aol.com>
From: Vanessa Trimble <info@LYCY.com>
Subject: London Young Comic of the Year

Dear Haylah,
You're in huge luck! Another contestant pulled out
yesterday as he's broken his leg, so we have one space left.
We've been looking through the 'near-miss' applicants and
couldn't decide who to put through, and then we watched
your video. You've got a great delivery and some hilarious
material – basically, we loved what you sent us! So we've put
your name down for tonight's competition.

Please turn up at the front desk between 6 and 6.30 p.m.
and collect a ticket for yourself and one other. You will then
be given a time slot in which you will perform one five-
minute comedy routine.

Good luck!

Vanessa Trimble

I read the email again and again.

They actually love my stuff! 'Great delivery'? 'Hilarious'? Argh, this is amazing!

My finger hovers over the reply button. I should tell them I don't want to come after all, and yet . . . I can't do it. I can't help being encouraged by their enthusiasm and I can't escape the feeing that this is a sign. I mean, someone literally broke their leg so that I could go – that's gotta be a good omen, right? A sign from who or what I don't know – maybe from the Gods of Comedy, smiling down on me and saying, '*Go for it.*' '*It's now or never.*' '*You can do this. You can show them all and you can beat him.*' Or maybe some kind of vengeful goddess, who just really wants to see me smash Leo. Either way, it's all good.

So I reply, thanking them and confirming my place. It's done. I can't back out now. I mustn't back out.

I try not to think about it.

I try not to think about getting up onstage in front of all those people.

In front of Leo. Argh!

Instead, I concentrate only on the next task ahead of me. On having a shower. On getting dressed. And then on getting Ruben there tonight. At least I now have a spare ticket for him.

While Mum and Noah are playing trains on the living-room floor, I sneak into her room and send a text to Ruben, using her phone. I know he didn't answer her phone calls after the break-up, but I'm hoping time and 'Mum' sounding quite desperate to see him will do the trick. So I write:

Hi, Ruben. I really want to see you
again. Could you come to the
Junction Theatre in the West End
tonight and meet me outside at
6.20 p.m.? Please don't reply – we'll
talk then. x

I figure he might think the 'don't reply' part a bit strange, but I don't want him sending a message back to Mum later and ruining the whole thing. I just have to hope he gets the text and likes Mum enough to come along tonight, no questions asked.

Before I go, I grab a quick, nutritious breakfast of a Bounty bar. (If you think it through, the coconut is basically a fruit, a nut and a seed all in one so what could be healthier?) Then, rushing out of the door, I see Noah lying on his own on the floor, playing with his trains. Mum's getting dressed upstairs and I know I don't have time, but I guess I could just have a quick play with him. I lie down next to him.

'Hey, Noah. You looking forward to going on a train later?'

'Yeah! It's going to be just like this!' he says, ramming a Thomas the Tank Engine along the track straight into the gurning face of another engine coming the other way so that the two derail in a horrific rail accident.

'Erm, well, hopefully not *exactly* like that,' I say. 'So, how are you feeling about that whole Dad thing now? You know, when he called the other day?'

He doesn't say anything – just keeps pushing the train round the wooden track and making choo-choo noises. I pick up one of the other trains and join in.

'You know, I miss him too,' I say. 'But when he's here he just makes us all feel a bit sad, so I think he stays away so that we don't get upset.'

'But doesn't he love us?' asks Noah and my eyes fill a little bit.

'Of course he does – who wouldn't love you? He just needs to stay away for a while. He'll see us again when it's the right time. When he can make us all happy again. Like Father Christmas! We don't see him all year, but we know he loves us, right?' I say.

'Everyone leaves,' he whispers.

And I well up some more as I feel a surge of fierce and never-ending love for this little man.

'No they don't. I'll never leave you. Mum will *never* leave you,' I whisper back.

'But Ruben left. And he was like Dad, but better cos he was here.'

'I know,' I say, not wanting to make any promises about bringing Ruben back, but feeling more than ever that the plan to reunite Mum and him *has* to work. 'I liked him too. But he didn't leave because of you. I love you, Noah. So much. I *promise* I'll never leave you, OK?'

'Yeah. OK,' he says, picking up a wooden tree and putting is across the track before speeding a train right into it. '*Boom!*'

'Just promise me you'll never be a train driver, OK?' I say, kissing him on the forehead before getting up off the floor.

'I don't want to be a train driver, I want to be a comedian,' he says.

'Really?'

And it's like the best news I've ever heard. That this perfect little guy would be inspired by something I do.

'Yeah, like you. I want to make people laugh. With chicken jokes. Make them happy.'

My heart melts a little bit with pride.

'Thanks, tiny man. You make sure you laugh super hard tonight, yeah?'

'I will,' he says. 'I love Leo!'

'Hmmm,' I say.

I turn to leave, but see Mum peering round the door at us, smiling proudly. And I want to tell her I'm performing tonight. But she'd probably talk me out of it, asking if I'm sure I'm ready, which of course I'm not. If I'm sure I'm doing it for the right reasons, which I'm probably not.

So instead I just say, 'OK, so I'm off to meet Kas and Chlo in town. We'll see you outside the theatre at six thirty, yeah?'

'Yep, fine,' she says. 'You OK, Hay? About Leo and everything?'

'I'm fine. Well, I will be. Thanks, Mum.'

And, like a fearless she-warrior, I bravely stride towards Primark and my next truly gruesome challenge. Shopping.

*

I meet Chloe and Kas in the store coffee shop next door.

'OK, so why are we here?' Chloe asks.

And I tell them I've put my name down for the competition.

'What? Pig, that's amazing! Oh my giddy God, you're gonna nail this, but I'm so nervous for you. You really think you're ready?' says Kas, dipping a gingerbread man head first into a flat white.

'Of course she's ready!' says Chloe, sipping on her smoothie. 'You are, right? I mean, it's not going to be like last time?'

'Dude, that's really not helping!' I say. 'No, I don't think I'm ready. But what I do know is I want to beat Leo.'

'Oooh, I love it – a revenge gig!' says Kas.

Then, as I had hoped they would, they start harassing me into letting them make me over. And, for once, I'm going to let them.

'*What?*' says Chloe, her face lighting up like I've just given her a diamond tiara. 'Really? You'll let us make you over? Yay!'

'But on my terms,' I say.

'Which are?' says Kas.

And I explain that firstly I wish to wear no make-up other than a bit of foundation to minimize spotlight shine, and maybe a tiny bit of eye make-up so when I'm frowning at Leo it really freaks him out. Secondly, if anyone comes at me with nail polish, I'm heading for the door.

'Oh come on, look at these beauties.' says Chloe, fanning out her fingers for us to admire. 'Wouldn't you love something like that?'

'You look like you've got a psychedelic fungal infection.'

Chloe retracts her claws, tuts and rolls her eyes. Then they both laugh.

Lastly I explain to them that I want to wear what *I* want to wear and, after a brief argument with Chloe, who believes, mistakenly, that she's seen the perfect dress for me in a 'size-diverse' (fat-girls') shop, they agree to my terms.

'OK, so tell us what you want to wear, Pig,' says Kas.

'Well, you guys look great, like pop stars or movie stars . . . well, maybe not movie stars, but at least a couple of chicks from *Hollyoaks*.'

'Aw, thanks,' says Kas sarcastically.

'Aw, thanks!' says Chloe genuinely.

'But that's not me, and those people aren't *my* heroes. My heroes are comedians and funny women like Sara Pascoe, Victoria Wood, Caitlin Moran, Kate McKinnon, Gina Yashere, Tina Fey, Josie Long, Jayde Adams, Susan Calman, Sofie Hagen, Susan Wokoma, Hannah Gadsby –'

'All right, all right! Enough already, we get it!'

'OK, but you know who they all are, right?'

'Course we do, Pig. We've been your friends for, like, centuries, and we've sat through all your birthday "popcorn and comedy" evenings in front of the TV! We like these women too, you know,' says Kas.

'Totally. And I think I know *exactly* the kind of look you're after. This is going to be awesome. How much money do you have?' says Chloe.

'Twenty-five pounds. Fifteen pounds leftover birthday money from Gran, and it's been a lucrative couple of weeks on the fake-parental-letter front, but that's all,' I say.

Chloe dramatically drains the rest of her smoothie, raises a fist in the air and announces, 'Then let's get out of here and hit the charity shops!'

'Charity shops? You're a fan of charity shops?' I say. And it's like the Queen just told me she really loves an Aldi bargain.

'Oh hell, yeah,' says Chloe. 'They're retro-chic and *so* in right now.'

'I guess we all still have some secrets from each other!' says Kas.

As we leave the coffee shop, I link arms with both of them and say, 'Thanks.'

'What for?' they say in unison.

'Just . . . everything.'

After trawling round the charity shops, we end up back at Chloe's, with music blasting out of her phone and a massive box of Maltesers keeping us going as they pluck, primp and preen me to within an inch of my life, with me taking every opportunity I can to beg for mercy.

And I don't think we've ever laughed more in our lives.

Then, with half an hour to go before we have to catch our train, I stand in front of the mirror and take it all in from my toes upwards.

Chloe's sister's shiny black DMs (part of her festival wardrobe, and more accustomed to being teamed up with a miniskirt and spangly boob tube) leading to dark red leggings, leading to grey, dog-tooth-patterned shorts, leading to an old black David Bowie T-shirt over which I wear a brown tweed jacket, with my hair cascading in twirls over my shoulders. My eyebrows actually have a shape that's recognizably eyebrow-like for once, and I even let them persuade me to wear a lipstick Kas had with her which matches my leggings.

'Wow,' says Kas, 'you really . . .'

'You look FANTASTIC!' Chloe shouts.

'Yeah? You sure?' I say.

'Totally! You look *cool*, you've got *curves*, you've got *style*,' says Kas.

'A-MA-ZING!' agrees Chloe. 'And you're right, *this* is you.'

I look again in the mirror. I don't look like Kas and Chloe, who are stunning in their dresses and girlie shoes, but for the first time I'm looking at myself and genuinely thinking, *I look good. I look like how I wanna look.* And it's not like a bit of lippy made me realize what a knockout beauty queen I am (that Ally Sheedy travesty of a make-over in *The Breakfast Club*? – almost spoils the whole film for me), and it actually doesn't have anything to do with my size, it's just that I finally see the outside of me expressing what the inside has always been.

I look sort of interesting, cool, confident even. I feel like if I saw me in a room I'd totally want to talk to me.

'Come on, girls! You've got a train to catch – I'll drive you to the station!' yells Chloe's mum up the stairs.

'OK,' I say with my fists clenched. 'Let's do this. Let's go and comedy the *crap* out of London.'

TWENTY-SEVEN

On the train down to London, I stare at my set – a printed side of A4 with various words underlined and others scribbled out with funnier words written above the scribble. I furiously read it over and over again on the journey, stopping only occasionally to focus on what Kas and Chloe are talking about, or to give my eyes a break by letting them look around the carriage for a moment.

There's a few other students from school sitting by us, including Grace, Poppy and Fajah (they do know it's comedy they're going to see, right? Not a crafting convention), who sweetly wish me luck, and Dylan, who keeps looking over at Chloe and grinning like a complete twonk.

But no Leo. Still blissfully unaware that I saw him and Keesha sucking face, he messaged me earlier to say he's getting a lift there with his dad and a few 'mates', which presumably includes her. My failure to reply to any of his messages over the last few days doesn't seem to have triggered any realization in his ball-bag brain that anything's wrong.

But I'm grateful he's not here as I don't really know what I'm gonna say to him anyway, and if he's with Keesha I fear I might just punch him in the face.

Oh, I so want to beat him this evening.

My new clothes feel great, and as I catch a glimpse of myself reflected in the train window it makes me think, *Yeah, I can do this. I can show everyone this is me. I might not look like the other girls, but it's because I CHOOSE NOT TO. I'm cool, I'm interesting, I'm funny. I'm . . .*

Then I catch Dylan looking over with his eyebrows raised and a smirk on his face, and I look again at the tweed jacket, and the make-up accentuating my eyes and my mouth, and I think, *Oh God, everyone's gonna wonder why I've come in fancy dress as Toad from* The Wind in the *frickin'* Willows. I should have just worn my invisibility cloak like I normally do.

I look away from Dylan and down again at my set, only now the words jumble themselves up on the page and I can't focus on any of them. *Stupid words.*

Sensing my nerves, Chloe leans over and says, 'You're gonna be great, Pig,' and puts a hand on my knee.

'Do you want to practise on us?' says Kas, wearing a seriously concerned face that's making me even more anxious.

'Good God, no. I mean, thanks, but . . . well, if you don't laugh, I might just chicken out altogether.'

'Fair enough. Did you send the message to Ruben?' asks Chloe.

'Yeah,' I say, glad to think about something else for a moment. 'I guess we'll just have to see if he shows up. If he doesn't, I'm not sure how I'm ever gonna make it up to Mum.'

I spend the rest of the journey trying to focus on my set and making notes on the back of my hand with a biro – just words or even initials to remind me what to say and in what order.

As the train approaches London, I can't resist staring out of the window: the fields and trees give way to factories, sky-scraping buildings and bustling streets exploding with life and activity. I look at my friends' faces, wide-eyed as they gaze out of the window too, and I know they feel the same as me: that, try as we might to keep our expressions cool, to look like we come here all the time (not just the handful of times we've managed to persuade our ~~jailers~~ parents), there's no escaping the tingling feeling that here anything is possible.

'I chuffin' love London!' says Chloe as we leave the train at Liverpool Street Station.

'It's like your brain lights up when you get here,' says Kas.

'I know,' I say with a smile. 'It's just so frickin' *Londony*.'

We go down to the underground station and get swept along with a herd of people, all seemingly in the biggest race of their lives to get somewhere, anywhere, NOW. Then we get on a random train because Chloe 'has a good feeling about it'. After eight train changes, which we later discover should have just been one – our 'good feeling' train has taken us in COMPLETELY the wrong direction – we get to our stop, and at the top of an insanely long escalator we're spewed out on to the swarming West End streets.

The colours, sounds and random drunk nutters with purple hair that can only be found in London ignite our senses as we walk to the theatre, open-mouthed, drinking it all in. Chloe and Kas stop to look in every shop window, but I soon find that with every step my nerves about performing this evening increase. I'm actually performing.

TONIGHT.

ON A STAGE.

When we stop for a McDonald's, I just stare at my burger. Go over my set in my head again and again as the nerves swim around my insides. I'm only vaguely aware of Kas and Chloe carrying on their conversations, and occasionally I offer a 'yep' or 'hmm' so it at least appears I'm with them and haven't gone completely nuts. But then I must have said a 'yep' or 'hmm' at the wrong time because I suddenly realize they're both staring at me.

I pause the rerun of my set in my head. 'What?'

'I said, are you all right, Pig?' says Kas.

'Oh yeah, just, y'know, terrified by a crippling, hellish despair.'

'OK, but still, I've never seen you off your food,' says Chloe as if worried about an elderly cat.

'I know, right? I should totally do this all the time. I'd lose so much weight.' I rest my head in my hands. 'Oh God, what was I thinking? This is going to be horrendous.'

Chloe puts her arm round my shoulder. 'Rubbish, you'll be awesome! And remember – you're doing this to beat Leo! To teach him he can't just use girls and get away with it.'

'Yeah, and the important thing is you're *doing* it – getting up there, showing him you can do this without him. I mean, even if it goes wrong, at least you tried, right?' says Kas, delicately dipping a French fry in barbecue sauce.

'What? So you think it's going to go wrong then?' I say.

'Wait, no!' says Kas, panicked. 'I'm just saying even *if* it does.'

'Oh God,' I say again.

'Don't worry about it, Pig. Come on, eat your burger,' says Chloe.

And I feel like I'm being fattened up for the slaughter.

We reach the theatre, a small ramshackle place with peeling paintwork and a couple of boarded-up windows. Not exactly the perfect setting for a night of glamour and entertainment. But it *is* the perfect setting for a grisly horror story.

So this is where it ends, I think. *My life, my dignity, my dreams.*

The girls hang around outside with a few other kids from our school and a load from other schools while I go into the foyer. The inside is surprisingly clean and stylish. There's a few other kids standing around with their parents. They must be other contestants – they all look as horribly nervous as I feel, shuffling their feet or pacing about, looking at bits of paper, staring up to the ceiling, possibly hoping for a bolt of lightning to wipe them off the face of the earth so they don't have to go through with this. I walk up to the front desk and give my name, and a posh woman who sounds like she's sucking a lemon when she talks says, 'Haylah . . . Swinton?'

'Yeah,' I say, 'but everyone calls me Pig. So can I be introduced as Pig?'

'If you insist,' she snorts. 'Right, doors open in around half an hour. There's a backstage area through that door for the contestants. A panel of four anonymous judges are in the audience and they will make the final judgement based on the quality of your material, not the amount of laughs you get –'

What the actual? Isn't that the same thing?

She seems to pick up on my scepticism, looks at me over her spectacles and says, 'It's because some contestants bring twenty people along with them, some only three, and people tend to laugh louder for the people they support, do you understand?'

'Yes, yep, got it.'

Yeah, OK, that kinda makes sense.

Pleased with herself, she continues. 'There are eight contestants, everyone will be introduced by Jonno, our compère, so do NOT go onstage until you've been introduced. You're on last, probably around nine o'clock. After that, the judges will convene for ten minutes before reaching their verdict. OK?'

Verdict. Like a court's decision on whether or not I should be executed for crimes against comedy.

This is all getting horribly real and scary now.

'Yep,' I say, trying to stop my voice from shaking. 'Fine. Thank you.'

She gives me my tickets.

'Haylah Swinton!' says a voice behind me. I turn to see a young woman in a silver jumpsuit and a top hat. She's just about the coolest person I've ever laid eyes on. 'I'm Vanessa Trimble – call me Van – from the email.'

'Oh right, yeah! Look, thank you for letting me in.'

'Just don't tell the others you got your application in late, OK?' she whispers with a grin.

I smile. 'No, of course not!'

'Wait here – James is so gonna want to meet you. James!' she yells and an equally cool young guy in a brown suit looks up from his chat with another contestant and comes over.

'Look, it's Haylah!' says Van.

'Haylah!' he says, reaching out to shake my hand, 'A pleasure. I'm James. Me and Van run this crazy night, plus a few other more regular comedy nights across town. Look, you've got such a natural style, we can't wait to see what you do this evening.'

My heart does a little forward roll of joy at being complimented by people who actually know what they're talking about.

We chat for a bit as I tell them how nervous I am and they tell me that's perfectly normal, that you need the nerves to do well out there.

'So who are the judges then?' I ask.

'Well, we keep them anonymous as otherwise the acts tend to play just to them, and if they're not laughing we've seen people just give up and totally die onstage. They're comedians and guys who've run clubs or been on the circuit in one way or another for years. But, look, don't worry about them. Just do your best and focus on your delivery and the laughs will come, yeah?'

Then they wish me good luck and I go outside to join the others, glowing a bit from the encouragement, but still shaking at the thought of actually doing this.

'I'm on last!' I huff. 'Can you believe it? I'm on bloody last!'

'What's wrong with that?' asks Kas. 'The audience will have warmed up by then. Oooh, and have you seen those two boys over there, Chlo? They're totally checking us out.'

'Oooh, you're right!' says Chloe, drawing herself up to her full height and giving them her squinty 'flirty' look over her shoulder, which always looks to me more like she has a retinal problem.

'What's wrong with LAST?' I say. 'It means I've got to sit there all evening, watching everyone else and getting more and more freaked out, and EURRGHH! Why am I putting myself through this? I should just go and tell them I can't do it. I should just –'

Then someone taps me on the shoulder. I spin round – and am relieved to see it's not Leo. It's Ruben.

'Hi,' he says.

'Hi! Erm, Ruben. Kas, Chloe, this is Ruben.'

'Hi,' they say, before they really obviously look down at his feet to see if he's wearing socks. Luckily, his ankles are hidden from view by great swathes of beige corduroy trousers.

'So, your mum sent me a message asking to meet her here,' he says with a look of bewilderment behind his beard. And actually I thought seeing Ruben would be dead awkward, but the truth is, I'm kind of glad to see him, and relieved to think about something other than my impending onstage humiliation.

'Yeah, erm, I need to tell you something about that . . .'

We walk round the corner and sit next to each other on the concrete back steps of the theatre.

'OK, look, so . . .' I take a deep breath. 'Mum didn't send you that message. I did.'

'What? Haylah!' he says.

But then, before he can get cross, I spill everything out. And he listens as I explain to him that although, yes, I thought he was a twonk when I first met him, now he actually seems all right. I tell him that I didn't know they were serious, and that I just wanted to keep everything the same for me, Mum and Noah. I tell him that since he left she's been a total sad sack and that I think she actually likes him. A lot.

'Oh,' he says when I'm done, running his hand over his beard.

'I know, I was horrible. And super selfish,' I say.

He thinks about it for a moment. 'No you weren't. You were looking out for your family, and there's nothing wrong with that.' He sighs. 'So, you want us to meet, right? Today?'

'Yeah. It's a comedy competition thing. I'm performing and . . . Mum's coming along in a bit, though she doesn't know I'm going onstage. I know she'd love to see you. So would Noah. So . . . you'll stay? Please?' I ask, hopefully handing him his ticket.

He takes it. 'Yeah, OK. I'll stay long enough to see what your mum thinks of me being here.'

Result!

'Thank you.'

We get up and start walking back to the front of the theatre, my nerves increasing with every step.

'So, wow, you're really performing tonight?' I can't tell if he's impressed or just as alarmed as I am about the whole thing.

I run my fingers through my hair and huff out a long breath. 'Yep, if I can force myself out there. But listen, don't tell Mum that I'm going on. I think she'll try to persuade me not to go out there. I've kinda had a crappy week and she's feeling a bit overprotective of me. She wouldn't think I'm ready, and she's probably right, but I don't need to hear it.'

Then Mum and Noah walk round the corner. Noah runs up to us, yelling Ruben's name in delight. Yay! Then I look at Mum. *Uh-oh.* She shoots me an angry, questioning look.

'Come on, Noah,' I say, refusing to meet Mum's glare.

'But it's Ruben! I want to stay with Ruben!' he says, wrapping himself like a lunatic koala around Ruben's legs.

'Come and say hi to Chloe and Kas – they're desperate to see you!' And, fickle little freak that he is, he detaches himself from Ruben and scampers towards them.

I feel Mum's eye-daggers pierce the back of my brain as I chase after him.

'Hey, Noah!' says Kas. 'How was the train?'

Noah rambles on, giving them a minute-by-minute account of his journey: how a man with only one leg sat opposite them, how Mum went for a wee on the train, but didn't shut the door properly and a woman walked in on her, how there were no fewer than three pieces of chewing gum stuck on his window, but he couldn't get them off, which was a shame because one of them looked like strawberry flavour, which is his favourite.

As he yammers on, I peer back round the corner. Mum and Ruben are talking.

What if it goes wrong? What if she tells him to get lost? What if this whole thing just makes her hate me?

Then, after a few agonizing minutes, they kiss. Which is both brilliant and utterly disgusting at the same time. All that beard. Ugh.

They walk back over to us, hand in hand. Mum is looking happy again. Ruben is looking like the bearded cat who got the cream.

'Ooooh!' says Chloe to them. 'Look who's a couple!'

'Chloe!' I say.

'What? They're so cute together,' she says.

Mum's beaming, but then turns and glares at me.

'Thank you, Chloe, but excuse me a minute while I have a quick word with my *daughter*.' She lets go of Ruben's hand and drags me back down the alley.

Oh, holy bumbags. This is bad.

'I'm sorry, Mum. I –' But before I can go off into a whole apologetic ramble she smiles, puts her finger up to my mouth to shut me up and then gives me a big hug.

Wait, what?

'Look, I'm not loving that you went through my phone or tried to meddle in all this, but, well, I am loving why you did it. I love you, Hay. I don't know what I'd do without you,' she says into my hair.

'Probably have lots of boyfriends and a crazy love life?' I say.

'Well, obviously,' she says, laughing.

I tell her I'm sorry, that I know I did a dumb thing.

She hugs me tighter and says, 'You so often do the right thing, Hay. You're allowed to do the wrong thing from time to time. You're amazing. Me and Noah are both so lucky to have you.'

She moves back from me, holding my face in her hands. 'Look at you! This new outfit, your hair, even the make-up . . . you look absolutely beautiful, you know that? My funny, gorgeous girl. *You* should be up on that stage, not Leo. Where is he anyway? You want me to smack him in the face?'

I suggest it's probably not the best idea. (Mum's got arms like a bricklayer and would probably send him into orbit.)

Then I decide to tell her about tonight.

'Truth is, I've thought up a better way to punch him in the face. I'm . . . well, I'm performing tonight.'

And, instead of warning me off, her eyes widen and she smiles at me. 'You're really going onstage?'

She actually seems pleased about it – does this woman have no compassion for me at all?

'Yeah, unless I just go home now, which actually might make a lot more sense.'

'Oh, no way! You're *so* ready, Hay. I thought it all along. When we were watching Leo perform your jokes, I was thinking, *Why's she writing for some other guy when she could be doing this herself?*'

'You did? So why didn't you say that!'

'Oh, love. Because I will never push you into anything you said you didn't want to do. And, well, I probably wanted to protect you –' she glances over at Ruben – 'like you wanted to protect me. Thing is, if we don't take risks, we never get anywhere, never do anything. Seeing my baby onstage in front of all these people . . . I can't imagine anything better. But, look, don't do this just to beat Leo. Do this for you, because you're talented and you deserve this. Even if you bomb, I'll be so, so proud of you.'

We hug again, both of us watery eyed.

'Am I really going to bomb though?' I say as we pull away.

'Course not, love! The amount of time you put into writing your funnies, how could you fail?'

'There's some stuff in my set about you and Noah – just funny stuff. Well, I flippin' hope it's funny stuff. Is that OK?'

She squeezes my shoulder. 'Of course! You can say anything you want about me, babe, as long as it gets a laugh. Be confident out there, like you deserve to be. Come on, shoulders back, boobs in the air and go get 'em, tigress!'

'Thanks, Mum,' I say, standing a little taller.

'Oh, but first fix that make-up of yours because you look like Uncle Fester.'

'Oh knobnuts,' I say, seeing the black mascara I just wiped from my eyes smeared over my fingers.

We go into the theatre and I'm told there's a special place for the contestants to sit, right near the stage, and a backstage dressing area we can use.

With a last set of 'good lucks' from everyone, I head backstage to try to save my smeared face and calm my frantic nerves.

But when I get there, of course, there's Leo.

TWENTY-EIGHT

'Hey, Pig!' he says. 'I've been looking for you and, God, you're rubbish at checking your messages – whoa, you look amazing! Check out the new look! So you've come to wish me luck?'

'Good luck,' I say coldly, sitting on a rickety chair in front of a mirror and raising a tissue to my panda eyes.

The other contestants are milling about, checking themselves in mirrors, reading through their scripts. One red-haired girl is doing what I can only hope is some sort of vocal exercise, although she sounds more like she's having a fit.

Leo walks over to me and looks at my reflection in the mirror. And the problem is, my stupid heart is still pleased to see him, even though the last time I did he was playing tonsil tennis with Keesha.

'Yeah, thing is, though, I don't think anyone's supposed to be back here apart from us performers,' he says with an apologetic smile.

'I know,' I say, refusing to look at him, trying instead to focus only on fixing my eye make-up.

'You all right?' he says. 'You're acting funny. You're not nervous for me, are you? Cos I'm gonna nail it, don't you worry.'

'I'm sure you are,' I say flatly.

Then a balding, round man with a face like a wobbly trifle, wearing a red sequined waistcoat, bounds in, followed swiftly by the lemon-sucking front-desk woman holding a clipboard.

The trifle throws up his arms and says, 'Well, hey, kids! I'm Jonno. I'll be your compère this evening (not just a nutter)! Y'know, introducing the acts, making a few jokes to keep the audience lively for ya, maybe dropping a few of my best dance moves – we'll see how the evening goes!'

At the end of every sentence, possibly in an attempt to fool the audience into thinking what he had just said was an actual joke, he puts on a strange nasal voice, not unlike Fozzie Bear. Except that compared to this guy, Fozzie Bear was the Oscar Wilde of joke writing.

The posh woman rolls her eyes and says, 'Right, let's do a namecheck, just to see that you're all present and correct.'

She starts to read out the eight names, each kid in the room responding, 'Here,' apart from Leo who answers, 'Always present, always correct.'

And now I do look at him, and for the first time I don't think, *God, he's charming!* I actually think, *Chuffin' smart-arse.*

The woman is equally unimpressed and glares at him over her half-moon glasses. After a few more names, she says, 'And, ahem, *Pig.*'

'Here,' I say.

'Right, that's it then,' says Jonno. 'Good luck, everyone. I'm sure you'll all be hilarious (though not as funny as me obviously)!'

And they leave us all to our nerves again.

Leo stares at me. 'You? You're performing?'

'Yep,' I say, glancing at his reflected face in the mirror before concentrating back on my own.

'Since when?'

'Last-minute addition. Don't you just hate it when you don't know something that everyone else knows, and you end up feeling a complete dumbnut?' I'm trying to keep my cool, but that was definitely said in way too high a pitch.

'Erm . . .' he says, slowly sitting down on the bench next to me. I can almost hear the cogs whirling in his head as he figures it out. 'What are we talking about here?' he whispers.

I carry on fixing my make-up in the mirror. 'How's Keesha?'

'Erm . . . fine.'

'Yeah, funny that. She looks fine to me too, which is weird as the last time I saw her you were giving her mouth-to-mouth RESUSCI-frickin'-TATION!'

'Oh.'

'Yes.' I turn to him. 'I saw you two. At it like blowfish,' I say, returning to my reflection and pretending to do something with my hair.

'When? What – oh, on the doorstep.'

'No, it was definitely on the mouth.'

'Don't joke,' he says, looking down at his feet.

'This is a comedy night, Leo – it's kinda what we're here for.'

'Look, I don't know what to say. Me and Keesha, we've known each other for years.'

He says that like it explains everything.

'And . . .? I've known my postwoman, Janet, for several years, but she doesn't expect that kind of doorstep service.'

'I mean, *known* known her. We're kind of a couple, I guess. Look, I-I thought you knew . . . I don't know what to say.'

'So that's it?' I say. Then, frustrated and unable to make any kind of sense of the rush of thoughts that are trampling through my mind, I blurt out, 'Not even a sorry? You just don't get it, do you? You come along with your – your *jokes* and *that* smile, and make me feel actually really *good* about myself for once – you raise my hopes, only to . . . to wipe POO all over them.'

And now my eyes are misting over again. Partly from embarrassment at the whole poo reference. Not exactly the sophisticated, calm riposte I had imagined.

I turn away and he reaches out to touch my arm. 'Pig, Haylah –'

But I shrug him off. 'And now you've made me smudge my sodding mascara again! I always knew make-up hated me!'

'Listen, Hay, I AM sorry. I didn't know you felt like that about me.'

I look at his reflection in the mirror – somehow I can't bear to actually face the real him. 'Yes you did. And anyway I don't, or maybe I did, but only because I thought *you* felt like that about me. Because *you* flirted with *me*,

289

because you –' I realize at this point that my voice has hit an unnatural volume and several other contestants are now staring over at us, so I whisper-shout, '*Kissed* me . . .'

Leo puts his hands behind his head and stares at me in the mirror with a frustrated expression. 'Look, I flirt with everyone! That's just how I am! And I kissed you because you grabbed *me* and kissed *me* and, well, I'm a boy and an idiot and you're a lot more attractive than you think you are, OK?'

Patronizing git. And, great, so now he's saying it was just me forcing myself on a guy who wasn't really into it.

'So it meant nothing. I get it. Just forget it! OK?'

'No, it wasn't *nothing*! I didn't mean that. It's just . . . I'm with Keesha. It's just the way it is. I've been with her on and off since we were, I don't know, eight or something. I guess I love her. I'm sorry. I thought you knew that.'

'I didn't. And doesn't she mind you tongue-wrestling other girls?'

'Other girl. Singular. You. Just you. And, yes, she would mind, and I shouldn't have done it. I just . . . I'm stupid. And I like you, Pig. A lot, you know?'

Yeah, right.

'No you don't. You lied to me and you pretend you don't know me when there's other people around. If you like me, you've got a really funny way of showing it,' I seethe.

He sighs. Lost for words for once. Then says, 'So this gig is your way of getting back at me? You think you're going to win? Cos these contestants all know what they're doing. I mean, some of them were at last year's competition

290

and they're good, you know – *really* good. And experienced, and . . .'

'And I'm not ready, right?' I say.

'Look, I just don't want you to make a fool of yourself.'

'Well, it's a bit late for that, isn't it?'

He sighs again, and is about to say something else when the posh woman announces that it's now time to take our seats. As I walk to my seat on the front row, next to all the other contestants (but luckily far away from Leo), I catch sight of Chloe and Kas a few rows back. Kas holds two thumbs up to her chest and Chloe mouths, 'You OK?' I nod back to them.

But I don't feel OK.

Angry, stupid, used, very, very nervous, completely out of my depth, but definitely not OK.

I try to shut my mind off and just concentrate on my set, which I run through in my head again, and the stage. The big, empty, lonely stage that I'm going to have to walk out on later.

OhGodOhGodOhGod.

First Jonno the compère comes out. He's surprisingly lively onstage, scampering about like an idiot, and asking a few people in the audience where they come from before taking the pee out of whatever they say. His jokes aren't particularly funny, but the audience laughs along politely and at least it sets the bar pretty low for the rest of us.

Then he introduces the first act, a girl who's so nervous she can barely get a word out to start with, but when she's warmed up she actually gets some big laughs. And it's great to see another girl actually being funny onstage, but at the same time, the funnier she is, the more I want to crawl into a hole and die rather than go up there myself.

Oh God, she's really good. What am I doing here?

She does a whole bit about her being British-Chinese, and how teaching her white dad to hold chopsticks was a bit like teaching a chimp how to crochet. When she's done, no one claps louder than me and the contestants along my row. We all know that anyone who's mad enough to put themselves through this deserves applause. And possibly a psychological evaluation.

Next up is a freakishly tall boy who talks mostly about football, and how to sound like you know what you're talking about to your mates when really you haven't got a clue. We laugh along, at least the front row does, but to be honest he's not that good, he fluffs quite a few lines and some of his material is kind of a private joke with his friends, who laugh raucously from a few rows back, though the rest of us are left baffled. Which is all great for me as I'm pretty damned sure I could do better than that. Right?

Then there's a guy who does a lot of impressions – some, like his one of Simon Cowell followed by Gollum from *Lord of the Rings* calling Cowell a 'fat little hobbit', are spot-on, whereas others, again, leave me and the rest of the audience bewildered. I'm still not sure whether his last impression was Arnold Schwarzenegger or David Attenborough.

Next there's a girl who brings a keyboard out with her and sings surreal songs, one of which is called, 'Your Pencil Case Tells Me You Heart Me So Why Won't You Lend Me

Your Biro'. She's really funny actually, so again I'm feeling nauseous about my own pathetic offerings.

Then it's Leo's turn. And after a bit of a nervous start he does nail it, of course. In fact, he blows all the others out of the running.

As he starts offstage, Keesha in the row behind me claps and laughs louder than anyone. I turn to stare at her, but she just offers back a friendly smile.

What a manipulative cow.

The hurt from seeing them kiss is fading though. I get that Leo and Keesha are together. And actually I'm strangely OK with that. Maybe I didn't want his love after all, at least not in a romantic way. Maybe all I wanted was his respect and friendship – I mean, forgetting the kiss thing for a moment, more importantly he was the first person I've ever shared my material with (not a euphemism). And that was a pretty big deal. At least to me.

But I can't worry about that now. Mum's right. I don't care if I beat him any more – it's not about that. This is about me, about doing something just for *me*.

There's only two more acts before I go on, and I can't sit in my seat any more because I'm just a big blob of rumbling nerves and swimming thoughts. So, with my heart and stomach somersaulting over each other, I make my way backstage to wait for my name to be called.

Leo's there. Sitting on a threadbare sofa in the corner of the room. Looks like we're in for round two then.

'You were excellent,' I say begrudgingly, 'but then you know that already.'

I start pacing around the floor, looking over my script, which I'm gripping with trembling hands.

'They're your words, Pig. I couldn't have done anything without you,' he says eventually, in an uncharacteristically serious voice.

Whatever.

'Look, I get it. You were just using me to write your set. It's cool – it's over now. No hard feelings,' I say.

I'm pleased to see him looking ashamed. 'What? I wasn't using you for material!' he says defensively as I shoot him a Very Hard Stare. 'No, OK, well, maybe I was using you at first. And that was crap of me, and I was a dumb-ass and I'm sorry about that – but seriously I don't wanna lose you as a mate, Pig. Nobody else gets the comedy thing like you do; no one else makes me laugh as much as you do. You're important to me, OK?'

'OK,' I say, not meaning it at all.

'Right, so we're cool, yeah?'

'Yep,' I say, my hands shaking.

'Great. So . . . don't go out there then. You don't have to prove something just to try to get back at me. Why put yourself through it? I'll win, and we'll share the money like we agreed. It's all good, yeah?'

Erm. EXCUSE ME?

'Oh, *I* get it.' I say, stopping my pacing and looking squarely at him. 'You're scared that I might actually win!'

'No!' He laughs at the very idea, but I can see his body tensing. 'Sorry, but not even a little bit. You heard the crowd – they frickin' loved me. But the truth is, I *am* a little bit worried you're going to go out there and do something stupid, like tell everyone you wrote my stuff. And I really don't need that, Pig. I mean, we agreed we'd do this together; we agreed you wouldn't tell anyone. So you just need to get past this – you can't let some *personal stuff* mess everything up for me.'

My hands stop shaking. I turn to look at him full on, and he actually flinches at the anger raging behind my eyes.

And this is it. This is what I actually needed. He's just pushed me into finding a new gear I didn't know I had, and I've just speeded up and overtaken.

My anger has overtaken my heartbreak.

My determination has finally overtaken my patheticness, turned round and put two fingers up to it.

Slowly, I walk towards Leo like a panther nearing its prey, and through gritted teeth I say, 'This will *mess everything up for you* – seriously? You're only doing this because you're a massive show-off, but you can't sing or dance – that's what you told me, right? Oh, and because it'll "look good" on your bloody Cambridge application.

'For me, this is everything – it's what I've dreamed about my entire life. Everything I've wanted to be is there for the taking, on that stage – it's not a stepping stone to some other glory. I don't even care about the prize. Oh, but I'm forgetting, it's all about *you*, isn't it, Leo?'

'Yeah, all right, Haylah, you've made your point,' he says, at least having the good grace to squirm in his seat.

'What *possible* other reason could there be for *me* to go out there?' I fume, starting to almost enjoy myself. 'I mean,

I'm just an irrelevant, fat schoolgirl! I can't possibly be as funny as the great Leo Jackson! No one wants to hear what *I* have to say, right?' I'm looming right over where he's sitting now, my hands on my hips in full Mum-rant power stance.

'No, come on, that's not what I'm saying at all! And I've told you – you're not fat,' he says with – UNBELIEV-ABLY – a wink.

'I'LL DECIDE IF I'M FAT OR NOT!' I yell down into his face.

And it does occur to me that I haven't actually thought about being fat for quite a while, which makes me feel pretty good, although shouting at him at the moment is making me feel even better. So I continue. 'And *I'll* decide what I say or don't say. And *I'll* decide whether I'm ready to go out there or not, and *I'll* sodding well decide if I'm going to forgive you or not. GOT IT?'

Leo holds his hands up to me in surrender, but I swear he still has a smirk on his face. 'Yeah, all right! Calm down, Pig.'

'AND MY NAME'S NOT PIG – IT'S HAYLAH!'

And with that the smirk disappears and he gets up and storms off, just as the lemon-sucking woman tiptoes into the room and whisper-scolds, '*What* is going on in here?'

'Nothing,' I say, my blood cooling again and leaving me with a fresh feeling close to elation. Like I've just freed myself from something that was holding me back, like I've just crawled out of an ugly chrysalis and realized I've got a set of kick-ass wings and I know how to use them.

'Well, can you make the "nothing" *quieter*, please? And you're about to go on.' She looks down at her clipboard and raises an eyebrow again. 'Pig, isn't it?'

I pause before responding with a nod. Time standing still, and in that still moment I think back to crying myself to sleep that first day I boldly told everyone to call me Pig, just to get the bullies off my back. It was the same week Dad left. Well, I'm tired of putting up with the bullies and quietly being whatever they push me into being. I need to reclaim myself, I need to stand up. And I want to do stand-up. As me. The real me.

And, right there and then, I make a decision.

'No, actually. Can I change that? I just want to be Haylah. Haylah Swinton.'

'Very well,' she says. 'I'll tell the announcer. I'm not changing it again though, so are you *sure* you don't want to be Pig any more?'

'Yeah,' I say, with my chin held high. 'I'm sure.'

TWENTY-NINE

Nerves are running through me like fire as I walk to the side of the stage, an actual stage with curtains and hot lights and an audience of faces staring at it and . . . *Oh God.*

My stomach churns its contents like a cement mixer, and I'm suddenly remembering playing one of the Three Wise Men in the school nativity aged five. Instead of giving gold to the baby Jesus, my nerves got the better of me and I pooped myself, started crying and loudly wailed out into the audience, 'Mummy! It's a code brown!' It's quite possible that that exact same scenario might present itself here tonight. And not even my mum's gonna think that's cute this time round.

As if I'm waiting to walk out in front of a firing squad, I wait for the compère to finish titting about onstage, making a few jokes at the expense of a couple of the parents in the audience, who squirm in their seats, and then he . . . *gulp* . . . introduces me.

'And finally tonight, ladies and gentlemen, give it up for . . . Ms Haylah Swinton!'

As I emerge from behind the curtain, everyone cheers, though no one louder than Chloe and Kas. Cutting above the rest is Noah's high-pitched voice shouting, 'Just tell chicken jokes, Hay! Chicken jokes, chicken jokes, chicken jokes!'

And hearing them and my name actually makes me smile and starts to put me at ease, although that message hasn't yet got to my legs, which are still shaking like a newborn deer's. I manage to get to the centre of the stage as Jonno leaves on the opposite side. And now it's just me up here. Alone. I grab the mic and look down at the huge audience of expectant faces, now hushed and waiting for me to talk: people from school, my two best friends, my mum, holding hands with Ruben as Noah sits on her lap. And *somehow* the nerves disappear.

And I feel like I'm home. Like this is where I'm meant to be. Like this is what I was made for. This is the *me* me.

And then I start talking. And they laugh. A *lot*.

'Hi, my name's Haylah, it's nice to be here. Before we get started, I should warn the front row that, although I look dainty, the last time I did a gig I turned round and my butt exploded all the stage equipment.

'Yeah, I can't even do the *stand-up* bit of stand-up comedy without making the audience feel nervous. It's possible that not only might *I* die up here, comedically speaking, but you guys might *actually* die.'

A huge laugh, the first of many, erupts from the audience and my brain jolts into overdrive, like I've just been injected with a heavenly heady mix of caffeine, adrenalin, chocolate and electricity.

'I'm not too nervous though cos I've got my family here for support. So I know if I get badly heckled . . . that'll just be my mum. And there's my little brother, Noah. Everyone give Noah a shout-out.

'Actually, I told Noah I was going to do this and he suggested some of his own . . . "jokes". He suggested I open with, "Who ate all the trees?"

'Treesus.'

Everyone gives the biggest laugh yet.

'Hmm, not bad. Thanks, Noah. Living with an under-five though. Yikes. It's a challenge, isn't it? Like sharing the house with a tiny little drunk fascist dictator. Stumbling about, yelling ridiculous demands while everyone runs about after him, trying to avoid a major conflict. When you live with an under-five, you don't live in a family, you live in a *regime*.

'Now, for those of you who *don't* have younger siblings – so those of you who *are* the younger sibling, or the only child of the family, YOU HAVE NO IDEA WHAT IT'S LIKE. Oh yeah, as the youngest in the family, you've *sailed* through your childhood in the *full* and *certain* knowledge that the world revolves around *you*.

'You know why? Because *you* were the dictator in your family! *You made the decisions, you ruled by force.* When your family went to a restaurant, YOU decided when they left.

'When your family needed to go out, THEY WAITED FOR YOU to find *your* shoe, to stop *your* random tantrum, for *you* to stop peeing in the laundry basket.

'It was *exactly* the same story when the Nazi Party had to wait for Hitler before going to a rally. Dictators and youngest siblings. Same thing.

'But I'll tell you something – it is *not* like that for the older sibling. Oh no. That's not how *our* childhood goes. We're the oppressed, downtrodden people trying to please YOU, because *if we don't*, your foot soldiers, Mum and Dad, *will make US suffer.*

'When you're kicking off, they're like, "Look, *you* need to help find his shoe NOW or he'll never stop screaming and we'll never leave this house and it will *all be your fault*! *I mean, you're SIX. For God's sake, take some responsibility!*"

'Very different childhoods. You younger siblings and only children, you're the Kim Jong-un of your family. The rest of us, at best, his older brother. You know, the one he had killed. Probably just for telling their mum and dad it was little Kimmy who shoved the shoe down the toilet.

'I'm kidding though. I love my little brother, although I am a *little* jealous of him. I mean, isn't it amazing what *little* kids *can* get away with in public? Like practising doing forward rolls in church, down the aisle. At a funeral.

'Apparently, I was being "inappropriate", but I mean, if *he'd* done it, it would have been *fine*. And, when *I* wear a Batman costume down to the local Tesco Express, it just freaks people out. Even when I tell them, "It's OK, I'm not Robin!" (That was one just for you, Noah.)

'But at least he's not a baby any more. I don't know, I just don't get that whole baby thing – dribbling, screaming, pooing everywhere. I don't know if anyone else has that reaction when they see a baby – it might just be me.

'My mum's the same though. She's not interested in tiny babies. She says, "I just like them when they start doing stuff . . . like leaving home."

'Nah, my mum's great though – we get on really well. I have to say that because she's here. But genuinely she doesn't nag me too much now I'm a bit older, a bit wiser. She's stopped asking whether I've brushed my teeth, had a bath or wiped my bum properly. She figures I've got that stuff down by now.

'*Shows how little she knows.*

'No, now she asks me about boys. "You got a boyfriend yet? Why not? Aw, you must have your eye on someone!" Until you actually *do* get a boyfriend, and then she's like, "Do NOT let him in your bedroom unless the door is OPEN, you have a panic button round your NECK and your knickers are *password protected* – you get me, girl?"

'But then everyone wants to know about your love life when you're a teenager, right? Your friends, your parents, even the cashier at Tesco.

' "Contactless?" they ask.

'Well, a boy kissed me once, but other than that, yes, if you must know.

'So I've taken to using the self-service checkout at my local Tesco Express, which is fine. I mean, they try to make it feel like you're dealing with a real person, don't they? It *talks* to you – they almost give it a *personality*.

'The problem is, the one in my local store is a complete bitch. She's lazy, can't be bothered to weigh stuff – if you want two carrots instead of a pre-filled bag, she just blanks you like you're beneath her, then throws your change at you, one coin at a time.

'Then, just as you think she's done, she throws a final two pee at your shin while sarcastically yelling, "I hope you enjoyed shopping at Tesco!" At least she didn't ask me about my love life though. Although, come to think of it, she did ask me if I'd had an "unexpected item in my bagging area".

'Truth is, and I know you'll be surprised to hear this, I don't get so much attention from the boys – not like my beautiful girlie friends do. Cos, y'know, I'm not a proper *girlie* girl.

'Any other girls in here not a proper *girlie* girl? Oh, nice, plenty of cheers and whoops from you guys. *I'm not alone!* Hurray!

'So I'm not sweet or dainty. I don't like the colour pink, can't be bothered to moisturize. Don't do skirts and dresses. Mostly cos I don't like the idea of there being nothing between my knickers and the outside world but air, y'know?

'And I used to think not being a *girlie* girl made me *less* than a girl, but now I realize you can't wear a bra the size of two dome tents lashed together and think yourself *less* than a girl. If anything, I'm too much girl. I mean, there's no getting around these two.

'Sometimes literally. The other day I wore a wonder bra in an open-topped vehicle and the police ended up giving us a "wide load" escort vehicle.

'So I've got girlie boobs and I do like romance, so I guess that's pretty girlie too.

'Give us a shout if you've ever fallen in love. Yep, a lot of you. It sucks, doesn't it? I don't know, I think we should have guessed it from the term "*falling* in love". I mean, no one *falling* into anything is ever good, right? No one who landed in anything pleasant would be described as *falling* into it.

'You *dive* into a cool swimming pool, you *plunge* into a warm bath, but you FALL into a *ravine*, an *industrial machine*, or a *pile of crap*.

'Anyway, I don't think I really *fell* in love at all. I just tripped over it and grazed my knee on the gravel of humiliation. But then, as a feminist, I shouldn't be obsessing about falling in love with a boy anyway, right?

'I mean, this is the problem for the teenage feminist girl. We're just this big hormonal bag of contradictions, right? We look in the mirror and we say to ourselves, "OK, you wanna be funny and smart, but not funnier and smarter than the boys because how are they gonna flirt if they can't belittle you?"

'You wanna be flirted with, but you don't wanna *look* like you wanna be flirted with because that makes you a needy, possibly slaggy let-down to the sisterhood.

'And are you even *allowed* to have boobs as a feminist? I'm pretty sure you are – but are you allowed to be *proud* of them? Again, I think, yeah – but I do suspect naming them is a no-no. So – Ant, Dec, keep your identities secret, OK?

'So you look in that mirror and you say, "You're a feminist – be yourself and be *proud* of who you are. Screw what people think! No, wait, you're a girl, be *ashamed* of who you are. What other people think is everything – how dare you go against the grain?"

'And, I mean, boys don't have this crap, right? They might look like the Elephant Man, have the brainpower of a trout and the muscles of a premature baby – but I bet you *they* look in the mirror and say, "Oh *hell*, yeah. You are *all* man. Go get 'em, tiger."

'They have the confidence of a warrior king even if it's based on literally nothing. And, I mean, they've got the right idea there, haven't they? We could take a leaf out of their book of never-failing confidence, right, girls? So, hang on, they're right and we're wrong on this? Which means that boys are better than girls.

'No, wait! Dammit!'

And then it's over. As everyone falls about with laughter, I feel pumped up and more alive than I've ever felt before. I step back from the mic to let the audience know I've finished my set. Cue even more applause. I take a deep breath and exhale slowly. Trying to remember every detail of this amazing moment.

Then I step forward again and say, 'My name's Haylah Swinton. This has been amazing. You're all amazing. Thank you all so much. Goodnight.'

The laughter, applause and whooping still thunders around the theatre audience and, as I replace the mic in its stand, unable to keep the massive smile from my face, I can clearly see my gorgeous little group of family and friends, who are all on their feet and chanting, 'Haylah, Haylah, Haylah . . .'

It is, without doubt, the best night of my life.

I make my way off the stage as Jonno takes the mic and tells the audience that all the acts are done and there will now be a brief pause in the proceedings. And for a few moments I'm backstage by myself. I just stand in the middle of the room, running my fingers through my hair, trying to take it all in. My brain is buzzing.

Did that really just happen? Oh, my good holy frickin' cobnuts, did that just happen!

Then James and Van come in, and Van actually hugs me and tells me I totally nailed it, followed by a few of the other contestants, who trickle in and tell me how good I was, and I, of course, return the compliment, and then, before I know it, I'm swamped with hugs from Kas and Chloe, Mum and Noah, who've all made their way in. Even Ruben follows on behind them, giving me a proud if lipless grin from beneath his beard. They all screech with excitement and yell, 'You were AMAZING!' 'You're SO gonna win!'

And, for the first time, I really kind of believe them.

THIRTY

As I walk back out into the theatre, everyone I know cheers for me again and my brain glows with a pure joy I've never felt before. All the kids from school, even Destiny and Jules, the crafting trio (and who knew their humour spanned further than cat memes?), and a load of guys from my year who've barely spoken to me before are gathering round and telling me how great I was, and then in the middle of them Leo walks over to me and holds out his hand to shake mine.

'You were amazing. You totally deserve to win,' he says.

'Thanks,' I say. 'I'm sorry I shouted at you. And, well, truth is, I wouldn't have done any of this without you – you showed me it was possible.'

'Then I'm glad I did something right by you,' he says and we hug. And he leaves. And I'm actually totally OK with that.

I'm not angry or hurt any more, I'm just excited. About my life, about my future, about being me, the *me* me, the me that was inside and is now outside, proudly dancing around like an unashamed naked toddler after a bath.

As everyone's milling about and starting to take their seats again, Dylan, of all people, pulls me to one side and I think, *Oh, please don't ruin this moment.*

'I just wanted to say, I mean, I just wondered . . .'

'What is it, Dylan? Because if you want me to ask Chloe out for you, now's not the time.'

He actually blushes and looks mortified. 'What? Chloe? No, I just . . . well, for a while I've . . . look, I just wondered if you wanted to go out sometime. With me. To the . . . cinema or something?'

What? Is this the same guy who normally at best has some smart-ass remark about everything I do and at worst is persistently a complete git to me?

'Go out? With you?'

'Yeah,' he says, kicking at the floor with his foot, unsure of himself for once.

And it genuinely doesn't even look like he's taking the pee. But, even if he's not, he's always a jerk to me. I mean, what does he expect me to say?

'Erm, thanks? But very much no.' I start to walk away, but he holds his hands up to me as if pleading for me to listen.

'OK, OK, look, I know what you're thinking. I'm always saying dumb stuff to you, right?'

'Well, duh.'

'And, yeah, OK, that's true, but it's because, well, it's because –' he scratches the back of his neck – 'I dunno, whenever I see you I just say *anything* to make you look my way. Because . . . I like you, Haylah. A lot.'

And I can tell he worked really hard to get that sentence out – like seriously there have been babies that were born more easily than that sentence – and I can also see that he, bizarrely, genuinely means it. Which is kind of shocking and also a bit lovely. But still. *Dylan?*

'*OK* but . . . You get that being a jerk is a really dumb-ass way to show someone you like them, right?'

'Right. But, hey, I wasn't just mean to you – I've flirted with you as well.'

'That was *flirting*?'

'Yeah, OK, so maybe that wasn't super clear. Look, I'm a guy, I'm stupid. I don't know what I'm doing, but I do know I think you're awesome, and funny and . . . argh, forget it, OK? I'm sorry, and we've gotta sit down again anyway, and this is your night – just forget it.'

He gives me a sweet, sad smile then turns to leave, but this time I stop him by touching his shoulder, just for a moment. He looks back at me.

'I'm not going to say yes now, but ask me again,' I say, 'in a week or so. If you can be cool to me at school, in front of everyone, for a whole week, then, well, ask me again and *maybe*. OK?'

His face lights up. 'A week?'

I nod. 'Then *maybe*.'

'That's great. I will. I'll do that.' He starts walking away from me backwards, then points at me with both hands like guns, before quickly putting them down again. 'Sorry, don't know why I did that! But, erm, yeah. In a week, got it.' Then, as the auditorium lights dim, he trips over a chair, gets up, raises his eyebrows at his own duffishness, turns and jogs away.

It's almost kind of cute.

As I take my seat, I look over to Chloe and Kas, who jointly mouth the words, 'WHAT. WAS. THAT?'

And I mouth back with a smile, 'I'll tell you later!' and they giggle.

'C'mon, Haylah! Darlin', sit down – they're going to announce the winner!' shouts Mum from her seat.

The compère bounds back on to the stage with a piece of paper in his hands as I sit back down. Apart from the odd random whoop and cheer, the atmosphere is tense, but I feel strangely calm about everything.

The crowd hushes as he starts thanking the audience, the contestants and Van and James for organizing the event and then tells a couple of weak one-liners, but even he can tell that at this point the whole audience is thinking, *Just get on with it!*

Then, as he opens the envelope, silence fills the place. Everyone holds their breath and he announces that the winner is . . . Ayesha Lewis. The girl who sang the surreal songs.

Everyone turns to me with a 'you was robbed!' look on their faces as she goes up to receive her prize.

And for a moment I'm almost disappointed. Then the other half of my brain merrily slaps that half round the face and I applaud wildly, whooping and hollering with a massive grin plastered on my face.

A grin which might, actually, never fade.

THIRTY-ONE

I'm performing an incredible magic trick onstage, which ends with me producing a laughing rabbit from my silent magician partner Batman's trousers. Spock, Henry VIII and Miss Piggy all love it, but Simon Cowell decides it's not for him so I throw the rabbit in his face. It claws him to death and Ron Weasley grabs my hand as we lead the world in a celebratory samba to 'La Cucaracha'. He gets carried away and starts using my boobs as bongos.

It's then that I come to and realize that Noah is sitting on my chest and repeatedly banging his little palms down.

'Ow – Noah!'

I bat his arms away, prise my eyes open, grab my phone and see that I've slept in. Again. Some things never change. Some things, on the other hand, really do.

Noah beams down at me, holding his arms out wide. 'Look at me!' he says.

'Wow, Noah, you got yourself dressed!'

I mean, everything's on backwards and inside out, and it's his school uniform even though it's a Saturday, but, hey, the boy done good. I give him a big smile and pull him down for a hug.

'I'm so proud of you!' I say. 'Come on, let's go get some breakfast and then I'm taking you to the park to meet someone!'

'Yay, park, park, park!' he chants as we march down to the kitchen.

'Morning, Hay,' says Mum, sitting at the kitchen table and crunching on a piece of toast, bleary-eyed after a night shift. 'After brekkie I'm just gonna get some shut-eye for a few hours, then Ruben's coming over this afternoon, that OK?'

'Of course,' I say, getting Noah settled in front of a bowl of Chocopops. 'He said he'd help me out with some homework actually.'

'Oh yeah?'

'I've gotta design a bird feeder for a D&T project and I figured with his saddo love of "twitching", or whatever it's called, he might actually be pretty useful.'

'Well, that's just great, Hay!' says Mum, her face lighting up. 'You guys will have great fun doing that together.'

'Yeah, all right, don't get too excited, Mum. I still find the man's lack of socks a massive strain on my gag reflex.' But I say it with a smile.

'Oh, shush, ya big sarky cow!' she laughs.

Then, just as I'm putting my bread in the toaster, she grabs my side and starts tickling.

'Aww, Mum! I'm way too old for tickling!' I recoil.

At the word 'tickling', Noah's put down his spoon and, with an evil grin, is now advancing on me with outstretched fingers.

'Never!' says Mum with a deranged laugh, and a split second later she's chasing me into the living room. 'Tickle Monster Mother will never retire from her mission!'

And now she and Noah are on top of me on the sofa and I'm almost wetting myself with hysterics.

After getting showered and dressed, I eventually get Noah into something more Saturday-ey and towards the front door. Though now he's refusing to let me help him put on his shoes while putting zero effort into actually putting them on himself.

'Noah, come on, dude – stop faffing. We need to go.'

'I'm not faffing!' he says, holding a shoe up to his ear. 'I'm just seeing if I can hear the sea.'

'You are SO faffing. You're like Bobby Faffage.'

'I am not Bobby Faffage!' he says with a smile.

'You're Colonel Faffington. Baron von Faffenhausen.'

And now he's laughing. And letting me put his shoes on for him. Isn't the power of laughter amazing?

'Hamish McFaff of the Clan McFaff.'

And *boom* the shoes are on. And we're out of the door. And, yes, we're going to be a little late, but you know what? That's OK. He can wait for me.

When we arrive at the park, we see Dylan sitting on a bench with his little sister. He's wearing a button-up shirt and smart trousers like he's actually made an effort. As we approach them, I feel a few nerves fluttering around inside me, but nothing I can't handle.

Stand tall, chin up, norks forward. You've got this.

Bigger than the nerves is the doubt that I'm doing the right thing. *Dylan? Really?* But, true to his word, he has actually been super nice to me at school for the last week, joking along with me rather than at me (and he's actually pretty funny). Even Chloe and Kas said they thought it was a good idea and that I should give him a chance. And, anyway, it's not like I agreed to go on a proper date with him or anything. It's just a play date in the park for our little siblings.

Truth is, everyone's been nicer to me at school this week. It's like a different place. Even those who weren't at the gig have congratulated me on the comedy competition, and people are actually starting to move from 'Pig' to 'Haylah'. A Year Seven even asked for my autograph. Actually, it was a request to fake her mum's signature on a note to get her out of PE, but that still counts, right?

Leo's spoken to me a few times at school, in front of his friends, and though it was a bit awkward at least I'm not at all doughy-eyed around him any more. Truth is, I don't know what I feel about him now. I think I just don't want to think about him for a while. But who knows, maybe we'll eventually come away from this as friends.

'Hey, Dylan.'

'Hey, Hay,' he says, standing up from the bench he's been perched on and looming over me.

Good God, he's tall.

'I bought you a Twix,' he says, sheepishly presenting the chocolate bar to me like a bear delicately presenting a diamond ring.

'Wow,' I say with my hand on my chest, 'my favourite. How did you know?'

He smiles. 'So this is my little sister, Ruby.'

A tiny pigtailed thing emerges from behind one of Dylan's calves.

'Hi,' she says in a small voice.

'Hi, Ruby, this is Noah,' I say, shoving Noah towards her. He frowns at her, and for a moment I think, *This is not going to work.*

Then Ruby says to him, 'I can do a cartwheel – you wanna see?'

She doesn't wait for an answer before putting both her hands on the ground and kicking her bent little legs in the air, showing everyone her knickers for a second before landing in a heap.

Noah seems impressed and applauds her.

Dylan leans down and whispers to me, 'I just hope no one ever shows her what a cartwheel really looks like.'

'I know, right? That's like the worst cartwheel ever. What is she thinking?' I whisper back with a smile before saying, 'Wow, Ruby, that's like the best cartwheel ever!'

Dylan laughs.

'I can run as fast as Flash,' says Noah in return, and immediately runs off extremely slowly to the sandpit. Ruby follows him.

The summer holidays aren't even here yet, but already I feel that air of change, of freedom and new beginnings and the sense that anything is possible.

Me and Dylan sit on the bench together and share the Twix as the two of them start playing and laughing in the sand like they've been best friends forever.

And I get the feeling that this might actually, just maybe, be the start of something really frickin' lovely.

ACKNOWLEDGEMENTS

So it turns out writing a novel is bloody hard. OK, not compared to, say, real jobs like firefighting, window-cleaning or accountancy. And yes, it's kind of fun too but still bloody hard.

There's simply no way I could have done it on my own. I'm not saying other people deserve more credit than me because frankly I deserve a little bit. I mean I did write *most* of these words myself but, seriously, it's without question because of the efforts, encouragement and love of so many people that this book came about.

I really have to start by thanking my agent Laetitia, who, thank God, saw some sort of spark in my writing and took me under her wing. With always the right amount of constructive criticism, she gently and tirelessly shaped, poked and prodded my work until it became something I could actually be proud of. She then worked her butt off to get me published by the best publisher in the world, making all my dreams come true. Genuinely, I can't thank her enough.

Massive thanks also go out to everyone at Penguin Random House for generally being awesome and working so hard on creating, producing and promoting *Pretty Funny*. Special thanks to my editors Naomi and Emma for believing in me and this book, having the patience to work with me on it, and sharing my passion and determination to get it published. Without them and Laetitia, I would never have discovered Haylah lurking in my head and now I'm utterly smitten with her.

I would also like to thank hilarious stand-up comic, top friend and podcasting partner Kirsty for all her help, encouragement and suggestions on the stand-up routines over so many glasses of gin. They were the hardest parts of the book to write and my already huge admiration for stand-ups is now off the scale.

I'm also so very grateful to the first readers of my early drafts of this and previous failed 'novels', Karen, Theresa, Marion, Sam, Helen, Clemency, Lucy, Ben, J, Micky – all of whom said nothing but nice things about my stuff, even though when a mate asks, 'Can you just read this book I've written? It might be rubbish', it must be a truly terrifying prospect.

I'm forever grateful to my crazy school friends, especially Rachel, Jen and Gem who made those days so much fun and etched in me a lifelong love of teenage friendships, making writing about them so much easier.

I would like to thank Stephen Fry for responding to my crazed fan-mail when I was a comedy-obsessed teenager and instilling in me an enduring love and respect for all comedians. I would also like to thank Caitlin Moran for hilariously inspiring a new wave of feminism and for responding to one of my tweets, which made me wee a little bit with excitement.

I want to send my never-ending gratitude to my wonderful parents for loving and supporting (and putting up with) me for so many years and always thinking more of me than I deserve. And especially my mum who reads and edits everything I do before anyone else sets eyes upon it and never fails to big me up and encourage me to keep going.

Big bagfuls of love and thanks also to my son Toby, who makes me laugh every single day, and my son Benjy, who let me write down everything he said for a year and allowed me to steal it for Noah. I will also never stop being grateful and thankful for my daughter Clementine, who I miss every day but who still inspires everything I do.

The person I really have to thank the most is my husband Matthew; my rock, my number one fan (though not in a sinister way), my gorgeous man, best friend and comedy partner through this thing called life.

Finally, I would like to thank all the girls out there who go out every day and insist on being themselves rather than bending to fit into a world beset with harsh expectations, prejudices and idiots. You're all total heroes.

ABOUT THE AUTHOR

When Rebecca was six, she precociously pronounced that she wanted to be 'an artist and a writer'. After a 'brief' detour from this career plan involving wanting to be Stephen Fry, a degree in philosophy and a dull office job, she fulfilled her dream in 2001 when she became a full time children's book illustrator. Since then she has become an award-winning and bestselling author of over 30 books for children, including her ongoing series Owl Diaries which has sold nearly 6 million copies worldwide. If she's not story-making Rebecca can be found reading, podcasting with her comedian best friend, drumming or singing in her band, making something (normally a mess), or just hanging out in sunny Suffolk with her husband, gorgeous children, moronic chickens and sarcastic cat Bernard.

DEAR READER DUDES,

If you've read this far then I'm guessing you're pretty invested in me, and frankly why wouldn't you be? I am awesome.

'So,' I hear you wondering, 'what's next for Haylah and her epic quest for comedic world domination?'

'Well,' I will answer between mouthfuls of KitKat, 'I think –'

Actually, do you know what? I'm gonna drop this whole pretend conversation thing as TBH it just makes us both sound like spanners.

Right, so, my plan . . .

I'm gonna keep writing the funnies, keep obsessively checking my emails for news of a proper gig from Van, keep experimenting with the kinds of clothes I wanna wear (I'm thinking accessories – maybe I'd look amazing with an old man pipe, what d'you think?), keep hoping for a snog from a boy for no other reason than he just wants to snog me, oh and . . . wait for it . . . I feel a thought forming in my head like a fart brewing in my stomach. And my thought fart is . . .

I'm gonna start a YouTube channel!

For why does the internet exist if not for saddos like me who think they're funny and want other people to think the same!?

Sorted. We have a plan. Hopefully nothing will randomly decide to mess with that plan like, oh, I dunno, **MY COMPLETE BUMHOLE OF A DAD COMING BACK AND FILLING OUR LIVES WITH CHAOS.**

That would be pretty crap, wouldn't it? Or maybe it wouldn't be so bad. I guess you'll have to find out. Now shut up while I enjoy the rest of this KitKat (remember people, thumb down the foil, break off and enjoy one finger at a time. Carelessly biting into the whole thing is JUST MORALLY WRONG.).

Later dudes. Miss you already.

HAYLAH. XX

(AKA THE COMEDIAN FORMERLY KNOWN AS PIG)

REBECCA ELLIOTT

PRETTY RUDE

COMING
SUMMER 2020